GRANDPA JACK

Jeff Thompson

GRANDPA JACK

JEFF HAMPTON

TATE PUBLISHING
AND ENTERPRISES, LLC

Grandpa Jack
Copyright © 2013 by Jeff Hampton. All rights reserved.

No part of this publication may be reproduced, stored in a retrieval system or transmitted in any way by any means, electronic, mechanical, photocopy, recording or otherwise without the prior permission of the author except as provided by USA copyright law.

This novel is a work of fiction. Names, descriptions, entities, and incidents included in the story are products of the author's imagination. Any resemblance to actual persons, events, and entities is entirely coincidental.

The opinions expressed by the author are not necessarily those of Tate Publishing, LLC.

Published by Tate Publishing & Enterprises, LLC
127 E. Trade Center Terrace | Mustang, Oklahoma 73064 USA
1.888.361.9473 | www.tatepublishing.com

Tate Publishing is committed to excellence in the publishing industry. The company reflects the philosophy established by the founders, based on Psalm 68:11,
"The Lord gave the word and great was the company of those who published it."

Book design copyright © 2013 by Tate Publishing, LLC. All rights reserved.
Cover design by Rtor Maghuyop
Interior design by Jake Muelle

Published in the United States of America

ISBN: 978-1-62295-105-5
1. Fiction / Political
2. Political Science / Political Process / Elections
13.01.18

PROLOGUE

Jack Dodger sat quietly on the hotel room sofa, his white hair and tired features illuminated only by the blue light from the television across the room. The volume had been turned down to a whisper, allowing him the only quiet he had enjoyed in months. From the other side of the closed door and through the eggshell-thin walls, he could hear the muffled murmurs of a dozen or more people in the next room. But mostly, he could just hear his own thoughts.

Like the images on the TV set that flashed and jumped with every passing second, Jack's mind jumped forward and backward over the past eleven months, focusing on brief images of people and places before moving to the next random destination. The scenes flew by so quickly in his mind that he couldn't quite get a handle on the reality of it all. Had he really crossed the nation from east to west and back again? Had he really shaken hands with thousands of people and looked into the eager faces of a million more? Had he really been the focus of countless newspaper articles and television interviews? Had he really been that close to power so vast that few people give it any thought, let alone pursue it? It was more than a semiretired barbershop owner from East Dallas could comprehend.

The flashing television screen—combined with his own dancing thoughts—made him dizzy, and he closed his eyes for a moment. As he did so, he heard the door open, the noise from the next room spill in after it, and then the door shut again. Then there was the soft sound of small feet on the carpet and the sensation of a tiny body sitting on the sofa beside him.

"What's the matter, Grandpa Jack?" implored the tiny voice beside him.

With his eyes still closed, he reached to his left and raised the warm little frame onto his lap. He opened his eyes and was met immediately by a wet kiss from Wendy, his best pal and keenly aware granddaughter.

"Oh, nothing, Little Blossom," he answered, calling her by the nickname he pinned on her when he first saw her little head protruding from the petal-like blanket she was wrapped in moments after her birth. "I was just thinking about all the nice people I've met in the past year and how I'm going to miss seeing them."

"But me and Mommy will always be with you," said Wendy, looking intently into his silver-gray eyes.

"That's right, that's right, Wendy," he said, smiling down at her little face. "And you know what? We're going to have a lot more time to spend together than we've had in a long while."

As he said that, the door opened again, and this time, it was Billy Briar. He closed the door quietly behind him so as to keep the noise outside for a moment longer.

"Is it time?" Jack asked, already knowing the answer.

"Yes, Jack, everyone's waiting for you. The hall is bursting at the seams with your friends. And all the networks have their people in place. All that's missing is you."

"Well, then, I suppose I shouldn't keep them waiting any longer. That wouldn't be right," he said. He took one glance back at the television screen, then lifted Wendy off his lap and back onto the sofa. "Why don't you stay here, and you can watch me on TV," he told her. "Then, you can tell me how I did. Just like always."

"Sure, Grandpa Jack. Just like always."

With that, he leaned down and kissed her on the forehead and then walked the few paces to where Billy was waiting.

"What will I say, Billy?"

"Just go down there and tell them what's on your mind. Just like always."

As Jack reached for the doorknob, Billy put his hand on his shoulder. "You'll do just fine."

Jack nodded appreciatively, pulled open the door, and walked into the light and noise. Billy gave a little wave to Wendy and then followed him out of the room. They walked silently through the sea of well-wishers gathered in the outer room, then into the elevator, down ten floors, around a corner, through a side door, and onto the ballroom stage. The waiting throng screamed and cheered and waved as Jack hesitated in the back corner of the stage. Any weakness he had felt coming to this place was vanquished by the buoyancy of the people who surrounded him.

Back in the quiet of the hotel room, Wendy watched as her grandfather approached the podium. Just then her mother came in and sat down beside her. "Oh look, Mommy, it's Grandpa Jack. He's on TV tonight."

"Yes, honey, he sure is."

They watched as he waved appreciatively at the ballroom crowd. Even with the sound turned down, they could read his lips as he said over and over again, "I love you. I love you."

"I love you too, Grandpa Jack," Wendy said, believing that his smiles and words were meant just for her.

CHAPTER 1

Few people among the hundreds of millions that have populated the United States have stood where Jack Dodger stood on that November night. The odds of anyone getting to that place in time were extremely high—even more so for a man like Jack Dodger. Just a year earlier, the notion had never entered his mind. Not once in his seventy years had he ever given thought to any kind of public office. And while some schoolboys say they want to be president some day, Jack Dodger never once made such a childish pronouncement. He had never even dreamed about it. His was not a life of dreams; his was a life of the here and now.

Jack Dodger took his first breath at 10:43 p.m. on New Year's Eve, 1929, in Dallas, Texas. What would become known as the Great Depression was just two months old, and the only child of John and Margaret Dodger was born into the turmoil of the times. While he was anticipated with joy nine months earlier, by the time he arrived, the joy was tempered by concern about how he would be clothed and fed.

When banks began failing in early 1930, John Dodger lost his position at a small downtown financial institution where he was a runner and an odd-jobs man. With nothing more than an eighth-grade education and jobs disappearing daily, he took to the streets like so many others to squeeze a living out of anyone who needed a hand. He ran errands, sold newspapers, dug ditches, and did anything else he could find to put bread on the table.

John Jr., or Jack as he was called by his parents, rarely saw his father during those early years, except for the times when he would come home for lunch between day labor jobs. The family lived in a little apartment on a side street off of Live Oak near Exall Park. Among the earliest sounds Jack heard were the streetcars on Live Oak, children playing in the park, and babies crying in adjacent apartments. As with the Dodgers, families continued to grow, Depression or not.

On Saturdays when John wasn't working, the Dodgers would take a streetcar out to the new White Rock Lake east of town, carrying sandwiches and fishing poles made from bamboo that John had helped clear from a building site. On Sunday mornings, they would walk downtown to the First Baptist Church. Afterward, they'd walk around downtown, looking in the windows at Neiman-Marcus, Sanger Brothers, A. Harris and Co., and other popular retailers. After a street-side picnic of crackers, cheese, and bologna, they would start the walk back up Live Oak toward home. All along the way, John would intently check shop windows for job notices and ask the occasional stranger if they knew of any part-time work.

So life continued until 1936, when Jack's dad got a job with an oil company, first working as a laborer installing pumping equipment at oil well sites and later as a foreman overseeing several crews engaged in that work.

Oil was flowing fast out of the East Texas and Louisiana oil fields, and the Dodger family enjoyed a considerable increase in income though nothing coming close to the fortunes of those who owned the wells. At first, John would send money back to his family in Dallas, but as he settled down into work near Marshall, Texas, his family joined him among the East Texas pines.

Jack fell in love with the outdoors and the natural world—the warm earth, the cool streams, and the glorious towering pine trees. On weekends when his father didn't have to work, they'd camp out in the woods and fish in a cove where pines and cypress trees had fallen into the water, creating shallow pools that the fish could only reach by literally "jumping over the pines." After dark, they would lay awake listening to the curious sounds of the night.

Jack prospered in the small country school where he and a gang of kids from grades one through six learned and played together all in the same room. Among his schoolmates was Franky Parker, a big redheaded kid who, although a bit slow for his age, was as friendly and loyal as a puppy. Some of the other kids made fun of Franky and played pranks on him, but Jack formed a special bond with him.

On a summer afternoon in 1939, Jack and Franky were wading in the creek down behind the house, looking for frogs and other forms of trouble when their play was interrupted by a terrible shriek from the house. Jack raced barefooted up the hill to find several men on the front lawn and his mother collapsed in agony on the front porch.

The men had brought terrible news: An explosion in the oil field had killed five well workers, including John Dodger. He had been training a new crew when one of them got careless with some equipment, creating a spark that ignited natural gas vapors. The men said that John had seen the accident about to happen and had pushed several men away from the well, saving their lives and losing his own. John Dodger was a true hero, they said.

It was of little consolation to Margaret Dodger and her son, who were not only husbandless and fatherless, but were also without any means of income. Fearing that the few skills she had were of no use in a small town like Marshall, Margaret believed they might do better back in Dallas. So with the few belongings they had and a little money from the oil company, they moved back to East Dallas to another small apartment off of Live Oak, not far from where they had once lived.

For Jack, who was just nine years old, readjusting to city life was difficult. While there were trees in the park that he could climb, the honking of cars and the fumes from exhaust were always present. The school was large and crowded, and there was nobody like Franky Parker with whom he could play. Nights were filled with sirens and horns rather than crickets and owls. Worst of all, there was always an empty chair at the dinner table.

While Margaret Dodger tried to put on a strong face for her son, she never quit grieving for John, and Jack saw sadness in her face that was present until the day she died. For his part, Jack tried to be the brave man of the house, choosing to work hard and help out rather than complain and pout.

For the next eight years, he studied hard at school, graduating with a solid *B* average in everything except for math, where he made an *A*-minus. In the afternoons after school and during the summers, he worked at a small men's store downtown while his mother worked around the corner running a cash register at a drugstore. The work was steady for both mother and son, especially in 1945 and 1946 as soldiers came back from the war and began buying civilian clothes and other goods again.

Jack graduated from high school in 1947 and began taking classes at a business school at night while working full time at the men's store during the day. Within a couple of years, he was made the assistant manager and was in line to take over management of the store some day, but then, America entered the conflict in Korea and all able-bodied men had to register for the draft. Jack's number was called in 1951, and after basic training, he was shipped off to Korea. At five feet eleven inches and 180 pounds, he was well suited for the infantry.

Jack was proud to serve his country, and there were times when nights out on patrol reminded him of camping with his dad. And while he faced real danger and saw his share of combat and true horror, any fear about his own safety was less a matter of clinging to his own mortality as it was preserving his mother's sanity. He knew that if anything happened to him, she would go over the edge. He was all she had.

The highlight of Jack's army service came one evening when, while going through a chow line back behind the front lines, he saw a face that he knew he'd seen before.

"Franky," he shouted. "Is that you?" While they had last seen each other as boys, and this man was nearly six feet tall and at least 250 pounds, his flaming red hair, his freckles, and the slight droop of his bottom lip were unmistakable. And so that evening after dinner, Jack became reacquainted with Franky Parker from Marshall, Texas. Franky had been called up like so many other young men, but the Army had determined that he was too slow and clumsy to carry a rifle. So they put a ladle in his hand and stationed him in a field camp spooning out hot grub to soldiers coming off of patrol or from skirmishes on the front lines.

Jack and Franky's paths crossed several more times during the following months, and they swapped stories over games of cards played late into the night. Franky's parents had died in a highway accident several years after Jack had moved back to Dallas. As it turned out, he too moved to Dallas, where he got the rest of his schooling at a children's home. He was never adopted and when he came of age, he stayed on at the home to do maintenance and odd jobs around the property. Jack told Franky to look him up when he got out of the service.

After the war, Jack went back to Dallas and, with the help of the new GI Bill, finished up his business education. He was smart and sharp and was able to get on at a large downtown accounting firm. Within a year, he had saved enough money for a down payment on a little house in East Dallas, up the hill in the Lakewood district. The house had two bedrooms—one for himself and one for his mother.

While the big firm certainly had its financial rewards, Jack missed the personal contact he had with customers working at the men's store before the war. So after he had saved a nice little nest egg, he moved out on his own and opened a little bookkeeping practice on Live Oak. Having grown up in that neighborhood, Jack knew the shop owners and was able to secure enough clients to get started. It was tight at first, but somehow, every month he had enough money to pay the office rent and the home mortgage and buy some groceries. He even was able to hire Franky—who had taken him at his word and landed on his doorstep after getting out of the service—to deliver documents to clients around town.

By 1960 business was going well, and Jack, now thirty, began to think more about his personal life—often with the nudging of his mother, who kept reminding him of his "advancing age." He dated sporadically, mostly young women he met in the performance of bookkeeping, but nobody really caught his attention. That was the case until 1964, when Franky talked him into going to an eastside ballroom for a sponsored Christmas dance. Neither one of them had a date, and neither one of them would have gone on their own, but together, they worked up enough nerve to give it a try.

Jack and Franky didn't get fifteen feet inside the door of the ballroom when Jack noticed a cute brunette girl with a quizzical look on her face sitting all alone at a table in the corner. Something about her gripped his heart and would not let him go. With all the courage he could muster and a good push from Franky, he made a long walk around the perimeter of the room until he reached her table. With his hat in his hand, he asked if he could join her. She did not object, and small talk turned into deep thoughts, and by the end of the evening, they were inseparable. Some years later when reminiscing about that night, neither one could recall whether or not they ever set foot on the dance floor. There was no question, however, that they had fallen in love that night.

Claire Budrow and Jack were married in June at the First Baptist Church. Claire moved in with Jack and his mother, and soon after the wedding, she surprised Jack with news that she was expecting a child. Within nine months of their wedding day, they were hovering around a brand new baby girl. Caroline Dodger was the spitting image of her mother Claire and was Jack's pride and joy.

With the little house overflowing, Jack began to look for a larger home and eventually found one near White Rock Lake. Sadly, Margaret Dodger never made the move. They were all set to move in November in time for Thanksgiving, but she became ill. A bad cold progressed into pneumonia, and before the doctors could get her settled into the hospital for treatment, she died.

Margaret Dodger was the one person Jack had known all his life, and the loss hit him hard. But in time, the hurt began to heal, and the sorrow slowly turned to laughter, helped along in no little way by the experience of watching Caroline grow up right before his eyes. The late 1960s and '70s was a happy time in the Dodger household with Jack's business blooming, Claire pursuing a belated college degree, and Caroline excelling at everything she tried.

Jack's life, if drawn out on graph paper, looked like a succession of peaks and valleys. Just when it seemed like he was on a steady upward trend, something happened that would plunge him to the depths again. In early 1986 Claire developed a nagging cough, and what first was brushed aside as bronchitis turned out to be lung cancer. The diagnosis came too late, and not wanting to miss a moment with Claire, Jack closed his business and spent his days and nights feeding her, reading to her, talking to her, and making plans for a future that would never come. On Claire's last night, Jack climbed into bed with her and held her close until she slipped away.

Following the funeral, Caroline went back to school at the University of Texas, and Jack turned within himself, desolate and lonely, the light of his life extinguished. There were regular phone calls from Caroline, and Franky and other friends made sure Jack was not alone for any great length of time, but these kind gestures in no way filled the void left by Claire. Jack would disappear for hours at a time, sometimes strolling the shores of White Rock

Lake. Caroline came home in December for the holidays, but Christmas proved to be a joyless event.

At the first hint of spring, Franky pushed Jack into his car and drove him away to the Piney Woods of East Texas for a week of camping and fishing at the hole that Jack and his father had frequented. Jack seemed to wake up among the towering pines, and he and Franky talked and laughed about their boyhood days. By the end of the week, Jack felt strong enough to suggest that they circle back through Marshall, and they got a real kick out of visiting childhood sites and talking about old times.

As they drove back to Dallas, Franky made Jack a proposition. Knowing Jack was at his best when faced with a challenge, Franky decided to provide Jack with just that. He had noticed a little diner with a "For Sale" sign in the window, and he suggested to Jack that they buy the place.

Jack was skeptical at first. Aside from Franky's knack at turning raw meat into steaks and hamburgers, what did they know about running a diner? But as he settled back into life in Dallas, he began to mull the idea over. The accounting business kept him busy during the day, but evenings alone around the house were pure drudgery. So he consented to the idea, but only if Franky would agree to be the operating partner, leaving Jack to handle the bills, purchases, and other noncooking tasks.

And so began the first of several ventures into small business—little operations like the diner, a flower shop, a laundromat. Sometimes Jack would buy the business and let the original owners run it. And other times, he brought Franky or another partner in as a manager. Being an accountant had given him a front-row seat to the success and failure of other businesses, but unfortunately, it did not give him any special knowledge of the vagaries of customer interests. As a result, some of the businesses had marginal success while others were outright failures, including the diner, which closed in 1990.

In 1995, as Jack began to think about real retirement, one of his longtime bookkeeping clients died, and in his will, he left to Jack his only two possessions of any value: a little barbershop and his Labrador retriever named Blackie. Jack didn't know the slightest thing about cutting hair, and he wasn't about to go to barber college at age sixty-five, so he let Woody and Paul, two of the shop's longtime barbers, run the place while he kept an eye on the business from a distance. The little building had been paid for decades earlier, so the only expenses were paychecks, barber supplies, and property taxes.

In time, Jack began to spend more and more hours at the barbershop, drawn by the quiet atmosphere and the congenial conversation of the men who wandered in and out throughout the day—some to get a haircut, and some to just get a cup of coffee and catch up on the news of the day. And then on Friday nights, there were the card games: sometimes poker, sometimes bridge, sometimes gin. Jack had never joined in these types of activities when Claire was alive, but once the barbershop became his, he took a lively interest in the weekly ritual. After all, he had to keep an eye on Franky. There wasn't a lot Franky was good at, but there were two for which he had no equal: short-order cooking and cards. And it was cards that brought them together on Friday night, New Year's Eve, 1999.

CHAPTER 2

New Year's Eve, 1999, was just another Friday night at the barbershop. While fifty thousand people jammed into downtown Dallas to welcome the new millennium, and the rest of the city partied in hotel ballrooms, celebrated quietly at home, prayed at church, or hid in their back rooms awaiting an undefined cataclysm, five men in East Dallas cared about nothing more than who would win the next hand.

Oblivious to the hype surrounding the change of the calendar, or even the fact that it was Jack Dodger's seventieth birthday, Franky, Woody, Paul, Jack, and Judson, another neighborhood old-timer, sat around a table in the back corner of the barbershop. Blackie, who had been raised among the barber chairs, was stretched out in the jumble of legs and feet beneath the table, snoring loudly yet peacefully. The venetian blinds were pulled down and drawn shut in front of the plate glass window and door, and the front lights were out, giving the shop a look of complete desertion from the street.

Illuminated by the three coned fixtures from a beat-up pole lamp, Franky dealt cards around the table while the others moaned and groaned as they picked up the cards that slid in front of them.

"Come on now, Franky, is this the best you can do tonight?" said Woody in mock disgust.

"Yeah, Franky," echoed Paul. "After all, the world may end in another fifteen minutes. Can't you deal me a winning hand tonight? Just one? So I can leave this life with a smile on my face?"

Judson was silent as always, while Jack just sighed. He knew from past Friday nights that those griping the loudest were the ones to be wary of when it came time to bet. Judson was always a wild card and had the best poker face in the room, and Franky was just plain wild.

"Okay, boys, let's see who has what," declared Franky, who reached into his pile of chips and tossed five into the middle of the table. Jack, Paul, and Judson followed his lead, while Woody bailed out.

Jack held up two fingers indicating he needed two fresh cards. Franky stood firm, while Paul asked for two, and Judson for three. Franky obliged them, and then a moan drifted around the table again as they eyed their updated hands.

"I'm out," said Jack, tossing his cards back toward Franky.

"Me too," said Paul.

That left just Franky and Judson. Franky tossed in a couple more chips, Judson called him, and Franky crowed as he displayed three tens and a pair of queens.

"Pshaw," scoffed Judson, and slid his cards across the table so they'd get mixed with the others without being viewed. "What's the point? What's the point?"

"The point, my friend, is winning." Franky laughed, dragging the chips from the middle of the table and stacking them neatly to his side.

The others resumed their gripe fest about Franky's dealing as he gathered up the cards. But it was really all in fun, as the stakes were low: the winner at the end of the night got a free lunch paid by the losers the following Wednesday.

Franky gathered the cards and began shuffling them when Blackie suddenly awakened and growled. Nobody noticed, except for Jack, whose feet had been cradling Blackie's head.

"Must be a rat or a raccoon out in the alley," he said to the others, who nodded but were paying more attention to Franky, making sure he shuffled well before dealing the next hand.

"The only rat I see is dealing the cards," said Paul.

Franky's honesty became a moot point when Blackie suddenly jumped up, tilting the table and causing Franky to sputter cards all over the place.

"What's the matter girl?" asked Jack, as Blackie's large bulk emerged from under the table. Jack's question was answered by the sound of breaking glass in the back storeroom, which had a door and a window to the back alley. The breaking glass was followed by the sound of heavy thuds and low shuffling.

"Somebody's breaking in," Jack whispered, by this time getting everyone's attention and making a gesture indicating that all should be quiet. "Let's all move to the corner," he said. As Blackie's growls became edgier, Jack pulled Woody and Paul by the shirtsleeves toward him and away from the door. Judson followed, but not Franky. He was emotional and impulsive and did not have a full sense of the danger that might be upon him.

Just then, the door from the storeroom swung open and a man in his midtwenties came through. Franky, who at sixty-nine was still as stout and strong as he had been thirty years earlier, lunged forward and picked up the man in a massive bear hug, pinning his arms to his sides and constricting his chest and the blood flow to his head. Not knowing that the intruder had passed out almost immediately, Franky spun him around in circles, which caused the man's legs to extend outward. As Franky made wild, awkward circles around the room, the man's feet hit one barber chair after another, sending each one spinning. And then his feet hit everything else in the shop—shelves of hair tonic, vats of blue Barbecide, trays of combs and brushes, boxes of tissue. All the while, Blackie barked and nipped at the man's heels each time they passed overhead. Above the din, shockwaves from the fireworks show downtown rumbled up the street to the shop and rattled the metal blinds.

Just when it seemed like Franky might spin the man till dawn, he slipped on a puddle of Barbecide and stumbled, causing his victim to kick a big bottle of talcum powder off a shelf. The bottle hit the ceiling, the top popped off, and white powder snowed down on the entire scene. Blackie yelped, and Franky, blinded by the talc, let go of his prey, who fell unconscious at his feet.

"That'll show him." Franky gasped and bent over to catch his breath, clear his eyes and get a good look at the man. The others remained huddled in the corner, with only Jack stepping forward to give Franky a hand.

"Well done," he whispered, putting a hand on Franky's shoulder, "but I don't think—"

Before Jack could finish his sentence, a second man burst into the room, this one no older than the first but armed with a small caliber handgun, which he pointed directly at Jack and Franky.

"Don't move," he shouted, with more panic than authority in his voice. The room became silent for a moment, and even Blackie quit barking. Then, the silence was broken by a talc-induced cough coming from one of the men huddled in the corner, which excited the intruder all over again.

"All of you, all of you, get on the floor now!" The five men followed his orders as quickly as their old knees would allow. Blackie sat too at Jack's command. "Okay, who's got the money? Where's the cash register? Now—where is it?"

Jack raised his hand and pointed to the cash register on the counter near the door. It was old and solid and was one of the few things in the shop that had survived Franky's heroics. Jack made a key-turning gesture, indicating that he could open it.

"Good." The man motioned for Jack to get up and go to the cash register.

Jack fumbled in his pocket for the key as he maneuvered through the scattered debris. He opened the cash drawer, and then stepped back.

"We really don't have much here," Jack said in a calm, apologetic voice. "We went to the bank this afternoon before we closed for the holiday."

"Shut up." The man pocketed what little there was, eyed the card table with the chips scattered on it, and went over to look for more cash.

"Sorry, but we don't play for money," said Jack. The man leaned over to verify that point, when Franky, covered in white talc from the shoulders up, got the urge to make another move. But he was stopped in his tracks as the man whipped up his gun and pointed it directly at Franky's gut.

"Okay, we don't want to get in your way." Jack slid between the man and Franky and backed Franky into the corner with the others. "We don't want any trouble. We'll just wait here, and you can be on your way."

Still pointing his gun, the man froze for a moment. He looked at his accomplice passed out on the floor and then at Jack. He pulled Jack by the arm and drew him to his side. "I need you to come with me, old man."

"Sure, whatever you say. You fellows don't wait up for me," Jack said to his friends, who stared back in shock. He gave Franky a wink and then walked out the back door with the gun-wielding intruder following him closely. The others heard a vehicle start up—they recognized it as Jack's Ford pickup—and roll away slowly down the gravel alley.

With the gunman gone, the others moved out of the corner.

"If that don't beat heck," said Woody, scratching his head. "Been here forty-five years and never been robbed. Must be that millennium bug or whatever nonsense. All the crazies are out tonight."

"So, Franky, what'a you suppose we oughta do with this one?" Paul asked, standing over the other intruder who was still in a lump on the floor.

"I'll tie him up while you get on the phone to the police. Gotta tell 'em Jack is missing."

Franky looked around for something to tie up the man and finally settled on an electric trimmer with a twelve-foot cord. He used the trimmer to make a knot around the man's neck and then used the remainder of the cord to bind up his wrists and ankles. "That oughta hold him for now."

"Wait a minute, wait just a doggone minute." Woody's face was red. "This feller wrecked our evening, wrecked our store. Heck, he even made us miss the fireworks. I'm gonna give him something to think about." With that, he plugged in another trimmer, and lifting the man's chin, he cut a big wide furrow down the middle of his head. "A little reminder of your visit to the barbershop."

It was two in the morning before the police had taken a statement from everyone, cuffed, and removed the abandoned intruder, dusted the back door and cash register for fingerprints from the other man, and checked the alley for evidence.

"Why don't you fellows go on home and get some rest?" said the investigating officer. "We've alerted other departments and the highway patrol about Mr. Dodger, and we'll call you as soon as we know something."

At four thirty, Jack Dodger's dark blue pickup rolled up to the curb in front of police headquarters downtown. He was driving. His assailant sat in the passenger seat.

Jack climbed out first and walked around and opened the door for the other man, who climbed out slowly and somewhat cautiously compared to his earlier bravado.

"Are you sure about this?" he asked Jack, a puzzling question coming from someone who had been in control earlier.

"You're just gonna have to trust me," said Jack, putting his hand on the man's shoulder and turning him toward the door. "It's not gonna be easy, but you're doing the right thing."

They walked side-by-side up the dozen steps and through the front door, where Jack introduced himself to the desk sergeant. "I believe you may have been looking for us. My name is Jack Dodger, and this young man here has decided he would like to clear up some business with you."

The man was escorted down a hallway for questioning. Jack was led down another hallway to an office, where he was given a cup of coffee, asked if he needed to see a doctor—he assured them he did not—and then was asked to give a statement detailing the previous four and a half hours.

That business was wrapped up by five thirty, and before heading home, Jack called Franky and then his daughter, Caroline. After Jack calmed Caroline's fears, and after she offered him a "Happy Birthday" and a kiss over the phone lines, he drove home to East Dallas.

The first day of the new millennium dawned as Jack pulled into his driveway. He stopped on the sidewalk, picked up the newspaper, and carried it inside where he was met by an excited Blackie. Again, Franky had taken care of everything, this time making sure Blackie got home. Jack was glad to see her, although he laughed when he noticed she still had a light dusting of talc on her short, black coat.

"Hey, good girl, did ya miss me?" He bent down to pet her as he carried the paper to the kitchen table. "If you don't mind, I'm gonna lay down for a few minutes. We'll take a walk later."

Jack plopped on the couch with a sigh, pulled his shoes off and then pulled his feet up and stretched out. Blackie sat on the floor next to him, blowing her warm breath on his face as he drifted off.

CHAPTER 3

The sheaf of paper was twice as thick as usual for a Saturday morning as Billy Briar walked up to the desk at the police station to sift through the photocopied incident reports from the previous night. It was a rookie job for a rookie reporter at the *Dallas Times*, but one that Billy approached with more zest than most. While his primary mission was to fill the paper's daily "Police Blotter" column, he always kept his eyes open for something with human interest potential—something that could be developed into a longer piece, perhaps even for the front page.

"Must've been quite a night," he said to the officer on duty as he picked up the stack of reports and carried them over to the table against the wall set up for reporters.

"Yep, wasn't quite the end of the world, but a few folks had a pretty bad time of it anyway," said the officer.

"Anything unusual?" Billy asked.

"No, mostly run-of-the-mill stuff—drunks, fights, accidents—just more of it since it was New Year's Eve. Had a couple of socialites who got in a catfight during the blowout at the Hanover Hotel. I heard furs and diamonds and purses went flying everywhere."

"Anybody important?"

"Nobody I've ever heard of. Might be the daughters of someone important. Beats me. It's all in that stack there."

Billy started leafing through the reports at rapid-fire speed. In his six months on the job, he had learned how to recognize at a glance incident codes and other jargon used by the arresting officers to describe an event. That way, he could breeze past those that were meaningless—traffic incidents, noise complaints, domestic squabbles—unless they were accompanied by a lot of text.

It was just such a combination of details that caused him to pause at a report that was coded for armed robbery and had a large block of text that covered the lower half of the page and continued down the back side. The narrative described a late-night armed robbery involving two men, one of which was disarmed at the scene and, curiously, was handed over to the police with a partially shaved head. Even more curious was the fact that the second man turned himself in at dawn, accompanied by one of the men he had apparently robbed. The report indicated that additional charges of kidnapping were pending further interviews with one of the victims, a John "Jack" H. Dodger Jr.

"Hey, Captain, what do you know about this one?" Billy asked, carrying the report over to the officer.

"Oh yeah, that was a strange one. Bunch of old-timers playing cards in the back of a barbershop had their game broken up by some part-time thugs. They subdued one of the intruders and apparently helped turn the other one in. The odd thing, though, is that there's a big gap in time between the incident and the return of the second man to the station. And this Dodger fellow here—they say he shook hands with the guy before he was carried down for booking, like they were pals."

"Hmmm ..." Billy scratched his head and returned to the table. He continued through the reports, made some notes for the "Blotter," and made a copy of the holdup-kidnap report.

"I'm gonna check this one out," he called over to the captain as he put the original back in the stack and headed for the door. "See you later."

"Good luck," said the officer.

Billy left the police station and drove east out of downtown toward Lakewood. At the succession of stoplights on Live Oak, he flipped through the pages of a city map book until he found the address and its grid location. With that information, he made a series of quick turns until he found himself on a street lined with stone-and-brick bungalows built in the 1920s. He came to the house matching the address on the police report, pulled toward the curb, and shut off his engine.

Inside, Jack Dodger snored peacefully on the couch with Blackie stretched out near him on the hardwood floor. Her ears perked up at the sound of footsteps on the porch, and the sound of the doorbell was followed by one sharp bark as she rose to her feet.

"Okay, okay, girl," said Jack, getting up groggily. "Let's go see." A glance at the clock in the living room let him know it was ten.

Jack paused to look through the little window on the door at the young man standing outside and then turned the deadbolt and opened the door.

"Yes? What can we do for you?" he asked, suppressing a yawn with his hand.

"Mr. Dodger?"

"Yes, I'm Jack Dodger."

"Mr. Dodger, I'm Billy Briar from the *Dallas Times*. I was wondering if you had a few minutes to talk about last night? You know, what happened at the barbershop?"

"Oh, how'd you find out about—"

"I'm the police reporter at the paper. I read the incident report downtown at the station. I just have a couple of questions."

"Well, I don't think there's much to tell, but sure, come on in if you'd like." Jack opened the door wide and gestured Billy in past him into the living room. "Me and Blackie were just taking a nap when you—have a seat there. You take coffee?"

"Sure, that'd be nice."

"Then, why don't you come on into the kitchen, and we can talk in there."

Billy followed Jack into the kitchen and sat at the small table. Jack set up the coffee pot and then sat down across from Billy at the table. Blackie lay in the middle of the floor, eyeballing the stranger.

"Long night, huh?" Billy said, seeing the fatigue in Jack's eyes. "That's what I wanted to ask you about. I was wondering if you could tell me what happened between the time you left the barbershop and the time you and the assailant, Mr. Walker, arrived at the police station?"

"Oh, that. Well, we got into my truck. He had me drive, and we headed east on Interstate 20."

"Did he ask you to take him anywhere in particular?"

"Well, not exactly. He really just wanted to get out of town. He seemed confused and upset and not really sure what he was doing."

"Were you scared? Did you think he might harm you?"

"No, I wasn't really scared. From the time he came into the shop, he just didn't seem like the type that would hurt anybody."

"Oh really." Billy scribbled in his notebook. "So where did you drive, and what did you do?"

"Oh, we just drove in silence for a while. I could hear him breathing hard, and his leg was shaking nervously, vibrating the whole front seat. I don't know who started it, but we just got to talking."

"About what?"

"Oh, just piddly things at first. And then I told him how it had been a long time since I'd driven east on that highway, out to the Piney Woods, and how there were a lot of things I hadn't done in a long time, like fishing. Turns out he used to like to fish too, but he'd been all bogged down with work and his family, which got us around to his situation."

Jack got up, walked to the counter, and poured two cups of coffee.

"And what was that—his situation?" Billy asked.

"Can't tell you that," said Jack, returning to the table and sliding a mug toward Billy.

Billy sat up straight, puzzled. "Why not?"

"Well, I made him a promise that I wouldn't discuss his situation with anyone."

"Oh really? And why not?"

"Well, we made a deal. My confidence for his going back to town and setting things right."

"But you told the police, right?"

"Nope. Didn't tell them nothing either. When they asked, I told them that all they need to know is that the boy made a mistake and that he knows he made a mistake and that he's ready to make it right. What got him to that point is really none of their business. What is their business is that he made a mistake, and now, he's ready to pay the consequences."

"Do you think they should let him walk based on extenuating circumstances—his 'situation,' as you call it?"

"No, not at all. He broke a window and scared a bunch of old men and Blackie here half to death and took our money and near 'bout drove me all the way to Louisiana, a trip that I didn't want to take last night. There's plenty of wrong in that string of events, and he'll have to pay whatever the courts require of him, but at the same time, he kept his word to me that he would take me home and turn himself in. And there's plenty of good in that, so I am going to keep my word to him."

Billy put down his pad and pen, picked up the cup of coffee, and took a long sip. He thought about it: such calm, self-assured talk out of an older man who just hours earlier had been in certain danger.

"Mr. Dodger, a few moments ago, you said that Mr. Walker didn't seem like the type who would harm someone. What made you so sure?"

"It just looked to me like it was amateur hour from the start. If those two had checked things out, they'd know that we play cards there every Friday night. Everybody in the neighborhood knows that. And they'd know we play without cash. And then there's the way they acted. The first fellow just stumbled in, and he wasn't armed. And when Mr. Walker came in, he had a gun but he wasn't in any position to use it. Never was."

"What do you mean?"

"Something I noticed back in the war in Korea. When you were in real danger, and you expected to fire your rifle, you'd keep your finger resting just so on the trigger. In fact, I built up a callous on my finger from rubbing it inside the trigger guard. But Mr. Walker, he held his gun loosely in his hand, and never once did I see his finger near the trigger. It was always wrapped around the grip. Seemed to me like he had no intention of ever using that gun. Probably wasn't even his."

"So you just trusted your instincts?"

"Not just mine, but his too. I trusted that his instinct wasn't about violence."

"So if you felt that way, why didn't you just try to talk to him there in the barbershop instead of out on the road?"

"Well, I thought I knew what Mr. Walker was about, and I certainly knew what I was about. But I had no idea what Franky and the other fellers might do, especially after what Franky did to that other man."

"No kidding," said Billy, "or what they all did to him after you left."

They both laughed.

"That's right, they told me about it down at the station," said Jack. "But seriously, with the one man down, I thought the other fellers would be in good shape if I got the boy out of the shop."

Billy took another sip of coffee and stood up. "Well, Mr. Dodger, that's some story. I appreciate your time and your candor. I'd like to check back with you later as the case proceeds."

"That'll be fine. But I don't think there'll be much of a case. I believe Mr. Walker will keep his word and take his medicine. Don't think there'll be need for a trial."

"Well, we'll have to wait and see." Billy's voice revealed a skepticism that came from months of following criminal cases through the courthouse. They shook hands, and Jack led Billy back to the front porch. He watched as the young man bounded down the sidewalk, climbed in his car, and drove away.

Still tired but too awake to go back to sleep, Jack showered, shaved, and got himself together. He called down to the barbershop where Woody and Paul were cleaning up in front of a crowd of the curious who had gathered to get a firsthand look at the crime scene. Word spread fast through the neighborhood, and Woody and Paul were more than eager to retell the story of how they had subdued a "gang" of armed bandits. Franky was due at the shop any moment, and no doubt, his agility and strength in subduing the first man would become more legendary with every telling.

"Why don't you come on down, Jack," said Woody. "The folks would love to hear your part of the story. Come to think of it, what is your part of the story? Where'd you go last night?"

"Never mind that," said Jack. "You just get things back together for business on Monday. Meanwhile, I think I'll stay home and rest." He was about to hang up when he added, "By the way, I suspect a young reporter from the *Times* will probably stop by pretty soon."

Jack wasn't one for the spotlight, and he didn't want to be a part of any circus at the barbershop, so he stayed home for most of the day. He watched part of the Cotton Bowl football game, and with the weather unusually mild, he drove Blackie over to White Rock Lake for a late-afternoon swim. Jack went to bed at ten, which was early for him, but he still had a lot of catching up to do.

As the clock struck midnight in Jack's living room, the weekend editor at the *Dallas Times* raced to finish the front page of the Sunday paper. He still had a large hole to fill, and after scanning the story queue on his computer screen, he plucked a story and a photo out of the inside of the metropolitan section and flowed it into the front page. With his mind racing and his fingers flying across the keyboard, he nudged words and phrases around until they formed a smarmy play on words: "Bandits Choraled by Barbershop Quintet."

CHAPTER 4

Jack Dodger was not a morning person, so it was not unusual that on that Sunday morning after the commotion at the barbershop, he didn't retrieve the newspaper from the front sidewalk until nine. And even then, he didn't dump it out of its plastic bag and begin perusing it. Instead, he put it on the kitchen table and tended to more important things: making a pot of coffee; throwing together a light breakfast of crisp bacon, scrambled eggs, and dark toast; and pouring some dog food into Blackie's bowl.

Jack was an old hand around the kitchen. When his father died, his mother depended on him to do his part around the house, and he learned early how to handle a skillet, a steam iron, and other household tools. And when he married, there was no "woman's work" or "man's work" in the Dodger home; there was just "work," and he and Claire went about it as a team. When Claire died, Jack did not have to spend time as most widowers do trying to figure out where things are or how to do things, especially not in the kitchen.

So it was that Jack prepared breakfast, just the way he liked it, and sat down to enjoy it. As he chewed and sipped and gazed out the kitchen window at what was shaping up to be a bright, sunny Sunday, he began to formulate a checklist in his mind of errands and chores to take care of during the day. He'd lined up a half-dozen items when his planning was interrupted by the telephone ringing. He tossed a scrap of bacon into Blackie's bowl and reached over to pull the phone off the kitchen counter.

"Daddy, you're in the paper!" Caroline shrieked at the other end of the line, not waiting for her father to identify himself.

"Huh … what … Caroline?" Jack stammered, startled by his daughter's excited outburst.

"You're in the paper. Your story's in this morning's paper!"

"What? In Austin? I don't understand."

Caroline tried to catch her breath. "There's an AP wire story in the Austin paper this morning about you and Uncle Franky and what happened Friday night. They must have picked it up from the *Times*. Haven't you looked at the paper this morning?"

"Well, no … wait just a minute." Jack set the phone down and dumped the paper out on the table. As he stared at the front page, he reached back and picked up the phone.

"Oh … my," he said. "Caroline, they've got it on the front page. That young man from the newspaper stopped by here yesterday morning." Jack took a long pause to bend over and read the first few sentences and look at a picture of the barbershop with Franky and the others mugging out front. "And they obviously sent their photographer to the shop." He took another long pause to read more. "I just didn't know it was going to be on the front page."

"Well that's exactly where it should be, Daddy. I'm so proud of you—for how you stood up and handled things, and especially how you treated that young man, Kevin Walker."

Caroline's voice faded into the background for a moment as Jack took in a few more sentences of the article. His attention returned to the telephone when he heard talking in the background at the other end of the line.

"Just a minute, Daddy, somebody here wants to talk to you."

There was a pause followed by the unpunctuated bundle of chatter that was Wendy, Caroline's six-year-old daughter. "Grandpa Jack, Mommy showed me in the paper and she read it and how you and Uncle Franky fought the bad men and how you won and everything's great and I love you and miss you so much."

"Well, hello there, Little Blossom," said Jack, setting the paper aside and giving his full attention to his only grandchild. "I love you and miss you too. When you gonna come visit?"

"Mommy says we might come in a week. Here she is now." And with that the phone was handed back to Caroline.

"Did you get all that?" asked Caroline. "We might try to come up later in the month, if Don can break away." Caroline had met Don Stone at the University of Texas, and they married soon after he graduated from law school. He now was a legislative aid in the state capitol. "Well, we better go or we'll be late for church. I love you, Daddy, and I'm so proud of you."

"Thank you, sweetheart. See you soon," Jack replied and gently hung up the phone.

Still stunned by the fact that he was on the front page of the *Dallas Times*—and in no telling how many other papers—Jack sat back down at the table and rubbed his forehead as he read the article from start to finish. He was generally pleased with the reporting by Billy Briar, but he was embarrassed by the attention that a front-page story would bring. He wasn't looking forward to going back down to the barbershop on Monday morning, or anywhere else in the neighborhood for that matter.

Jack cleaned up the dishes and then puttered around the house, working on his list of chores. By early afternoon, he had managed to not think about the whole affair for several hours when a new source of worry knocked on his door. This time, it was one of the local television stations; before he had time to object, the cameras were rolling, and he was being taped.

Before the end of the day, two more TV stations made the pilgrimage to Jack's front porch, and Jack accommodated their questions, all except for their inquiries about his relationship with Kevin Walker. As he did with Billy Briar, his answer was firm and to the point: "Can't talk about that."

That night, all three stations broadcast the story. Jack winced as he scanned the channels with his remote control.

After that, the floodgates just seemed to open wide, and for the next two weeks, Jack and his friends were the subject of countless interviews and articles locally and around the state. A Dallas radio talk show host dubbed them the "Dodger Gang," and Franky, Woody, Paul, and Judson enjoyed playing the part. As for Jack, he tried to duck the spotlight the best he could, but his reserved, unassuming manner endeared him to a growing audience.

In mid-January, Jack was asked to tell his story to the local Rotary Club. He obliged their request, although he was visibly uncomfortable standing before a microphone. With the weight of everyone's eyes on him, he found himself fighting a slight stutter that he had not experienced since the first time he had to recite a poem as the new boy at the little school in Marshall.

At the end of his talk, there was a brief question-and-answer session, and Jack loosened up in this less formal format. One of the younger Rotarians stood up and asked, "What do you think this incident says about the state of our society, and of people in general?"

Jack was surprised by the weight of the question, and he swallowed hard to keep from offending the man with a loud burst of laughter. "I doubt seriously that this says anything about our society," he answered. "I think the only thing it says is that a bunch of old men might better look for a safer location to play cards."

A chuckle drifted through the audience until Jack spoke again, this time more seriously. "I don't know, maybe it says that some of these young folks might want to think twice. Just 'cause we've got gray hair and round bellies, that doesn't mean we can just be pushed around." Jack closed with that comment and thanked them for their kind reception.

The Rotary talk led to invitations to visit other community groups, and Jack was shadowed everywhere he went by Billy Briar, whose newspaper reports played a major role in Jack's growing popularity. Someone would read Jack's latest words of wisdom in the morning paper, and by that afternoon, they were on the phone inviting Jack to speak at their next meeting. As often as he could, Jack would invite Franky to come along with him to provide moral support and to deflect some of the attention. On a few occasions, the entire "Dodger Gang" was invited to attend a luncheon or dinner. But in the end, it was always Jack who they wanted to hear.

Through repetition, Jack's story about how they subdued their intruders evolved into something entirely different. It wasn't planned; it wasn't something that he practiced. It wasn't even something that he noticed. It just happened, as if that wild night at the barbershop dredged forth feelings and emotions that had long been suppressed—fear, danger, struggle, action, friendship, trust, faith—and he found himself speaking with passion for the first time in years.

"In the end, we have to trust that the other person is going to do what's right. I believe our neighborhoods and communities are eaten up with distrust—folks avoiding each other and harboring suspicions based on nothing more than a lack of information. And while I believe that trust must be earned, it's not right to make someone a slave to the process. You have to unlock the shackles, step back, and give them enough room to prove themselves trustworthy."

Soon Jack's words began to creep into Sunday sermons and Monday school lessons. In early February, when the president made a fundraising stop in Dallas, his advance team read about Jack in the paper and made sure that the president cited him as an example of courage and resourcefulness.

Jack's words even penetrated the concrete walls of the Dallas County Jail, where Kevin Walker awaited his sentence for the barbershop affair. While other inmates may not have been listening, Walker quietly absorbed every word from his unusual, unexpected mentor, and he committed himself to becoming worthy of trust, not just Jack's trust, but his family's and his friends' trust.

As Kevin kept in touch with Jack through the daily paper and TV reports, Jack likewise followed Kevin's movement through the court system, which Billy Briar covered with equal tenacity. As Jack had predicted, Kevin did not fight the charges, he pled guilty and threw himself on the mercy of the court. While the prosecutor recommended that Kevin serve time in jail for commission of a crime with a firearm, his otherwise clean record led the judge to sentence him to two years probation and one hundred hours of community service. However, he did issue a stern warning for Kevin to never set foot in the courthouse again, with the exception of serving on a jury.

The story was different for his accomplice, who had prior arrests and was wanted in connection with a series of similar burglaries of businesses in East Dallas. Billy's investigative reporting revealed that Kevin needed money and had met the man just two days earlier, when he was recommended by a third party as someone who could "get things done." As it turned out, the man did not live up to his resume. He missed by one back-alley window the computer services company that had been his intended target.

In mid-February, Jack was invited to speak at the winter banquet of the Dallas Chapter of the Golden Eagles senior citizens organization. Jack's speech was met with appreciative applause, and he found himself surrounded afterward by individuals who thanked him for his words of encouragement.

"You're a credit to our generation. We seniors are well represented by a man of your character," said one woman.

"Well, I'm afraid some folks think me and the other fellers are just a bunch of 'characters,'" said Jack. "I may be doing more harm than good."

"No, not at all. You keep it up. We're counting on you." She reached out and patted his arm.

As the last of the well wishers thanked Jack and made their way through the sea of tables to the door, Jack was approached by Wilton Harris, a short, distinguished man with a name tag that identified him as secretary of the Dallas Golden Eagles.

"Mr. Dodger, I was wondering if we could talk a moment." He gestured toward the nearest table. Jack nodded and they sat down. He didn't know what this man wanted, but he appreciated the invitation to get off his feet for the first time in forty-five minutes.

"Mr. Dodger, I'm an officer here with the local Golden Eagles, but I also sit on the board of the national organization. We're having our convention later this month in Kansas City, and I was wondering if you would consider coming as our guest and addressing the convention?"

Jack sat silently for a moment and stared at his crossed fingers on the table. He was excited and terrified, and the two emotions fought for control of his tongue. The result was an awkward stammering confusion of words that betrayed the eloquence and ease that he had displayed earlier in the evening.

"Well now … I … I don't know about … this is all rather … I'm not sure I … this is all very … are you sure you think … good gosh …" He would have continued but Wilton rescued him.

"Mr. Dodger, I know it's a big question. Why don't you think about it? I'll call you in a few days and give you the particulars. We'll pay for your trip, of course. Bring one of your friends along for support if you like." Wilton stood up and offered Jack his hand. "You've got something to say that I think needs to be heard."

Wilton left Jack to ponder the proposition. He stared blankly at the white tablecloth for a moment and then was roused by the sounds of rattling dishes and slamming tables. He looked at his watch and was surprised to find that it was ten thirty.

Jack pushed back from the table and as he began the long walk across the banquet hall, he spotted Billy Briar sitting in a chair against the wall. Billy rose to his feet and met Jack at the double doors to the hallway.

"That was some talk you gave tonight, Mr. Dodger," Billy said.

"Don't they let you cover anything besides me?" The annoyance in Jack's voice was evident to Billy, who had no way of knowing that Jack was more troubled by the decision Wilton had dangled in front of him than he was about the prospect of another article in the newspaper. In reality, Jack was comforted in a way by Billy's presence. Billy had become a kind, friendly face among a sea of strangers that he was encountering more and more frequently.

"I'm sorry, I hope I'm not intruding. I've kinda made you a special project," said Billy.

"I see, a special project," said Jack. They walked side-by-side in silence through the hotel lobby and out to the valet parking stand.

"Tell me, Mr. Briar, you seem to have a good sense of what is newsworthy and worth telling—these folks want me to come talk to their national convention. I'm flattered, but I'm not sure I understand why folks are making such a big deal about this. I'm wondering if I should just kind of fade back into East Dallas where I came from."

"Well, Mr. Dodger, I think you've reminded them of who they are, who they can be. You've broken down the stereotype of the old—how should I say it … the senior citizen who sits at home behind burglar bars watching TV and waiting for the postman to deliver their social security check."

"Hmm," Jack mumbled. "That's interesting. I suppose there are folks who live like that. Well, here's my truck. You gonna report about tonight, too?"

"Umm … yes, sir," answered Billy. Jack tipped the driver, gave Billy a tap on the shoulder, climbed into his truck, and drove off into the night.

Billy walked down the street to where his car waited at a curbside meter. He could see from twenty yards away that the meter had expired, and he hissed when he leaned forward and saw the ticket waving in the breeze under his windshield wiper. "Violation," he read aloud as he stuffed the ticket into his shirt pocket and fell into the front seat.

As Billy began the short drive across downtown to the newspaper office, he repeated that word *violation* again, but in a new context: was he making too much of this Jack Dodger business? Was he out of line to follow Jack around town? Had Jack's privacy been violated by all the attention and publicity the newspaper coverage generated?

Those questions would not be answered tonight. Billy ran upstairs to the newsroom and headed to his desk. "I need sixteen inches, and you've got thirty-five minutes," the night city editor shouted from across the room. Billy nodded and got down to business.

❦

Wilton Harris kept his promise and called Jack the following Tuesday morning. "I've talked to the rest of the board and they all are eager to have you address the convention. In fact, they're quite insistent. You're not going to disappoint us now, are you, Mr. Dodger?"

Jack had really known what his answer would be when the question was first posed at the Dallas banquet. The growing momentum of the whole affair dictated that he indeed should go to Kansas City.

"What day do you want me there?" he asked.

CHAPTER 5

Chilly air and threatening rainclouds greeted Jack and Franky as they climbed out of a taxi in front of the Kansas City Convention Center on the leap year morning of February 29. Jack was uneasy and nervous, and it had nothing to do with the weather or the extra day on the calendar. Franky, on the other hand, was just along for the ride, and he was animated as usual.

As the two men made their way up the sidewalk, they fell into line behind what to Jack looked like thousands of people filing into the convention center. A gusty breeze from the south pulled and slapped at a large banner draped above the entrance that announced, "Kansas City Welcomes Golden Eagles 2000."

The Golden Eagles were an up-and-coming organization of people who were retired but who were not content to sit on the sidelines of life. Born in the American Corn Belt as a small-town volunteer league providing support to seniors in need who had no local family, the organization spread to other regions and crossed all economic and ethnic lines. The only firm rule was that members had to be at least sixty-five years old.

As with any expanding movement, the Golden Eagles were going through growing pains. Specifically, there was mounting pressure from within for the Eagles to begin flexing some political muscle. Indeed, some local chapters had openly taken sides in local elections, and in a few cases, they had run some members as candidates under the Golden Eagles banner. Wilton Harris, who had invited Jack to speak to the convention, was among those who believed it was time to expand the mission of the Eagles to include political activity, and not just at the local level. What was lacking was a charismatic leader for the organization to rally around. The Eagles' officers, for all their hard work and dedication, lacked the kind of magnetic personality it usually takes to steer a large diverse group in a new direction. Jack Dodger, on the other hand, had a quiet charm that Wilton had witnessed move several hundred people in Dallas. He now wanted to test that magic before thousands of people in Kansas City.

Jack and Franky walked to a registration desk from where they were escorted to a visitors' lounge and were met by Wilton. He in turn led them to a meeting room that had been set up for use by the Eagles' board of directors. Inside, they found a handful of people huddled in discussion at one end of the table. Wilton made the introductions.

"Jack Dodger, Franky Parker, this is Bob Reynolds, our treasurer; Elizabeth Bell, our vice president; and Hank Simmons, our president." The five of them then proceeded with the obligatory, octopus-like handshake routine with knuckles bumping and hands missing until everyone had been properly acknowledged.

Everyone stared awkwardly at one another until Hank Simmons took charge.

"Mr. Dodger, we're so pleased to have you with us. We've all been following your story in the newspapers and on TV, and we can't wait to hear what you have to say. We Golden Eagles like to think of ourselves as people of action, and so you're going to fit right in. We've got a lot of newcomers at this year's convention, and so I think you'll add to their motivation to get involved."

"Well, Franky and I appreciate the invitation." Jack cleared his throat. "Maybe we can say something that'll be of worth." Jack then sought an answer to a question that had been bothering him since they first saw the crowd outside. "So how many people are you expecting?"

Treasurer Reynolds piped in with the details. "At last count we had four thousand registered, but we expect that to swell to about five thousand by this afternoon for your keynote address."

Jack stood silently, shaping words that never got past his lips. The size of the crowd had tied his tongue, but that word *keynote* puckered his mouth like a sour lemon. All he could do was look into the eyes of one person after another, eventually coming around to Franky, who was grinning from ear to ear. "That's a lot of folks," said Franky.

Hank continued. "Now I don't know if Wilton told you, but you are helping us fill a large hole in our program. We invited what we thought were going to be the two presidential candidates to come and provide keynote addresses, but as you know, there are still four candidates fighting it out. And with primaries today and Super Tuesday coming next week, none of them felt they could afford to spend part of a day with us. Seems shortsighted to me, since they're going to need our vote. But anyway, that's how you've come to be our main event this afternoon."

Jack looked at Wilton, who in fact hadn't explained the agenda at all, and who shrugged back at Jack in make-believe innocence.

Jack regained his composure and squeezed out an uncertain promise: "We'll do the best we can."

"You'll do just fine," said Hank. "Now why don't you just take it easy. You can relax in here. You can look around the exhibit hall a bit or walk across the street and check in at the hotel. We'll need you on the platform at three o'clock."

"Thanks," said Jack. "I think we'll go on over to the hotel. I'd like to get my thoughts together."

There was another round of handshakes, and then Wilton escorted Jack and Franky back out of the room.

"I'm so glad you could come," said Wilton out in the hallway, hoping to ease Jack's fears. "Don't you worry about a thing, you're gonna do fine. Now why don't you go and relax, and we'll see you back here around three."

Jack and Franky, each carrying a small overnight bag, crossed the street to the hotel and checked into adjacent rooms. Franky stretched out on the bed in his room and clicked through the cable television offerings, which were a novelty compared to what he pulled out of the sky at home with his rooftop antenna. Next door, Jack also lay back on his bed, but he was not interested in seeing what was on the tube. Instead, he closed his eyes and started whispering softly through some thoughts and ideas. His mind kept circling back to the potential size of the audience, and he found himself whispering a soft, simple prayer: "God help me."

Jack and Franky had a light lunch in the hotel coffee shop and then spent an hour walking around the exhibit hall. Various Eagles chapters had booths displaying some of their activities over the past year, and vendors exhibited items and products of special interest to seniors. Jack and Franky eventually came upon the Dallas Chapter's booth where they were reacquainted with people they had met in Dallas.

The sight of a few familiar faces eased Jack's nervousness a bit, and he was thankful for the send-off they gave him as he departed for the stage. "Can't wait to hear you this afternoon," they said in unison.

Jack and Franky met Wilton at the side door to the stage, and they were led to their seats, with Jack seated next to Hank. He and Hank made small talk as the auditorium slowly filled. Jack certainly had been in larger crowds before, but he had never sat on a stage facing them in this way. The experience made him slightly dizzy as he tried but failed to focus on individual faces.

Jack gave up on that exercise as the lights in the auditorium dimmed, leaving him to stare into the darkness. From directly above him, the heat of the stage lights pulled beads of perspiration onto his forehead.

The convention program kicked off with a color guard of veterans presenting the US flag, followed by the Pledge of Allegiance and the singing of the national anthem to the accompaniment of a lone trumpeter. Various board members made announcements and comments about the morning's activities and the next day's agenda, and then, it was Hank's turn to introduce the featured speaker. Jack's mind was racing by this time, and he didn't hear a word that Hank said until he heard his name called. Jack looked up and saw his host waving him toward the lectern.

And then Jack was standing, all alone, at the microphone. He instinctively gripped the edges of the lectern to steady himself.

"Uh … thank you … uh … Mr. Simmons," Jack said, adjusting his volume with those first few words. "Thank you, that was very kind."

Jack paused and tried to form another sentence, but the spotlight aimed at his face created a fierce glare that blotted out the audience and caused him to scrunch his shoulders and lower his head.

"Uh … thank you, I'd like to say … " Jack tried again, but it was useless. He couldn't function under these conditions. He backed away from the lectern and was met by Wilton. Jack whispered into his ear, and Wilton walked back behind the stage curtains. Within seconds, the spotlight dimmed and the house lights came up. Jack's eyes cleared, the intense heat from above subsided, and he returned to the lectern.

"Thank you, yes, that's much better. As I told Mr. Harris just now, I've never spoken in a large hall like this before, and, well, I couldn't see you. And I want to be able to see you. I didn't come all the way from Texas to speak into the darkness. I can do that any old night at home."

Jack heard soft laughter and applause, which calmed him considerably. He was ready to do what he had come to do. Without notes or outline, he spoke from a place deep inside and with words that spilled out as easily as when talking with the boys at the barbershop.

"I'm told that your agenda says you should be seeing a presidential candidate or two standing up here at this hour. The fact that you're looking at me should be a pretty strong hint that none of those gentlemen are here. I suppose that's to be expected, since they've got a lot on their minds right now.

"Oh, I suppose it would have been interesting to hear what they've got planned for the future, if they've actually got a plan. It seems to me these contests have become less about what they want to do and more about what they want you to believe the other feller wants to do. The Republicans would have us believe that the Democrats want to make us seniors slaves of the welfare system, while the Democrats say the Republicans want to cut us off completely.

"The fact is that neither side truthfully represents what their opponents actually stand for. But they gotta keep talking and troubling people in order to drum up votes. The press calls it negative campaigning, but I call it just plain disrespectful. And I'm not talking about them being disrespectful of each other. I'm talking about them being disrespectful of us, the voters. They talk to us and about us like we don't have a lick of sense.

"I think it might be refreshing if they'd quit talking for a while and do a little listening. I think they'd find that with our experience, we might just have a thing or two to tell them about how the world works.

"I'm guessing that by now many of you have heard about how me and a few friends got into a little tussle down in Dallas on New Year's Eve. A couple of young kids broke into our shop, and we sorta took care of things. There's been a lot said and written about it since then, and we've been called courageous and brave and some other fine things. But the truth is there wasn't anything courageous or brave about it. A psychologist might call it survival instinct, and a doctor might explain it as a dose of adrenaline, but really we just acted. Something had to be done, and we did it.

"Now I've been thinking about that for the past couple of months, and it seems to me that the reason we acted is because that's what our generation was taught to do. Most of us in this room were born and raised up during the Depression, a time when nothing came easy. Our parents struggled to keep food on the table, and quite often, us kids had to pitch in and work too. And we couldn't be choosy either. Nothing was below us, as long as it was honest work.

"Then came the wars, and those of us who didn't go to Europe or the Pacific or Korea went to work in factories and plants, often working double shifts to make sure America didn't fall behind. And between the wars, our generation built the cities and the suburbs and the interstate highways. Nobody seems to remember it, but it was our generation that invented the first computers and other gadgets that have changed the way we live and do business. So I don't think I'm being too bold to say that we know a little bit about living and about getting things done.

"These young people wake up every day to a world that we couldn't have dreamed of when we were their age. They drive cars that tell them where they're going and live in houses that are automated. They take medicines and additives that add years to their life, and they sit in front of computers that put the world at their fingertips. But do they know that none of that would have been possible without the hard work of people like you and me?

"We have a lot to be proud of, and we've sure enough earned our retirement. But while it's one thing to retire from a job, I see some of us that are retiring from life, and that's not good. We hole up in our houses or gated communities and stare at the TV all day and only get up to go to the mailbox, the dinner table, the bathroom, or the bed.

"What's worse, we've entrusted our personal well-being to total strangers, and between you and me, I think America is suffering as a result. We've got people leading us that have the money, the good looks, and the energy to get elected, but they don't have the character or experience it takes to lead. Not the kind of experience that comes from real life in the real world. They look for short-term solutions to long-term problems. They want instant satisfaction rather than long-term commitment.

They tell feel-good tales because they're afraid of the criticism that comes from telling the hard truth.

"Now Franky Parker and I spent some time earlier today walking around the convention center, and I think it's great what you folks are doing in your own neighborhoods. You're doing what I'm talking about—you're putting your life experience to work—and I applaud you for that. But don't be afraid to spread your wisdom and energy a little further. If you see something going on at city hall that isn't right, go downtown and straighten 'em out. If one of these politicians shows up on your doorstep to ask for your vote, sit 'em down and bend their ear for a moment. When they ask you why you're so sure, tell 'em you've got sixty-five or more years of living that says you're sure.

"Most important of all, if it's not getting done—whatever it is—then get out and do it. Thank you and God bless you all."

Jack backed away from the lectern, and for a moment all that could be heard in the auditorium was the sound of his leather soles scuffing the stage decking. The silence—caused in part by Jack's sudden conclusion and in part by the weight of his words—was broken when Hank stood up and greeted Jack with a double-fisted handshake, which prompted the audience to relax into enthusiastic applause.

"I hope that was okay," Jack shouted into Hank's ear.

"Great. It was great. Well done, Jack. Well done."

Jack nodded his appreciation to the audience. Across the stage, the board members were all applauding except for Wilton, who with folded arms and a broad smile was observing it all. He hadn't told Jack what to say, and yet, Jack said precisely what Wilton had wanted him to say. Whether it was fate or just good fortune, he couldn't tell. All he knew was that Jack had delivered a speech—a call to action—that played right into his political plans. Wilton was pleased, but he knew the work had just begun.

Jack's speech concluded the day's official business, and as had become a regular ritual, Jack spent the next thirty minutes accepting words of thanks and appreciation from audience members as they left. Hank invited Jack and Franky to dinner, but Jack was exhausted and declined the offer. He and Franky went back to the hotel and had supper before heading up to their rooms. Their flight back to Dallas was to leave at midmorning, and they wanted to get a good night's sleep.

As they walked to the elevators, Jack was not at all surprised to see Billy Briar standing in the lobby.

"Another Jack Dodger speech, another story." Billy greeted the two men.

"How'd we do today?" asked Jack.

"Terrific, although, I'd be careful if I were you."

"How's that?" Jack's brow wrinkled.

"You get around enough, and someone's gonna want to put your name on a ballot somewhere."

"Naw, that'll never happen," said Jack. "I'd never let it happen. No way. But I'll take that as some kind of compliment."

"Oh, by the way," said Billy, changing to a more serious tone. "I spoke with Kevin Walker this morning after his probation hearing. He's been looking for work but hasn't been able to find anything yet. He seemed really worried."

"That's unfortunate," said Jack. "I'm sure the publicity has worked against him. That's just another example of what poor judgment will do to you." He scratched his head for a moment. "Well, we're gonna go upstairs. See you back in Dallas I'm sure."

"I'm sure you will," said Billy.

Up in his room, Jack got out of his suit and gave Caroline a brief call to report on the day and to get his usual dose of love from Wendy. Then he stretched out on the bed to watch television for a while, but he was distracted by his conversation with Billy Briar downstairs. He climbed out of bed and fumbled through his suitcase until he found his checkbook. He sat down at the little desk in the corner and wrote out a check to Kevin Walker in the amount of three hundred dollars. He wrapped the check in a piece of hotel stationery and then sealed it in a hotel envelope. From one of the inside pockets of his wallet, he pulled out a scrap of paper and copied the address written on it onto the face of the envelope. He put the letter and his wallet on the dresser next to his watch, keys, and other valuables, and then crawled back into bed.

Jack zapped through the television channels for a few more moments then turned it off and reached over to turn off the bedside lamp. Next door in Franky's room, the telephone rang, and the muffled sound of conversation through the walls quickly lulled Jack to sleep.

CHAPTER 6

Jack was slow to get up and get going on the morning of March 1 after all the excitement of addressing the Golden Eagles convention the night before. When he finally got dressed and knocked on Franky's door, there was no answer. He put his ear to the door and heard no sound inside either.

His intimate knowledge of Franky and his habits told him that his friend was already downstairs at breakfast, and that was confirmed when he stepped into the coffee shop and found Franky grazing in the buffet line.

"Got a little sleep, did you?" said Franky over his shoulder to Jack, not missing a beat as he scooped up generous helpings of scrambled eggs and hash brown potatoes.

"Yep, I guess I was really drained." Jack looked over the morning's offerings, picked up a plate, and went through the line. By the time he got to the table with his food, Franky's plate was already half-empty.

"I already got you some coffee," he said as Jack slid into the opposite side of the booth. "You better down those rations fast."

Jack looked at his watch and then shrugged. "No big rush. We've got plenty of time to get to the airport."

"Forget the airport. Gotta go back over to the convention hall," said Franky between bites. "Big meeting this morning."

"What meeting … whadaya mean?" Jack asked.

"They called me last night. Wilton Harris—he said the board wants to talk to you."

"Talk to me, what about? What about our flight?"

"Flight's taken care of. They wanna talk."

"About what?"

"They'll tell you."

"I don't understand? Why'd they call you?"

"Your phone was busy."

"Hmm … must've been while I was talking to Caroline," said Jack. "So when do they want to see us?"

Franky pushed up his shirtsleeve and glanced at his watch. "Fifteen minutes."

"Fifteen minutes? Good grief! Why didn't you say something sooner?"

"Quit talking and eat," Franky admonished. "You're gonna need your strength."

Jack's stomach was churning by now, and his plate-load of food didn't look so appetizing. He ate a slice of toast, took a few sips of coffee, and the two headed for the cash register.

Jack and Franky dodged traffic and crossed the street to the convention center. Once inside, they walked at a fast clip through the crowds of people toward the conference room, though the traffic inside was relatively light. This was the final day of the convention and attendance had dropped off somewhat. Or, like Jack, many people had decided to sleep in a little later.

Jack slowed his pace as he approached the boardroom door and turned the knob, but Franky failed to brake, which served to catapult Jack into the room and almost onto the board table itself.

"Good morning, Jack, Franky. Why don't you gentlemen have a seat there, and we'll get down to business," said Hank. "Would you like some coffee?"

"Yes, please," said Jack, having only taken a few quick sips at breakfast.

"Jack, we have a few questions, and you may think them odd at first, but by the time we finish here today, you'll understand. Jack, what is your political philosophy?"

"Political philosophy? I'm not sure I understand what you—"

"Are you a Republican or a Democrat?"

"To be honest, I can't say that I'm either. Not that it's anyone's business, but I've voted on both sides of the fence. Truman, Eisenhower, Kennedy. Voted for Nixon once. Voted for Carter once too. I was all the way for Reagan. And it's been much the same my whole life."

"So you're an independent?"

"Well now, if that means that I've never registered with a political party, then I'd say that would be right."

Jack looked at Franky, asking with his eyes for a meaning to this inquisition. Franky just shrugged.

"Jack, have you ever considered running for an elected office?"

"No, can't say I ever have. Always been too busy trying to make a living and taking care of things at home. It always seemed to me that I could do more good right in my own neighborhood than I could sitting behind a desk in a courthouse somewhere."

"Would you consider running … if you thought there was a need and if you thought that you could make a difference? And if you had the support of a good number of people?"

"Well now, I don't know." Jack paused for a moment. Hank was beating around the bush, and Jack knew it. He didn't have much patience for twenty questions.

"Mr. Simmons, no offense, but perhaps you better go ahead and make your point."

Hank looked around the room at the others and nodded. Then he leaned forward as if to meet Jack in the middle of the table.

"Jack, you said some things yesterday—and in fact you've been saying some things over the past few months—that lead us to believe that you have some strong feelings about the direction in which our nation is moving and the way in which individuals have an obligation to get off the sidelines and get into the thick of things, to help straighten things out, make them better. Am I characterizing your feelings correctly?"

"To be honest, a lot of these feelings I've had are brand new to me, born of the moment," said Jack. "Until two months ago,

I hadn't given much thought to any of this. But sometimes, something dramatic happens to a person, and it changes their perspective, and I suppose that's what I've been working over lately. But I've never thought that politics was—"

"Jack, the board met last night—late and long, in fact—and, well, considering all of the things that you said and the way you were received by the members, and considering the fact that the mission of the Golden Eagles is evolving, we'd like you to consider running for public office."

Jack pondered that idea for a moment. *Politics?* While he liked to stay active, politics was not exactly the way he had envisioned spending his retirement years.

"I don't know," he said. "I'm sure you've got some members in Dallas who have been watching things a little more closely and would probably be better qualified than me."

"Jack, we're not talking about the Dallas City Council."

"You're not?"

"No, sir."

"Well, state office has never—"

"We're not talking about state office either, or Congress for that matter."

Jack heard what was being said and shook his head in disbelief. He cast a glance over at Franky, whose big curly eyebrows twitched over a toothy grin.

"Aw no, Franky, you've gotta be kidding," Jack said. Franky smirked and shook his head. Jack was stunned, because he knew that Franky never lied.

Jack leaned forward and rubbed his forehead as his mind stepped up the political ladder from city council to county commissioner to state representative to legislature to—and his thoughts froze right there on the ladder. The next rung was out of his mental grasp, so Hank finished the climb for him.

"Yes, Jack, we're talking about the highest office—president of the United States."

Jack sank back into the padded boardroom chair. He wasn't just speechless now—he was breathless. His lungs felt compressed, and it was all he could do to draw air into his nose. His eyes moved around the table, focusing sharply on each person sitting there. As his gaze moved from one person to the next, it was met with a smile and a nodding head. The last face he met was Franky's. The sight of that big goofy smile triggered something in Jack, and he burst out in an uproarious laugh. Franky joined in, and the rest of the board loosened up like an over-tightened spring, and for a moment there were smiles and giggles and table thumping all around the room. Even Hank uncoiled for a moment, but he soon brought the room back to serious focus.

"I know it sounds far-fetched, perhaps even ridiculous, but we're serious about this, Jack. We had a long meeting last night, and the conclusion that we came to is that it's time for the Golden Eagles to let their voices be heard, and we believe you are just the man to provide that voice."

Jack was still speechless, so Hank continued.

"Now we all heard you speak out there yesterday, and I believe we're all of the same mind. We believe that while we've earned our retirement and it's time to give the younger generation the reins, we don't exactly like where they've been driving us lately. We're of the opinion that we'd like to spend a little bit of the energy and time that we've got left to give these young people a few reminders of what is important, while we still can.

"The difference between you and us, Jack, is that you've been given a gift. Call it luck or fate or even God's divine will, but you've been given a platform from which to speak. It started with that ruckus back in Dallas and with how you handled those boys. You let people know that we old folks still have strength and stamina, but more important than that, we've got wisdom and character. And those are two things that I think have been lacking in the public arena.

"So the question for you, Jack, is: Are you going to turn your back on this gift you've got, or are you going to embrace it and do something meaningful with it while you've still got the time to do so?"

Jack's head cleared, and he found his voice again.

"Mr. Simmons, I appreciate your view of things, but I think your assessment of my qualifications is way out of touch with reality. I'm just a retired bookkeeper and barbershop owner from Dallas. This is the first time I've been out of Texas in ten years. I don't keep up with current events as much as most folks. I couldn't tell you who's the president of this country or that. The only laws I know about are those with regard to small business and taxes."

Jack paused for a moment, trying to conjure up more negatives.

"And besides all that, I've only got one suit in my closet, and you've seen it now for two days in a row. I really don't think there's anything to recommend me to run for dog catcher, let alone what you've got in mind."

"Don't be so sure, Jack," said Hank. "Some of our best presidents came from humble beginnings, and what they lacked in book knowledge and worldly experience, they made up for in wisdom and character. But don't just take my word for it. If it's a second opinion you want, we've asked all the members to assemble at eleven. Why don't you wait and see what they've got to say about it before you make your final decision."

Jack sat quietly for what felt like ten full minutes, staring at his hands wrapped tightly around his coffee mug on the table. "I just don't know," he muttered. "I just don't know."

Franky, who had sat quietly through the encounter up to now, couldn't hold back any longer. He slapped the table hard with the palms of his hands as if to shake the reluctance right out of Jack's head.

"Come on, Jack, don't be so pigheaded," he said. "Of course you know. You always know what to do, and you know what to do now. Sure, it sounds like a lot of work and a lot of headaches, but you've faced that before. Besides, you're not gonna be alone. We're all gonna be right there with you, aren't we?"

"That's right," said Hank, a little nervous that Franky's nudging might push Jack in the wrong direction. But he didn't know the history of the relationship between these two men. He didn't know that Franky was the one person that Jack trusted without question. And this time was no different.

"So what comes next?" asked Jack, relaxing his grip on the mug, and with it, his nerves.

Hank, sighing with relief, looked at his watch. "Next? Well, the first thing we need to do is go and consult your campaign committee—all five thousand of them."

※

By the time Jack, Franky, Hank, and the rest of the board reached the auditorium, it was already full and buzzing with excitement. Wilton had leaked a few tidbits of the previous night's board meeting to a handful of key people, and word had spread rapidly through the hotel and the convention center that the Eagles were going to launch a political campaign, and that Jack Dodger was the probable standard-bearer. Wilton had also placed a few calls to the local media that morning, and several camera crews had arrived on the scene. So by the time Hank got to the microphone to address the crowd, they were already primed and ready, with some chanting softly, "Run, Jack, run! Run, Jack, run!"

Hank quieted the audience and briefly explained the board's deliberations of the night before and the gist of the morning's discussion. A few shouts of "no" from somewhere in the room indicated that there was some opposition to the Eagles' new political agenda. That was not unexpected, and so Hank pressed on.

"Folks, as I see it, this organization has a rare—and brief—window of opportunity to make a lasting contribution to our country. And we on your board of directors believe that the man best suited to give voice to our contribution is Jack Dodger."

And with that, Hank asked Jack to step to the microphone and address the crowd.

"Well, I'm not quite sure what to say, except that I'm honored and humbled beyond words," said Jack. He paused a moment, scratched his head, and glanced sideways at the board. Then he did something that was completely unexpected.

"Friends, I understand that this is not a political party, and as such there is no formal nominating process. And while your board has the authority to select a candidate, it seems to me that this may need the consideration of more than just a dozen people. And quite frankly, I need to know whether you really want me or not. So if you think I might be suited to represent you, then raise your hand in the air."

Even Jack was astonished by what happened next. The crowd didn't just raise their hands—they raised their bodies, standing in what appeared to be a near unanimous show of support. They didn't applaud or cheer. They just stood, silently, as if to say they not only supported him, but they were ready to march with him out into the streets.

"Well then, it looks like I'm your man," said Jack. "I can't promise that I'll be as polished as the other fellers, or as knowledgeable as they are on the big issues, but I can promise that I will always be straight with you, and I'll give this thing everything I've got. On that, you have my word."

With that, the dam of emotion broke, and the room filled with thunderous applause.

"That was brilliant, Jack. Just brilliant." Hank patted Jack on the back.

"Brilliant? Nothing," he responded. "I had to know whether or not I'm climbing out on this limb by myself."

Seven hundred miles away in Austin, Texas, little Wendy Stone was at a card table coloring as the noon news came on the television. She looked up and saw a face she knew as well as her own. Her smile lit up the room like a lamp and her little voice filled the house.

"Mommy, Mommy, Grandpa Jack's on TV! Grandpa Jack, look, look!"

Caroline rushed into the den from the kitchen where she had been making sandwiches for lunch, just in time to see a video clip of her father at the microphone in Kansas City, and to hear the local anchor say: "So if all goes well for the Golden Eagles this spring and summer, it looks like voters will have three choices for president in November. America, say hello to Jack Dodger."

Caroline clasped her mouth in shock, and then she fumbled for the remote control and clicked to other stations. No, she wasn't hallucinating; other stations were talking about her father also. She dropped the remote on the coffee table and rushed to the telephone in the kitchen to call Don at his office.

"Don, that trip to Dallas that we've been putting off ... we're leaving first thing in the morning ... Yes, first thing ... It's Daddy ... He's gotten himself involved in something ... I don't know ... Something very strange."

CHAPTER 7

"Uh-oh, looks like I'm in trouble," Jack said as he turned the pickup onto his street and saw Don and Caroline's Lexus parked at the curb in front of his house.

"Yep. I'd say *you've* got some explaining to do," Franky quipped from the passenger seat. "I'm sure they're just dying to hear all about your new career."

Jack turned into the driveway and pulled to a halt. He and Franky climbed out of the truck, and both reached into the bed to pull out their overnight bags. They had only packed for one night, so they were ready to change after spending almost three days in their suits.

Following the big announcement the day before at the convention, they had spent most of the rest of the day meeting with the Golden Eagles board to hash out some strategies and game plans for the upcoming campaign. Jack had insisted that he and Franky go home for ten days to take care of personal matters. Jack promised that they would be back in Kansas City by March 12 to get things going.

Tired and disheveled, the two men walked slowly up the steps. Jack reached for the front door knob, but before he could grasp it, the door jerked opened, and he stood face-to-face with Caroline.

"Hi … uh, darling. Uh … great to see you. Everyone here with you?" Jack's voice faltered. He knew Caroline was about to begin the inquisition.

"Yes, Daddy, we're all here. And what, may I ask, have you been doing these past couple of days?" she asked sarcastically.

Before Jack could answer, Don came into the living room from the kitchen. "Yes, by all means, Jack, tell us. How was your trip to Kansas City? Anything special happen?"

"So you saw the news last night?" Jack asked.

"Last night, and this morning, and on the radio all the way from Austin, and just ten minutes ago on CNN," Caroline said, her voice growing louder and her face turning redder with every word. "Yes, we've seen the news, and now we want to know: *What does it mean?*"

"I'm gonna go out back and see Wendy," said Franky to nobody in particular. He could hear Wendy playing outside with Blackie, and he felt it might be safer out there for the time being.

Jack watched Franky slip out of the room, envious of his detachment at this particular moment. He turned back to Caroline and caught her red-hot glare.

"Well … what does it mean?" she asked again, this time a little more calmly.

"First, Caroline and Don, you have to understand that this is not something that I pursued. It just sort of grew out of the progression of things. I spoke here in Dallas and then in Kansas City and one thing led to another, and the next thing I know, they're endorsing me for president."

"Well, I can see that part," said Caroline. "The part that I can't see is that you said yes."

"Well now," said Jack, "if you had told me a week ago that they were going to ask me to do this, I would have said not just no, but 'hell no.' But in the context of what has happened in the past few days, it seems to make sense."

Jack had not had an opportunity to put down his bag or even enter the room before the interrogation had begun. Now, while Caroline and Don mulled over his last comment, he took the opportunity to set his overnight bag on the floor by the door, walk over to the sofa, and collapse into the soft cushions.

He continued. "Caroline, nobody is more surprised or anxious about this whole affair than me. My head is spinning and my ears are buzzing. It sounds so difficult and impossible and all consuming, and common sense tells me that I should get as far away from this as I possibly can. But in my heart, something keeps telling me that I should go ahead and follow this road wherever it takes me."

"Where this road is going to take you is to towns with names like Embarrassment and Foolishness and Nonsense," Don chimed in with a tone of authority that outweighed his brief experience in the state political arena.

"And what about your privacy?" asked Caroline in a more gentle tone. "Daddy, you've always enjoyed a quiet, private life. You've always enjoyed going wherever you want to go, doing whatever you want to do. All that's going to end. If you lose, you'll be known the rest of your life as that foolish old man from Dallas. And if you win—"

"Ha, if he wins?" Don interrupted. "That's what's so foolish about this whole thing. There's no way you and your Golden Eagles are going to win anything. So why waste your time and money trying?"

"This isn't necessarily about winning," Jack said defensively. He genuinely loved his son-in-law, but sometimes the young man had an air of superiority that was annoying. "It's about making a difference. Having a voice. Contributing to the process. Leaving this world better than we found it."

He turned his attention back to Caroline. "Honey, I don't know how else to explain it, except to say that there are larger things at play here. And while it may look to you like my life is out of control, there seems to be a logical plan to all of this. Call it fate, God's will, or whatever, but I don't feel like I can turn my back on this thing and just walk away."

"Yeah, you can't walk away from those Golden Eagles," said Don. "You've given control of your life to them, and in return they're going to use you up and then just toss you aside."

Jack sat up straight on the edge of the sofa and spoke with a new intensity that caused Don to take a step backward.

"Don, you're a smart young man, and you're getting a lot of good experience down there at the state capitol building, but I've learned something in my years that apparently you haven't yet. You can't use someone who won't let himself be used. I've got my eyes wide open, my ears to the ground, and my hands on the wheel."

Jack slapped his knees and stood up. "Now, if you two youngsters are finished lecturing this seventy-year-old, I've got things to do, not the least of which is to get out of this suit."

Jack picked up his bag and walked down the hall to his bedroom, leaving Caroline and Don to whisper quietly in the living room. From out in the backyard could be heard the sounds of Blackie barking, Wendy giggling, and Franky egging them both on.

Caroline went to the kitchen to look out the window. Jack joined her there a few minutes later after changing into some old khaki pants and a well-worn plaid shirt.

"They're quite a threesome, aren't they?" Jack said, looking out the window to find Wendy sitting on Franky's broad shoulders and Blackie jumping up in the air, trying to lick them both.

"Yep, just made for one another. That Franky—nothing seems to ever bother him. He's just like a big kid."

"No, not always," said Jack. "I'll admit that he's never had the smarts that most people seem to think are an important measure of a person's worth. And that big ol' grin of his does tend to add a childlike quality. But he's got a deep, serious, wise side that most people have never seen. He just doesn't waste it on trivial matters like most of us do. He saves it for the most important things."

"So has he said anything about all this campaign business, or is this just trivial" Caroline asked.

"No, he knows there's nothing trivial about it," said Jack. "He says this is the most important thing I've ever faced, aside from family matters, and it ought to be treated thoughtfully and seriously. And he says that nothing is more serious or more important right now than to stay true to myself and follow my gut instinct. And that's what I intend to do."

"So we can't talk you out of this."

"No, honey, I don't think you can. I don't think you should even try."

About that time, Don walked in. "So what happens next?"

"Well," said Jack, "I've got about ten days to take care of some things around here, and then, I'll go back to Kansas City. The board has planned some strategy meetings, and we'll talk about how to proceed with this thing. And I've arranged for Franky to come with me—kinda help me keep myself straight."

"Are you scared?" asked Caroline.

"No, not scared. Scared is when you're sitting in a foxhole at night in the freezing rain with a deadly enemy lurking somewhere out there in the darkness. But this—no, I think *anxious* is a better word—even *excited*."

Caroline put her arm around her father's waste and gave him a big hug. "Well, if you're for it, then we're for it, right, Don?"

"Sure, why not." He extended a somewhat begrudging congratulatory handshake. "But just be careful. I realize I don't know as much as you do, but from my short tenure in Austin, I do know this: politics can be brutal. The media, the public, even your own advisors will pump you up for a while. But then there'll come a day when something happens and you'll find yourself all alone."

"Well, not completely," said Jack. "I'll still have my family, won't I?"

"That's right," said Caroline, hugging her father again.

The next ten days were a blur of activity as Jack put his affairs in order. He caught up on bills at home, had his mail diverted to the barbershop where Woody and Paul would take care of it, and stopped his newspaper delivery. He finished and filed his tax return, and did the same for the handful of clients who were still on his list and who had their documents in order. For the few who were still dragging their feet, he arranged for them to meet with other accountants in the area. As for Blackie, she rode back to Austin with Caroline, Don, and Wendy. Don wasn't thrilled with the arrangement, but both Blackie and Wendy were ecstatic.

In between these personal chores, Jack was able to accommodate some interview requests from the local media, including Billy Briar, who was still following Jack's every move. The national media seemed content for now to watch Jack from afar, rehashing whatever coverage the Dallas media generated.

And then on the afternoon of Sunday, March 12, Jack arranged a brief meeting with Kevin Walker. It was the first time the two had seen each other since the morning of New Year's Day when Jack drove Kevin to the police station to turn himself in. Jack was interested to see how Kevin was doing, and the news was mixed: Kevin had found work as a construction laborer, but he was deep in debt, and there didn't seem to be any hope of digging himself out. Jack encouraged him to keep working hard and even look for a second job in the evenings.

"You can never do too much or fight too hard for your family," he said. "Don't give up. It's a battle worth winning."

At dawn on Monday, Jack and Franky tossed their bags into the back of the pickup again. Instead of flying, they decided to make the ten-hour drive to Kansas City. For Jack, the pickup represented independence, and he thought it might come in handy if he and Franky found need to break away for a while. They filled the long hours on the road with talk about old times and old places and a good amount of speculation about the future and what might happen in the coming months.

"So if you get elected, can I come sleep in old Abe's bed?" Franky joshed.

"If I get elected," Jack said, "I'll make sure you have a room right next to mine. I've got to have you there every minute of the day and night. After all, I blame a lot of this on you."

"Now just what do you mean by that?" Franky asked, not sure if Jack was making fun or was being serious.

"Well for starters," said Jack, "if you hadn't surprised that first feller who broke in, they probably would have just stood us up against the wall, robbed us like they planned and left, leaving us with nothing to be famous about. And in the second place, when Wilton called you at the hotel that night, you should have told them right then and there that they were crazy and that there was no point in talking about it any further. That would've ended the whole affair right then, and we'd have been on a plane home the next morning just like we planned."

"Now come on, Jack, is that what you really wanted?"

Jack had no answer for Franky. He kept his hands on the wheel and his eyes on the road ahead.

They arrived in Kansas City and settled in at the hotel just across the street from the convention center. The next morning, they followed Wilton's directions and walked a half dozen blocks to the Golden Eagles headquarters, situated in a small suite of offices.

Golden Eagles president, Hank Simmons, opened the meeting by introducing some of the other Eagles staffers—all seniors themselves—who would be working on the campaign. Then he laid out the strategy for the next few weeks. While Jack honed his message and campaign skills, the staff, led by Wilton, would help organize Golden Eagles chapters to get signatures for the petitions that were required to get Jack on state ballots in November. It would be a daunting task, with many states requiring petitions by June 2, others due in July and August, and the remainder due by early September. However, the most urgent and immediate challenge would be to get the 37,381 signatures that Texas required by May 2. Still, with Texas being Jack's home state, Wilton pronounced his organization up to the task.

After a lunch break, two men in dark suits with briefcases joined the group: James Abbott and Nelson Costello, professional campaign consultants with a reputation throughout the midwest for getting candidates elected to state and national congressional offices. The pairing of their surnames was a curiosity whenever they were introduced, and their physical appearance was not unlike their Hollywood counterparts: Abbott was tall and thin, and Costello was short and round. But the comparisons ended there, and it was clear to everyone in the room, and especially to Jack, that this was no comedy team. Abbott was stiff and uptight with a near strangled look from a necktie pulled too tight. His short cropped hair, bland colorless suit, and starched white shirt reminded Jack of the oil company executives who had come to his East Texas home to announce the death of his father. Costello, on the other hand, was more at ease and was obviously not afraid of splashes of color, as evidenced by his bright blue shirt and electric yellow tie.

"Mr. Abbott is going to help sharpen your policy positions, and Mr. Costello is going to coach you on how to express those positions," said Wilton.

"Yes, that's correct," said Abbott. "Our goal is to make you television friendly and sound-bite coherent. By the time we're finished with you, the public's going to know exactly what you stand for and why they should support you."

"Well," said Jack, "I appreciate all the help I can get, but I don't think I need any help explaining what I stand for."

"Oh, yes, that's fine," said Costello congenially. "We're not here to put words in your mouth or change your views. We're just here to help make sure you express those views in a way that is—well, politically expedient. And that'll start with us finding out just which way you lean. If you don't mind, I'm going to go down a quick laundry list of topics, and I want you tell me the first thing that comes to mind."

"Sure, I guess that's all right," said Jack.

"Okay, what's your view on abortion?"

Jack whistled softly through his teeth and winced at the abruptness of the question. "I wasn't expecting such a harsh—"

"Abortion?" Costello repeated.

"I'm against it."

"Education?"

"I'm for it."

"Public prayer?"

"Sure, pray whenever you want to. I'm praying right now."

"Campaign finance reform?"

"If people want to vote with their checkbooks, let 'em."

"Taxes?"

"Cut 'em to the bone."

"Gun control?"

"People control would be better."

"Capital punishment?"

"A necessary evil."

"Welfare reform?"

"Personal responsibility and community action are the keys."

"The role of the federal government?"

"Defend our borders, protect our constitutional rights, give folks a helping hand when they've got no other choice, but mostly stay out of the way."

Abbott turned to Costello. "Iron-clad conservative, but I sense some wiggle room for moderation." Then he turned to Jack. "Well, Mr. Dodger, I think we have a pretty good idea of what you're about. Those are good, strong, concise answers, but we'll have to flesh them out and shape them a bit to make sure we—"

"Make sure we what?" Jack interrupted. "I've kinda been calling my own tune for most of my life, and I thought that was what you folks wanted—for me to express my own views."

"It is, Jack. It is," Hank reassured.

Abbott added, "But if you lean too hard on some of those views, if you're too strident, you may turn some people away. And no offense, but I think we're going to need all the help we can get."

Jack could feel his face flush with heat. It was day one of the campaign, and he was already wondering if he had made a terrific mistake. Maybe Don had been right. Maybe they were out to use him already. But then he looked at Franky, who gave him a calm smile and a wink, and Jack remembered what he had told Don: *"You can't use someone who won't let himself be used."*

Jack took a deep breath.

"All right," he said. "You fellers will have to bear with me. I've never done this kind of thing before, and I obviously have a lot to learn. I'm going to do everything I can to be cooperative."

"That's great, Jack," said Wilton, breathing easier. "This is new to all of us, and we've all got a lot to learn. That's why we've brought these gentlemen in to help us. They've been through this before, and they know how it works. Trust me, Jack, you're in good hands."

And that day marked the beginning of Jack's education in the fine art of professional campaigning. Over the next two weeks, Jack spent long days with his trainers. In the mornings, Abbott worked Jack through two dozen black binders detailing the history and current status of major domestic and international issues. In the afternoons, Costello worked with Jack on expressing his views on those issues, on how not to be so blunt, and on how to be vague without sounding so on topics with high volatility ratings.

Costello also worked with Jack on his delivery—projecting his voice, keeping his head up, maintaining eye contact, gesturing naturally, ignoring hecklers, and projecting optimism and confidence through body language. There were even lessons on politically correct hand shaking, woman hugging, and baby kissing. All of this seemed overblown to Jack, but he held his tongue and went through the drills like a good student. Franky was even put into service during role-playing sessions to portray everything from overzealous supporters to underwhelmed skeptics.

On a few evenings, there were trips to local men's stores to get Jack outfitted in a half dozen new suits that would wear well during long days on the campaign trail. Each was accessorized with an assortment of shirts and neckties that would help expand his wardrobe to several dozen different looks.

Weekends were filled with trips to local Golden Eagles groups throughout the Midwest and back to Texas to help rally the troops and generate enthusiasm for the state petition drives. Jack lived for these outings. The warmth and generosity of the volunteers energized him and reminded him why he had embarked upon this journey. And the laughter and honest conversation he enjoyed with these people had an effect similar to taking a long hot shower; Jack could feel the insincerity and falseness of the week's work being washed away.

By early April, Abbott and Costello called the board together and pronounced Jack ready for his first big test: a press conference.

CHAPTER 8

Wilton Harris looked through the gap in the door and was thrilled by what he saw. All fifty chairs set up for the press conference were full, the back wall was lined with video cameras on tripods, and the lectern at the front of the room had sprouted a bouquet of colorful microphones decorated with call letters from radio and television operations from coast-to-coast. Finally, after weeks of preparation, it was time to show America what Jack Dodger and the Golden Eagles were all about.

Back in the greenroom, Jack was being given a light dusting of makeup to absorb the glare of the camera lights while Abbott and Costello circled him nervously like bees, black binders in hand. Franky leaned calmly against the wall, taking it all in.

"Now, Jack, remember what we've talked about. Today is not so much about giving full answers as it is about making a strong first impression," said Costello. "If someone throws you a curveball out there, the best thing to do is to bunt it with something like, 'That is something we will be giving serious attention to in the coming weeks,' or, 'That is a very serious issue that demands thoughtful consideration before we firm up our position.'

"The worst thing you can do," he added, "is to answer like the governor did and say, 'I don't know.' Even worse is to just shrug—that smells of 'I don't care.'"

Wilton burst into the room, rubbing his hands with excitement. "Well, gentlemen, we couldn't have asked for a better turnout. It's standing room only in there."

Jack sat dead still, partially from nervousness but mostly to prevent an accident with the makeup technician. Nothing moved but his eyes, which followed the four men around the room. When the makeup job was finished, Jack stood up and stretched out his back. Franky handed him a plastic cup of water to wet his mouth. "How you feel?" he asked.

"Oh, about like a blind tightrope walker at the circus. I know there's danger out there, but I can't see it."

"You'll do fine," said Wilton.

Abbott, who had been silently poring over his notes, looked at his watch and then came over and stood in front of Jack. "Now, Jack, these press conferences have a limited lifespan, and they always come to a point where there is no sense in going on. The media starts churning the same ground, the speaker gets tired and begins to babble, or worse, he strays into controversy and torches the room. You won't know when that time comes, but we will. And at that time, one of us will come to the lectern and announce that there is time for just one more question."

Jack thought a moment then asked, "Has that ever happened after the first question?"

"No," said Abbott, smiling nervously, "and that's not going to happen today either, is it?" He looked at his watch then glanced around the room at Jack and the others. "Looks like it's time to go. Any last questions?"

"None from me," said Jack. Wilton shook his head. Franky made no indication one way or the other.

"Well then, let's go," said Costello. As they moved out the door and down the hallway, they were met by Hank, who was to introduce Jack.

Costello continued to coach Jack all the way down the hallway to the pressroom. "Now, Jack, there's nothing to worry about. Just remain calm, and above all else, just be yourself. You can never go wrong that way."

"What was that again?" asked Jack, distracted by his own thoughts.

"Just be yourself," Costello repeated.

At that moment, they reached the room and took their positions as had been previously practiced: Hank at the microphone, Jack just off of his right shoulder, Costello between Jack and the side wall, and Wilton, Abbott, and Franky against the side wall in a position where they were not part of the photo opportunity, but rather in a strategic position to observe Jack and the media simultaneously. Golden Eagles staffers and interested parties lined the other walls.

"Good morning," said Hank. "I want to welcome you to Kansas City and to the home base of the Golden Eagles. For almost a year now, there's been a growing feeling within our organization that it was time for us to become more actively involved in the political life of our nation. After all, there are more than thirty-four million people over age sixty-five in the United States today, and there is much going on in Washington that is of interest to us. But up until recently, we did not feel that we had a unified voice or, for that matter, a unified direction. And then along came Jack Dodger, and we found a strong voice quite literally overnight. Jack has reminded us about who we are, what is important in life, and that we still have much to contribute despite our age. In return, we have imposed ourselves upon him, and he has graciously and courageously accepted our challenge. And so, without any further to do, I give you Jack Dodger, our candidate for the presidency of the United States of America."

By now, Jack was almost conditioned to receive applause following an introduction, but there was none today. Rather, the media sat quietly in their typical fashion, like medical students waiting for the first view of the patient in a surgical theatre. The silence caused Jack to hesitate a moment, and Costello leaned forward and whispered in his ear, "You're gonna do fine. Just be yourself."

Jack acknowledged Costello with a nod of the head, winked at Franky, and walked up to the lectern. Lights flashed and shutters clicked as Jack rested his hands on the edges of the lectern and cleared his throat.

"Good morning, folks. I'd like to make a brief statement, and then I'll answer some questions. Just about four months ago, I was a private citizen doing what private citizens do: living my life, earning a retirement income, paying bills, and spending free time with family and friends. And then this unusual event happened, which most of you have already reported, and now here I am, a political candidate for the first time in my life, and for a pretty big office at that. I can't begin to tell you how proud and honored I am to be asked to represent my generation in the upcoming election. But I want to tell you that I don't want to be known as just the senior citizens' candidate, because the things that we seniors care about are the things that all Americans should care about. We've just been around a little bit longer than the rest of you.

"Now, I know there are certain rules to this game, and I've spent some time with some good people learning how these things work. I'm going to try real hard to abide by those rules, but I hope you'll be patient with me as I muddle through this today. Okay now, does anyone have a question?"

Hands shot up in the air, and reporters chanted for attention like grade-schoolers. "Mr. Dodger, Mr. Dodger!" With a nod from Costello, Jack began picking people at random.

"Mr. Dodger, what do you think is the greatest danger that our country faces today?" came the first question from a tall, earnest-looking man on the front row.

"I think there's a lot of individual problems out there: violence, greed, drugs, hate, poverty, abuse of all types, just to name a few. But I think those are all symptoms of a bigger problem, and that is a simple lack of respect—for each other, for our ideas, our desires, our ambitions, and our rights. Too many people spend too much time thinking just about themselves."

Jack pointed to another reporter, a middle-aged man to the right, who asked, "What would be your first action if elected president?"

"Now that's a tough one. I can honestly say that I haven't thought that far ahead. Perhaps the best place to start would be to haul all the White House staff into a big room and tell them that there's not going to be any monkey business on my watch. And I'd tell 'em that there will be no second chances. They do something foolish or dishonest and they're out the door—immediately."

"Have you thought about a running mate?" The question came unsolicited from someone sitting in the middle of the pack, and Jack paused to make sure he could see who he was talking to.

"No, we've really not gotten that far yet. We're still building our organization and working on getting on state ballots. And I've heard that process is moving along nicely. Certainly, we'll need to choose a vice presidential nominee by the end of the summer after the other folks have their conventions so the public can compare apples to apples."

Jack pointed to another reporter, who asked: "How do you plan to run your campaign? Will it follow the model set by recent national campaigns with debates, town-hall meetings and television advertising?"

"I suspect it will touch on all of those elements, but certainly not at the levels set by the vice president and the governor. We don't have and won't have nearly as much money as they do, but then I don't think we will need as much."

"Can you elaborate on that last statement?"

"Sure can. Because the Golden Eagles have chapters in every state now and are well organized in most major cities, we're going to use that network to help generate interest and support. Certainly, I'll be traveling as much as possible, but not in big jets like the other two men. And television time will be purchased at the local levels where the rates are much more reasonable. We haven't talked about debates, but if the other two men will let us on the stage a time or two, we'd like to be there with them. Okay, let's see, there in the back." Jack pointed to a woman in slacks standing behind the back row of chairs.

"Considering the amount of money the vice president and governor have raised, do you feel at a disadvantage? And while you're at it, what is your position on campaign finance reform?"

"Well first, no, I don't think we're disadvantaged at all. We're going to use as many free opportunities as possible, including our network of chapters. As for the reform question, this notion that the person with the most money has an unfair advantage is a bunch of hooey."

Abbott and Costello looked at each other. "Uh oh, we didn't even discuss that," Abbott whispered.

Jack continued, "The way I see it, fundraising is simply the election before the election. People with money give it to the candidate with the ideas and the resume that they find most attractive. But you know what? Come November, the man who gave a million dollars and the man who gave ten dollars are on the same footing, because they only get one vote each. Now, I do believe that the amount of money folks are throwing at this thing is obscene. I've been thinking about that lately, and I've got a solution for our campaign anyway. I'm going to ask that our supporters give no more than ten dollars each."

Abbott's black binder slipped out of his hand and crashed to the floor. Jack looked over to see his entire campaign team, including Franky, slack-jawed with quizzical looks on their faces. "Where did that come from?" whispered Abbott to the others as he bent down to pick up his papers.

Jack brought the attention of the room back to the lectern by continuing, "If we work our network well, we should do just fine. Heck, like Mr. Simmons said, there are thirty-four million people in America over age sixty-five. If we could get a little ten-dollar donation from just one percent of those folks, we'd have more money than we'd know what to do with. Meanwhile, parents can use the money they don't throw at me to put food on the table, and businesses can use it to provide more opportunities for their employees or to contribute to local charities."

Standing and scratching his head with his pen, a rumpled reporter on the left asked, "Mr. Dodger, I don't mean any disrespect, but that seems a bit naïve, which would lead me to wonder whether you are serious about running for president. Or is this just an opportunity for the Golden Eagles to raise their profile and their agenda?"

"Well now, I wouldn't be standing here if this was all just for show," said Jack, visibly annoyed by the question. "I can get that sitting at home in front of the TV. No, we're very serious about this, and I am very serious about this. Who's next?"

Costello elbowed Abbott. Jack didn't know it, but he had just broken one of the primary rules of the "game" that he had mentioned in his opening statement—don't get impatient with the media.

"Mr. Dodger, do you think that the American public will feel comfortable being led by someone of your age?" The question came from a young woman midway back.

"I don't see why not? My health is good, my head is straight, and my age has exposed me to experiences that the vice president and the governor have only read about in books."

With that, Jack delivered his first quotable sound bite that made mention of his rivals. Costello smiled. It was a good, competitive statement. Abbott was less than thrilled that Jack had shown he could be provoked, and the media continued to probe for his hot buttons.

Wanting more, the young woman asked, "What about your lack of political experience?"

"If politics is about lying and deceiving and pressuring, as it has been defined in recent years, then I would agree that I don't have the necessary experience. But if politics is about looking at a problem, observing its various facets, getting together all the possible solutions, and then reaching a consensus on what should be done, then I believe I can handle that. I've been practicing that kind of politics my whole life—in my businesses and even at home. It's good politics that keeps a family working and living together."

A gray-haired man in a white shirt, red tie, and matching suspenders stood from the second row and interjected with gravitas in his voice, "And what about the issues, sir? Do you think you have a grasp of the key issues that are necessary to lead?"

"I'm not a certifiable expert, if that's what you mean, but like most citizens, I have followed the important issues of our day, listened to what is going on, and I've formed an opinion or two."

"Okay then, Mr. Dodger, what is your opinion on abortion?" he pressed.

"I'm against it. But I don't really—"

"In all situations? Are you against abortion completely?"

"I'm against it."

"But what if a woman is—"

"Still against it. As I was trying to say, I don't believe that is a key issue in a presidential campaign. It is, however, a key issue in our homes and our churches and in our communities. That's where the hard decisions must be made. The president can harp on it all day, but that's not going to have a wit of impact on what's going on in the mind of a young woman."

"That's enough," whispered Abbott heavily, and he began to make a move toward the podium. But Costello grabbed his sleeve and held him back. "Let's give him a little bit longer. See if he can get himself out of this."

Jack scanned the room and pointed to a casually dressed young man, who stood and asked, "What do you think is the best way to eliminate pornography on the Internet?"

"Well this is all new to me, because I've never visited the Internet. But if I understand correctly, to get pornography, you have to actively seek it out and select it. It isn't just there on the screen every time you turn on the switch. As far as I'm concerned, if an adult wants to waste his or her time and money on the computer looking for that garbage, then they have that right. I'm not condoning it, but I'm not going to stop them if that's what they want to do. But now if you're a parent and your child is upstairs in their room all alone looking at one of these sites or chatting with some stranger in Idaho, then I think the problem is you're not being a good parent. When my daughter was growing up, we told her what she could and could not watch on TV. Same should be true with computers. Limit their time, install blocking programs, put the computer downstairs in the den—whatever it takes. Once they turn eighteen, they're free to do what they want, but if you give 'em good guidance up to that point, then I don't think you'll have too much to worry about. Okay, someone else?"

A woman in a tailored suit stood in the middle of the room. "Mr. Dodger, what do you think should be the role of our military in problems around the world?"

"I think the role of the military should be what it's always been—defend our borders and defend our allies who are threatened by aggression. Because our borders are safe, our troops have got a lot of time on their hands and so the politicians keep looking for new ways to use them, such as these humanitarian missions. While the goals are admirable, the military is the wrong vehicle. Soldiers, by definition, are trained to fight and kill. That is their ultimate purpose. That's what we were trained to do in Korea. Any activity that takes them away from that primary task is misguided."

"And what about women in the military?" she asked.

"As support personnel, sure. But to put them in combat is barbaric."

"Okay that's enough," said Abbott to Costello. "I'm gonna pull the plug on this thing right now." Abbott walked to the lectern and leaned in front of Jack. "Folks, we have time for just one more question."

The hands went up again, and scanning the room thoroughly for the first time, Jack came upon the familiar face of Billy Briar from the *Dallas Times.*"

"Yes, sir, what is your question?"

Billy stood up. "Thank you, Mr. Dodger. I was just wondering, why do you want to be president?"

"I'm not here because I *want* to be president," said Jack. "I'm here because a good number of people have asked me to run, and I've always been one to say yes when asked by good people to do something that is honest and honorable. Up until a few months ago, I wanted to retire. But now I've been asked to do this. It may be silly to a lot of the younger crowd, but I'm still patriotic enough to feel like one should answer a call to service when it comes."

"That's all, folks," said Abbott. "We appreciate you coming out."

Jack backed away from the lectern and watched as the media began to pack their belongings and disperse. A few attempted to approach him but Abbott and Costello intercepted them and told them there would be opportunities soon enough for more questions and even individual interviews.

As the room cleared, Hank and Franky stepped forward to shake hands with Jack and congratulate him, but Wilton decided to hold his comments until they'd had a debriefing session with the consultants. Wilton thought in his own mind that Jack had handled himself reasonably well, but he had some concerns about some of the hard lines that Jack was already drawing on certain topics.

Wilton was anxious to get back over to the Golden Eagles office and begin evaluating the press conference. What he didn't expect was that it would begin as soon as the last reporter left the room.

Franky brought Jack a cup of ice water, and he was chewing on some ice when he asked innocently enough, "So, how'd I do?"

Abbott's critique was immediate and sharp. "You were terse, impatient, abrupt, and almost rude. In case you weren't paying attention to the primaries, the voters don't much care for terse, impatient, abrupt, and rude. But that's not the worst of it. You showed too much of your hand too soon. This was supposed to be an introductory session, and you already pushed yourself into a corner—actually a half-dozen corners. After the media file their stories tonight, they're going to start planning their next round of questions based on what they just heard. And next time we do this, they're going to tear into us even deeper."

Jack turned to face both Abbott and Costello, with Hank, Wilton, and Franky right behind like a two-tier choir.

"What do you mean, 'the next time *we* do this?'" Jack asked loudly and with an ample dose of sarcasm. "Unless I missed something, it was me, alone, facing that crowd."

"Yes, that's true, but a successful campaign is a team effort," said Abbott.

"Yes," said Jack, his voice rising in anger, "and like a team, we all have different roles. Your role is to coach me, and my role is to perform as best I can."

At this point, Costello jumped in. "Well, apparently you've been ignoring our coaching this past month. Whatever happened to being friendly and conciliatory and not being reactionary?"

Jack countered, "Mr. Costello, the last thing you told me before I stepped up to the microphone was to be myself. In fact you said it three times. And by God, that's exactly what I did."

Jack took a deep breath and then rattled his cup of ice thoughtfully. His next words came much more softly and gently.

"I hate to let you down, but the person you've been trying to create the past month just isn't me. What you saw in there *was* me. That's who I am. I don't know how to be anyone else, and I won't be anyone else.

"Hank, Wilton, it seems to me you have a decision to make here. Do you want me to be your candidate, or do you want the man that these fellers have invented? If you want me, then I'm ready to go. But if you want their man, then you need to go and find him because he ain't me. I'm just Jack Dodger from Dallas."

Jack turned and walked out of the room and down the hall toward the greenroom. Franky nodded silently to the others and followed Jack. They disappeared around the corner, leaving Abbott, Costello, Wilton, and Hank frozen in place.

CHAPTER 9

Jack and Franky stepped out of the convention center into the bright midday sun. Jack stopped just outside the doorway and grabbed Franky's upper arm.

"Hold up," he said. He'd had his fill of attention for the moment, and he wanted to make sure that no media were standing around before they crossed the street to the hotel. It was clear, and they crossed the street undisturbed, but they didn't get far inside the hotel lobby before they were accosted by a handful of media people who were staying there overnight. They rushed up to Jack and Franky and peppered them with questions.

"Mr. Dodger, will you be holding regular press conferences?"

"What's your campaign itinerary?"

"Where do you go next?"

"Is this campaign for real?"

Jack held up his hand in a plea for silence. "At the moment our itinerary says we're going up to our rooms. I'm sure we'll be seeing you again real soon." He and Franky pushed their way through the lobby to an awaiting elevator.

After the doors closed, Franky pushed a half dozen random floor buttons along with their own destination. "In case someone follows us," he told Jack. "Seen it in the movies."

"Good job," said Jack.

After stopping at four different floors, they got off on the twelfth floor, and Franky punched another handful of floor buttons before letting the doors slide shut. The two men scooted down the hall to their rooms, which faced each other. Jack started to open his door, but Franky was still in full bodyguard mode and he stopped Jack from going in. "No, you better bunk with me for now. They may get your room number and come looking for you."

Jack was tired and in no shape to argue. They entered Franky's room, and like twin brothers, they simultaneously took off their suit jackets. Franky kicked off his shoes, and Jack did the same. Neither of the men had a plan at this point. Franky disappeared into the bathroom, and Jack switched on the television. As mentally tired as he was from the press conference, his curiosity wasn't dampened at all, and he switched to CNN and sat on the edge of the bed to watch. He watched a report on the stalemate with the Cuban refugee boy, and then the latest campaign pronouncements of the front-running vice president and governor. From there, the news anchor segued into a report about alternative candidates, including the Reform Party hopefuls, the Green Party's top pick, and finally, "Jack Dodger, the outspoken candidate of the older generation."

The report included footage from the press conference.

"I didn't know we had CNN there." Jack called out loudly. Franky came back into the room just at that moment and sat down on the edge of the second bed.

"You look good."

"Yeah, but how do I sound?" asked Jack. "Abbott and Costello seem to think I fouled things up. But what was I supposed to do? People ask direct questions, and they want direct answers. I just can't play the game they want me to play."

"Then don't," said Franky. "Don't play their game."

They watched the news a few minutes more, and then, Jack turned down the sound. He lay backward on the bed, his feet still on the floor. He locked his fingers on his breastbone and stared at the ceiling. Across the hall in his room, the phone rang several times. It stopped, and after a minute it rang again. Jack closed his eyes while Franky stared at the soundless television picture.

"You know, those fellers weren't so bad," Jack said reflectively. "They did teach me quite a bit. I sure know a lot more about some of the fine details of these issues than I did before. But they want to control how I talk about them and when I talk about them, and that's just not gonna work."

"What you need, is someone who knows something about the news business, but who also knows who you are and likes who you are," Franky said.

Jack thought about that for a moment and then opened his eyes, turned his head, and looked at Franky.

"Oh no, not me. I'm not talking about me." Franky laughed. "No, that'd be a wreck like you don't want. No, I'm thinking of someone else who knows you real well and who's been following you around like a pup."

Jack's brow bunched up as he strained to make sense of Franky's riddle. The phone rang across the hall again, and Jack rubbed his forehead in an attempt to block out the distraction; he knew who was probably on the other end of the line. Then suddenly his mind clicked, and he sat upright. He slapped his palms on the mattress and might have jumped up and touched the ceiling had he not been so wrung out from the press conference.

"Franky, you're a genius. Of course, young Billy Briar—he'd be perfect. He's been writing about my every move, and he's done a good, fair job of it. He's got no bias as I can tell. He's been reporting things just as they've happened. He's like us: he's never done this kind of thing before, so he doesn't come to it with a lot of formulas and procedures. But he's intelligent, energetic, and he seems to have good instincts. I think he'd be perfect."

Jack stood up and stretched, feeling reenergized.

"Not gonna be easy," said Franky, tempering Jack's enthusiasm.

"You're sure right about that," said Jack. "On the one side, I've got to convince Billy to come give us a hand. And on the other side, I've got to convince Wilton and Hank to let Abbott and Costello go."

"I think getting things straight with the Golden Eagles will be the easier part of it," said Franky.

Okay, Franky, Jack thought to himself. *Now's a good time for one of those sparks of brilliance I was telling Caroline about.* "How do you figure?" he probed aloud.

"Well," said Franky, "no offense, but I think this campaign may be a little more amateur than what Abbott and Costello are used to. I just bet they're up in their own hotel rooms talking like we are, except they're thinking up an excuse to leave town."

"Yeah, you may be right, Franky. They weren't at all pleased with my performance this morning. But what about Wilton and Hank? They've probably got these men on some kind of contract."

"Even if they do, they did it in private, so they can probably kill that deal in private. But you, they hired you in front of a convention hall full of people. I'm sure they'd rather send the campaign pros away in private than argue with their candidate in public. I don't see them squawking too much if you decide you'd rather work with someone else."

Jack thought a moment. Franky had dug into a rare vein of common sense.

"Tell you what," Jack said. "Since you did such a good job acting as my emissary back when the Eagles first called me to run, why don't you play that role again and go let them know that I'd like to choose my own advisor."

"Be glad to," said Franky, standing up to put on his shoes and suit coat. "I've been feeling like a spectator around here. About time I earned my keep."

Jack gave Franky a smile and a nod, and Franky was out the door. Meanwhile, Jack called the hotel operator to find out if Billy Briar was checked in, and he was. Jack called his room, and when there was no answer, he left a voicemail message asking Billy to come up to Franky's room as soon as possible.

Jack was napping lightly when there was a knock at the door. He got up and looked through the peephole to see Billy

Briar waiting. Excited, he unlatched the lock and swung the door open.

"Billy, good to see you. I'm glad you got my message. Come on in, and let's talk a bit if you've got time."

"Sure. I'm not going back to Dallas until tomorrow morning. I was sort of waiting to see if I could find out what you folks plan to do next so I could add it to my story before I file it."

"Well, that's kinda what I wanted to talk to you about. Come on in, have a seat." Jack motioned to the plush chair next to the window and facing the bed. "Can I get you something—a soft drink or some ice water?"

Billy declined, and Jack sat down on the edge of the bed where he could talk to Billy face-to-face. Billy started to open up his reporter's notebook.

"Oh, you don't need that right now," said Jack. "This interview is gonna be a little bit different."

Billy looked surprised and set his notebook and pen on the side table.

"Billy, you were there at the press conference this morning. How do you reckon it went? And I want your honest opinion."

"Well in general, I thought it went pretty well. The questions were good, and you were open and honest—perhaps more so than what was expected."

"How do you figure?"

"Well, I haven't been to a lot of political press conferences, but they generally seem more staged than this one. And the candidates hardly ever raise their voice, and it was clear that you were irritated there at one point."

"Do you think that is a problem?"

"Not if you continue to answer the questions. Remember back when Dallas's own computer billionaire was running? He'd get irate and start whining and wouldn't answer the questions, which turned the press against him—made him look crazy." Billy paused for a moment and chuckled. "You got testy, but you answered the questions, and it was clear that your campaign folks were not real pleased."

"It was that obvious?"

"It was to me."

"Well, that's what I want to talk to you about. You see, those fellers have a way they want to do things that is probably just perfect for a professional politician. But I'm not a professional politician, and so I think we're going to be crosswise on this thing."

Billy nodded in agreement. "Yes, I think you probably need someone with a more lenient touch—someone who knows who you are and will let you be who you are, with a little bit of reining-in only when absolutely necessary."

"Well now, that's just what I was thinking, Billy. I think it would be helpful if that person has some good media experience too—someone who has been on their side of the fence and knows how they think."

Jack locked his gaze on Billy, and Billy stared uncomfortably back, puzzled at the intensity of Jack's eyes.

Just then, a key entered the doorknob and Franky strode in, interrupting Jack's sales pitch.

"How'd it go?" asked Jack.

"It went just fine," said Franky. "Just like I thought, the campaign boys have already decided you're a little 'unorthodox' for their taste. So they've decided to move on." Franky dropped his key on the dresser and plopped down beside Jack on the edge of the bed. "So how's it going here?"

"I was just about to close the sale," said Jack. He turned back to Billy. "So what do you think?"

"What do I think? About what?" Billy asked.

"What do you think about being my new press advisor?"

Billy's jaw dropped to his neck, and he was speechless. Franky chuckled and nudged Jack with his elbow. "Looks like he's choking. Want me to give him that Heimlich squeeze?"

"Naw, he's just chewing on our proposition. Well, Billy, got any questions?"

Billy found his voice again. "Yep, I've got a big one. Are you completely crazy?"

"Not at all, just real practical," said Jack. "Listen, Billy, I can't think of anyone I'd rather have on my side for this thing. From what I've read, you're a dang good reporter—fair and detailed. What's more important to me, I feel like you know me pretty well by now, and I think we've developed a good rapport. And I really need that. So, whadaya think?"

Billy nervously rubbed his chin for a moment. "I'd have to quit my job. You'd pay me, right? I've got bills like everyone else."

"You bet," said Jack, standing up with an enthusiastic sense that Billy was going to accept. "We'll work that out with the Golden Eagles. So do we have a deal?"

Billy stood up, and Jack grabbed his hand for a presumptive congratulatory handshake.

"Mr. Dodger, Jack, you're asking me to do something that most people in my profession only dream about. But at the same time, you're asking me to change the course of my career before it really gets started. Once I leave newspapers for politics, I don't know if I can ever go back. People in the business tend to think of it as selling out—going to the other side."

"Who knows, you might find you like this side better," said Jack. "I'm bettin' you'll find that you're good at it."

Billy stood with his arms crossed, looking down at the floor. "I don't know. I just don't know."

Jack patted Billy on the back. "I know it's a lot to consider. Why don't you file your story, go back to Dallas, and then call us from there in a day or two, but don't wait too long. We need to give the Golden Eagles a plan *B* soon before they come up with one of their own. If we're gonna run, I want to run my own way."

"Fair enough," said Billy. "I'll let you know day after tomorrow."

Billy walked to the door, pulled it open, and stepped out into the hallway. He stopped and turned back to look at Jack and Franky.

"So what happens if you win?" he asked.

"I guess you'll have to find someplace to live in Washington," said Jack.

CHAPTER 10

By suppertime, Jack and Franky had come out of hiding and were back at the Golden Eagles headquarters sorting things out with the staff. Wilton was furious with Jack for disappearing, even if it was just for five hours, but Hank chalked it up to "opening-day jitters." He told Wilton, "Lighten up. No harm done. It's all behind the scenes where it belongs. Let's keep pushing forward."

Jack smiled at Hank. While Wilton had designs on making the Golden Eagles a national political force, Hank was simply interested in leaving the world better than he found it. And like Jack, he wanted to do that by restoring some common sense, honesty, integrity, and honor to public service. If the mainstream political parties weren't up to the task, then the Golden Eagles might as well give it a try.

At Jack's insistence, the campaign team took a break on Sunday. Jack and Franky slipped into the back pew of a downtown church, and then they enjoyed a leisurely lunch and a drive around town to visit a few local attractions. Afternoon found them at the Nelson-Atkins Museum of Art, and Jack was impressed by the quiet contentment and cheerfulness of the people roaming in and out of the galleries and relaxing out on the grounds.

"It's interesting, Franky," he said as they sat on a bench in the sculpture garden and watched the parade of people go by. "Here I am running for president, I've been on the news countless times locally and nationally, and yet nobody here is paying me the slightest bit of attention. No questions, no autographs, no congratulations, no jeers—just quiet. It's a beautiful day, and people are just interested in living their lives. They could care less about politics and issues and who wants to do this or that. It's all irrelevant here. I think that's what the folks in Washington seem to forget—that most of the time folks just want to be left alone to live and enjoy their lives. They don't want the shadow of government hanging over them all the time. They just want to sit in the sunshine."

※

Jack awoke Monday morning feeling refreshed and relaxed, and then came news that put a literal spring in his step: Billy Briar would join the campaign.

"I asked my editor for a leave of absence, but he said I was ineligible because I haven't put in enough time," he told Jack on the phone. "I thought about that for about thirty seconds, and said, 'I quit.' Then he told me to leave—immediately. So I'll be ready to get to work first thing Thursday morning. What the heck—I'm young, single, and I may never get an opportunity like this again."

Jack could hardly wait to share the news with Wilton and Hank. Wilton allowed that while Billy was young and had no political experience, his knowledge of the media would be good for the campaign. And secretly, Wilton appreciated the fact that he would not have to pay Billy nearly as much as he would have paid out to Abbott and Costello through November.

Wilton was the treasurer for the campaign, and so these kinds of considerations weighed heavily on him. He knew it was going to be a tricky balancing act: running a campaign that was visible and effective without spending more money than was available.

By mid-April, the Golden Eagles had contributed one hundred thousand dollars in seed money, and another fifty thousand dollars had come in from outside contributions—what one of the mainstream candidates might collect from one table at a single fundraising dinner. For the Golden Eagles, fundraising efforts had taken somewhat of a back seat to the state-by-state balloting drive, but Wilton was confident that money would come in at a faster rate as the emphasis shifted. Still, he believed the effort was forever crippled by Jack's early pronouncement that no more than ten dollars should be collected from any one person. Looking at the contribution logs, it was clear that most people were following Jack's wishes.

On the brighter side, without all the big political party overhead, the campaign was destined to be lean and efficient. Jack and Franky were both living off pensions and social security. Any Golden Eagles staff devoted to the campaign would earn their regular salaries or stipends, which were already budgeted. Billy Briar would get less than he made as a rookie reporter at the *Dallas Times*, which was about two thousand dollars per month. And out in the trenches, the campaign was being staffed entirely by retiree volunteers. That meant that the bulk of the donations could be devoted to travel expenses and advertising.

Billy Briar rolled into Kansas City on April 20, and he, Jack, and Wilton got down to business right away. Hank came in and out of meetings as time allowed, but he still had a large national organization to run. Franky sat quietly and offered moral support, as well as doing the occasional odd job and running errands—bringing in lunch or manning a campaign hotline.

Topping the list of things that needed to be done now that Billy was on board was to plan a strategy for the next few months. Jack was still making some short trips to outlying communities to talk and drum up support, but he and everyone else were getting cabin fever in Kansas City, and they all agreed it was time to take the campaign out on the road.

There was a consensus right away that the campaign should not charter an airplane, but for different reasons. Wilton said it would be too expensive, and Billy reasoned that an airplane-bound campaign would overfly too many opportunities. Franky chimed in that airplanes make him sick, and that was enough to rule airplanes out for good.

Wilton was in favor of renting a large, full-sized van, since there wouldn't be many people traveling with Jack. A driver would be needed, of course, and Franky quickly volunteered.

"My record is clean, I've never had a wreck—not a bad one—and I like to drive," he said.

Wilton was keen on the idea—he was counting costs again—but Jack wasn't so sure that his friend was up to it. He worried to himself that the grind of driving long hours, day after day, might be better left to a younger man.

"Franky, I appreciate your offer, but don't forget I'm gonna need you with me at other times. I think it might be better if you save yourself as a relief driver if we need one."

Billy agreed, but for a different reason. "I was thinking that we need something bigger than a van. I'm thinking a bus, or a large RV might work better."

Billy saw Wilton grimace, and so he quickly explained.

"Here's my reasoning: First, with a bus or RV, we don't have to look for a hotel every night. We can just pull off the road or into a parking lot. Save a lot of money right there. But also, that would allow us to keep moving, even when Jack needs to rest, and he's going to need lots of rest. We all will. I bet we can find a used bus or RV to rent for a reasonable price."

"What about all those campers here in the parking lot last month?" Franky asked Wilton. "Where'd those rigs come from?"

"Yes, yes, that's good. That's real good," said Wilton, somewhat surprised at Franky's logic. "We did have a bunch of our members come in RVs for the convention. I'll go down the list and see what we can find. Good. That's a great idea, Franky."

Jack smiled at his old pal. Then Billy turned to him and continued.

"Yes, that'd be great. Now, Jack, there's another reason I think a rig like that would be good. I know how uncomfortable you were at that press conference. Now I don't think there's any way we can completely avoid that, but whenever possible, we should arrange one-on-one interviews with the media. That would help deflect some of the tension, and it would give the media a chance to get to know you a lot better than they will by shouting questions at you. And an RV like that would be a good place to do it. It'll be relaxed and casual, like that first time I interviewed you at your kitchen table. We can also keep moving by holding some of those interviews en route. Pick 'em up in one town and drop 'em off in the next."

"Sounds like a wonderful plan," said Jack, pleased with the work of his new media advisor. "What do you think, Wilton?"

"Sure, great. All we need is a driver," said Wilton.

"Hmmm," Jack said. "I've been thinking about that too, and I know someone who's young and energetic, who has experience as a truck driver, and who also is desperate for a steady job."

"Good, give me his name and number." Wilton pulled out his pen.

"His name is Kevin Walker, and I better be the one to call him," said Jack.

Wilton wrote the name down in his notebook, and when he saw the words on the page in front of him, he looked up at Jack. "Wait a minute, isn't that the kid who—"

"Yep, he's the kid who held us up, but he's okay. He's paid his dues, and he's ready to make something good of himself. I'll vouch for his character. I've already trusted him with my life, so trusting him to drive us cross country is easy."

"I don't know," said Wilton. "How's that going to look: a convicted felon driving a presidential candidate across the country? What do you think, Billy? You're the media expert."

Billy scratched his head for a moment. "Well, it is unusual. I'd say this whole affair is unusual. But if Jack trusts him, then I do too. Anyway, outside of Dallas nobody has really seen him. And with the schedule we'll be keeping, he'll be in the rig sleeping a lot of the time while we're out campaigning. I don't think any media will even notice him. I would, of course, but I'm no longer in the media."

"That's right." Jack laughed. "You sold out."

Billy nodded sheepishly.

Over the next week, Wilton worked the Golden Eagles membership roster and was able to get the use of a sleek new Winnebago. It had room for seven passengers and would comfortably sleep four.

Meanwhile, Billy, Jack, and Franky mapped out the first few weeks of a road tour. The RV was based in New Orleans, so the campaign party would fly to New Orleans by way of Dallas. In Dallas, they would pick up Kevin. And not wanting to miss an opportunity, they planned a rally in downtown Dallas and then a send-off at Love Field.

On the morning of May 1, they flew to Dallas and were met at the airport by Kevin, who embraced Jack with a hearty handshake and a quiet thank-you for the job. Jack introduced him to the rest of the team, and they began walking to baggage claim when a familiar voice cut through the terminal noise.

"Grandpa Jack! Grandpa Jack!" Wendy and Caroline had driven up from Austin for the day to surprise Jack and to help send off the group. Jack and Wendy were full of chatter as they made the short drive from the airport to downtown. Kevin had borrowed a van and was already earning his keep behind the wheel.

Thanksgiving Square was chosen as the site for the rally. It was a fitting location in that one of the key themes of Jack's speeches had been giving something back to his country in gratitude and thankfulness. And because the park attracts a lot of office workers at lunchtime, high noon was the chosen hour.

Several hundred local Golden Eagles and their friends and family were waiting in the square with placards and balloons, and curious lunchtime pedestrians swelled the crowd to approximately five hundred. Billy had contacted local media and he recognized a few familiar faces. He knew that they would pass their stories along to the wire services and networks.

The crowd was larger than Jack expected, and in order to be seen and heard, he climbed up on a short retaining wall but lost his footing. He would have tumbled into the shallow fountain and perhaps killed the campaign right then and there had Franky not been at his side to pull him back. Jack turned to face the crowd, and with his right hand on Franky's shoulder for support, he made a brief address.

"I just want to thank you all for coming out today. We're getting ready to set out on a great adventure, and I want you to know that we won't be traveling alone. We'll be taking your goodwill and good thoughts with us.

"I wanted to start this trip here in Dallas because I grew up in this town, and it's the place I'm gonna miss the most. I walked these streets as a small boy with my mother and father, and later with my wife and daughter, and more recently, with close friends. Dallas is a great city—it's been very good to me, it's helped make me who I am.

"Likewise, this country has been good to us, and so that's why we're setting out on this trip. We want to share some thoughts and ideas that we think are still important. We want people to know that America is still a great country, but we've all got to work hard to keep it great. Our work begins here today and will take us to as many places and people as will have us and time will allow. And so we thank you for your support, your kind wishes, and most of all, your prayers for safe travel. Thank you and God bless you all."

Jack stood on the wall and waved for a few moments as the partisan crowd cheered their approval. Out at the perimeters, office workers in business suits and bright dresses stopped to look down at the scene before shuffling off to lunch or noonday errands. A yellow transit train glided by and sounded its horn at onlookers that had spilled from the sidewalk onto the street.

As Jack climbed down off the wall, he was greeted again by Wendy, who ran past the media shouting "Grandpa Jack, Grandpa Jack." Someone in the crowd heard her and began chanting "Grand-pa Jack, Grand-pa Jack." The refrain spread up the sidewalks and soon the air was filled with a rhythmic "Grand-pa Jack, Grand-pa Jack." Jack lifted Wendy up and shouted over the crowd, "Little girl, I think you've started something."

"What was that all about?" Wilton asked later in the van. "Grandpa Jack?"

"I think our candidate has just been crowned with a brand new identity," said Billy, smiling with the knowledge that a catchy, endearing name would be good for business. "If George Washington was the father of our country, America's about to meet its new grandfather."

Kevin drove the party back to the airport where they were to board a Southwest Airlines flight to New Orleans. Banners spanning the door to the loading bridge announced "Jack Dodger for President" and "First Stop Dallas, Last Stop Washington." More well-wishers lined the concourse.

By the time they reached the gate, Jack was teary-eyed with excitement. The past month in Kansas City had been rather clinical: planning and strategy and theory and lots of what-ifs to think about. But now, the reality of the campaign was upon him. From here on out, it would be spontaneous and free flowing and personal—as spontaneous and personal as a crowd chanting "Grand-pa Jack."

Jack saved his final pre-board hugs and kisses for Caroline and Wendy.

"Hey, I've been thinking, why don't you two join us out on the road in a few weeks? We've got plenty of room. I need a personal secretary, and Wendy's a shoe-in for the job of chief morale officer."

"Sure, we'll see if we can work it out," said Caroline. "Now go and have a great trip and don't let them wear you out. When this is all over, we still need you to be our own Grandpa Jack."

They shared a last hug, and Jack walked down the ramp and boarded the plane.

A little over ninety minutes later, they were on the ground in New Orleans. They were greeted at the gate by several dozen sign-waving, bead-wearing Mardi Gras–type revelers. A large banner bore an adaptation of the well-known New Orleans motto, "Dodger for President: Let the good times roll." Jack gave a short impromptu speech in the terminal before being hustled away.

The RV was waiting in the parking lot of a private air terminal, and the team was delighted with the accommodations. There was plenty of room for Jack, Franky, Billy, Wilton, and Kevin, with enough seating left over for Caroline and Wendy later on. The donor of the camper had added a few finishing touches: a large US flag hung from the back end, small flags waved from the side mirrors, and magnetic signs on either side announced "Dodger for President" in bright red, white, and blue.

Everyone pitched in to load luggage and boxes of supplies, and then Kevin climbed into the driver's seat, made a quick scan of the controls, and adjusted the seat and mirrors. Franky took the shotgun position, and the others took seats back in the spacious cabin. Large side windows provided Jack a panoramic view and later would allow him to hang out and greet people from a slow roll.

As they rolled north out of New Orleans, with the sun glaring brightly off of Lake Pontchartrain on the west and the Gulf of Mexico on the east, Jack looked around the RV cabin and surveyed the various activities under way.

Sitting across from him on the sofa were Billy and Wilton. Wilton was speaking softly on a cell phone and flipping through calendars and notes. With his hands at the controls of a political machine, albeit a small one, Wilton was definitely in his element planning "the great campaign of 2000."

Meanwhile, Billy sorted through newspaper clippings and scribbled on a page of his ever-present reporter's notebook. Free from the manipulations and second-guessing of an eternally surly night editor, Billy was enjoying getting to do things his own way for a change.

Up front, Kevin had both hands firmly on the wheel as his eyes circled from roadway to gauges to mirrors and back again. On one of these circuits Kevin caught Jack's eyes in the rearview mirror. He smiled and took his right hand off the wheel just long enough to offer an enthusiastic thumbs-up. Jack was glad that Kevin had taken the job. It was important for him not just to work for the sake of his family but also to regain a sense of self-respect and trustworthiness. Jack figured that some time spent away from Dallas and out in America would give Kevin a new sense of being part of something good and important.

Jack turned his attention finally to Franky. It hadn't taken long for the rhythm of the road to coax the hulk of a man into a deep sleep, with only the shoulder belt keeping his dead weight from spilling down onto the floor. As Franky's head bobbed back and forth, Jack imagined that he was dreaming of childhood days in East Texas—of a hot summer afternoon, bobbing in the cool waters of a slow-running creek.

Jack was bemused by the incongruity of the whole scene. Was it possible that the hopes and dreams of an entire nation were rolling north out of the Mississippi Delta in the back of a borrowed Winnebago?

Jack chuckled out loud, which caused Billy and Wilton to look up from their respective tasks.

"Nothing, it's nothing," Jack said waving them back to their work. "I was just daydreaming."

CHAPTER 11

Billy Briar awoke to the sound of laughter in the midsection of the RV, and he stumbled out of the back sleeping room to see what was up.

"How long've I been out?" he asked, rubbing his eyes behind his glasses.

"About ninety minutes," said Jack. He, Franky, Wilton, and a reporter from Charlotte were sitting at the tiny table playing cards.

Billy was not especially pleased by what he saw.

"Now, Jack, this is not what I had in mind when I suggested we show the media a little hospitality. And you, Wilton, you've encouraged this?"

"Relax, Billy, we're just playing a dignified game of spades," said Jack. "There's no money on the table."

"And good thing," said Franky, shuffling the cards. "Turns out Wilton is some kind of grand master. He's winning every hand."

Wilton turned and grinned at Billy. It was a rare sign of ease and informality for the otherwise uptight campaign treasurer.

"Well, at least you got Wilton to loosen up a bit," said Billy. He patted Wilton on the back as he slipped past the table and made his way up front to check on Kevin.

It was dusk and the highway ahead was scattered with approaching headlights. Kevin was launching into a big, gap-mouthed yawn when Billy slipped into the passenger seat, causing him to quickly cover his mouth with his hand and force the yawn out of his nose, which made a hissing sound.

"How's she running?" Billy asked.

"Like a rabbit on cabbage. Smooth and making good time," said Kevin.

"How 'bout you? Need a break?"

"Naw, I'm okay right now. I got some good Zs while you were in town this afternoon. I'm good till we get to Raleigh to drop off the reporter."

"Well, you just let us know if you need relief. We've got nothing scheduled in the morning so we can pull off the road later if we need to."

The reporter in Billy wanted to engage Kevin further and find out a little bit more about him, but he resisted. The campaign had settled into a comfortable, enjoyable rhythm, and he knew better than to do anything that might risk upsetting the chemistry by putting even a minor player like Kevin on edge.

༺༻

For four weeks, the campaign had rolled along almost flawlessly, cutting across the heart of the Gulf Coast states, dropping down into the Florida Panhandle and then turning north into Georgia and the Carolinas. The journey was marked by planned rallies and speeches in the state capitals and larger cities and unplanned stops in smaller towns where it looked like they might be able to find a dozen or so people. This worked especially well around lunchtime, as every small town had a diner where the local folks gathered at noon. Standing in the parking lot or behind a lunch counter, Jack would deliver his simple message of responsibility and respect.

At the planned stops, they were greeted more and more by signs and banners that said "Grandpa Jack for President." Just as Billy had anticipated, the public had found an affectionate name that suited Jack's image well. Because of the potential issue of Jack's age, it was not a moniker that the campaign actively promoted, but Billy was not about to discourage it as long as the connotation continued to be maturity and wisdom and not simply age. When word came down that a Golden Eagles chapter in Tennessee was making signs that said "Codgers for Dodger," Billy told Wilton to make sure the signs were destroyed and never seen.

The question of age was raised in at least one women's magazine, but it wasn't Jack's health that they were interested in. Under the headline "A Step Back in Time?" a writer asked, "Why aren't there any women on Jack Dodger's campaign team? Is it because in his generation women were supposed to stay home and take care of the kids? Is that his vision of America?"

Wilton wanted to counter immediately with a letter to the editor listing the women who were in leadership positions throughout the Golden Eagles. Billy reasoned that they should hold off until Jack was confronted with the issue in a face-to-face interview. Jack agreed with Billy. He had been raised by a strong woman, was married to a strong woman, had fathered a strong woman, and had always encouraged each of them in their various endeavors. "I've got nothing to hide, my life speaks for itself," he said.

As Billy had predicted, the one-on-one interviews with the media were proving to be a big success. With Jack at ease in what Billy jokingly referred to as his "natural habitat"—sitting at the kitchen table in the RV—reporters one by one became acquainted with his insight, intelligence, and warmth. As a result, these reporters were more likely to write about Jack's "wisdom" and "maturity" rather than using the "A" word.

Still, Jack had weak spots in his resume that could not be totally brushed aside, and these were handled with calm honesty, as prescribed by Jack himself. Most prominent of these weak spots was foreign policy.

The subject came up in earnest one early afternoon just outside of Greensboro, North Carolina, as Jack was being interviewed by a local reporter.

"Mr. Dodger, I know that you've won a lot of admiration and support for your common sense approach to life and your desire to restore some dignity to the political scene here at home, but as you are well aware, the president of the United States is looked to for leadership in matters around the globe. And quite frankly, there's a strong feeling out there that you are woefully lacking in your knowledge of foreign affairs."

"Woefully lacking?" Jack asked with a soft chuckle. "Are those the actual words that people on the street are using? 'Woefully lacking?' Or is that what the reporters and editors are saying up in your newsroom? I'm always a little skeptical when the media tells us what people are saying 'out there,' because I don't think the media spends much time 'out there.'"

"Okay, okay," said the reporter, surprised at Jack's backroom media knowledge, "but you've got to admit that it is a valid concern. Don't you?"

"Well, sure it is," Jack said. "I'm admittedly light on my knowledge of foreign affairs. Haven't been outside the country in years, and that was just to Mexico. Before that, my only real experience with foreign affairs was in the Korean War, and I was a bit player in that show."

Jack leaned forward to make sure his next point was heard.

"But look at the presidents we've had over the past half century. How many of them had a lick of experience with foreign affairs before becoming president? Most have been governors or congressmen. Heck, the most successful president of the past forty years was an actor turned Hollywood union leader turned governor, and yet, he forced the Soviets to their knees and ended the Cold War."

"I understand your point," said the reporter, "but how do you propose to bring yourself up to speed?"

"Same way the others have done it," said Jack. "Surround myself with good people."

The reporter paused a moment to look around the RV. Kevin was at the wheel, his scraggly hair hanging from beneath a faded ball cap. Franky sat in the front passenger seat, his head bobbing in the midst of one of his signature afternoon snoozes. Billy looked like the green twenty-four-year-old that he was. Wilton had the polished, patrician looks of a senior advisor, but the illusion was shattered when his cell phone buzzed, startling him and causing him to spill his notebook on the floor.

Aware of the reporter's visual survey, Jack spoke up.

"Of course, there are those who help get you elected, and those who help you lead. And if I were to get elected, I think there's a wealth of good men—and women—who would be willing to pitch in. We've got bona fide world leaders in retirement right now who still have a lot to contribute."

"And what would *your* role be, Mr. Dodger?"

"It would be the same as any president. Listen to the advice of the best people available and, then, make a decision based on common sense, practicality, and a sound philosophy."

"And how would you characterize your philosophy?"

"Well, first and foremost, we've got to stop this business of basing our activities abroad on personal ego or political legacy or public opinion polls. And we've got to be more consistent. Why do we rush in to help one group of people, but then, we sit back and watch this other group over here starve or get slaughtered? Makes no sense."

"Are you suggesting that we help everyone? Or that we help no one?"

"I'm suggesting neither at the moment, because I don't know all the details of these situations. I'm just saying we need to be consistent."

The reporter shrugged and scribbled in his notebook. Jack stood up for a moment, stretched, and then pulled open the refrigerator door. He fished around and pulled out two bottles of iced tea, handing one to the reporter.

"You know," Jack said as he sat back down, "we Americans have this notion that we can fix everything. We always have. It's one of the things that sets us apart—makes us special. But our population is getting larger and older and more diverse, and we've got to be careful not to overextend ourselves. We're gonna end up like a doctor I knew in East Dallas who worked night and day to help indigent patients, all the while neglecting his own health. One day, he had a massive heart attack. Now he's not helping anyone. He can't, because he's dead. We've gotta take care of ourselves here at home too."

Jack always tried to ease these "kitchen table chats," as they came to be known among the media, into lighter discussions before they came to an end, and the session with the Greensboro reporter was no different. By the time Kevin pulled the RV into the airport parking lot in Richmond, Virginia, Jack and the reporter were engaged in a lively discussion about the merits of different breeds of dogs. Jack extolled the virtues of Labradors and in particular his adopted Blackie, while the reporter was partial to the frantic liveliness of spaniels.

"Well, thankfully, God saw fit to give us a lot of different breeds to choose from," said Jack. "He knew our needs for companionship would be very different."

"And leadership too?" the reporter queried. "Everyone's got a different idea about what type of leader the country needs, don't you think?"

"Yep. That's a fact. And that's another thing that makes America unique. We've got a real choice when we go to the polls. Some might think it's not a very good choice, but it's a choice just the same."

The RV pulled to a stop, and Jack and the reporter stepped out into the parking lot. It was well after dark, and the air was quiet except for the drone of a turboprop somewhere on the other side of the terminal.

"Mr. Dodger, it's been a pleasure," said the reporter. "I appreciate your candor and hospitality. I have to be honest, though, I think you've got an uphill drive in front of you."

"Ever driven to the top of Pikes Peak?" Jack asked. "I did it once. Almost burned up my engine on the way. Had to pull over every few minutes to cool it down. But when I got to the top, the view was magnificent."

Jack extended his arm, and the two men shook hands before the reporter hustled into the terminal to catch his commuter flight back to Greensboro.

The campaign rolled up the Atlantic Coast, bouncing from town to town. With each group of citizens he met and each reporter he engaged, Jack gained name recognition and familiarity. By the time they reached Virginia, national polls indicated that 56 percent of the electorate knew the name of Jack Dodger, and, more importantly, they knew he was running for president. Less promising, however, was the fact that only 4 percent of the respondents said they would vote for Jack if the election were held tomorrow.

"The numbers are lean, but we can build on them," Billy reassured the team. "We've just gotta keep pushing forward."

Jack's low poll numbers kept the mainstream national media from giving him anything more than a wink and a nod. Television coverage of the campaign painted him as a "curiosity" and a "political oddity" on the sidelines of the main event. The coverage often came as a thirty-second tongue-in-cheek coda to the newscasts before the anchors signed off, shuffled their papers, and rolled the credits.

Interestingly, Jack got more serious attention abroad. Some of the European, Middle Eastern, and Asian press expressed concern about what a man like Jack Dodger might do with regard to their region's hotspots: Kosovo, Israel and Palestine, China and Taiwan, Iraq, Iran, Russia. At the other extreme, a French newspaper was preoccupied as the French so often are. "Any old girlfriends we should know about?" they asked.

Outside of the Golden Eagles and other senior groups, endorsements were nowhere to be found, although the campaign did receive some congenial advice and encouragement on some editorial pages. The publisher of a small-town daily in South Carolina wrote:

> I like Jack Dodger a lot, but the presidency is more than one man. I'm concerned about his ability to field a competent cabinet and executive branch staff. Based upon what I know now, I'd have to wish him well, but reluctantly vote for an established pol. I'm specifically nervous about his lack of foreign policy experience. Maybe he should seek out a retired general, or even a retired former president, as an advisor on foreign policy matters. He needs to somehow develop, in the minds of the voters, a sense of confidence and credibility that he can assemble a team to run the country successfully, to go with his captivating patriotic down-home personality. If he can do that, I'd be with him in a heartbeat as the most refreshing, exciting candidate in years. We'll be back to the idea of a 'statesman' vs. a politician, and public service vs. a chance to grab personal power—but only if he has the right people with him. Otherwise it's politics as usual.

Another publisher provided a more cautionary analysis—directed at both the candidate and the electorate:

> If the campaign picks up steam, the two big parties will begin to paint Jack as an incompetent old man who has no business leading the country. They'll say it will be dangerous and irresponsible to elect him, even if you like his quirky personal style. They'll say that even if Jack Dodger is well-intentioned, others will take advantage of his inexperience in office and control the country from

behind the scenes, or other countries will run roughshod over us.

And such was the political "Catch 22" that the "Grandpa Jack for President" campaign faced. As long as Jack's poll numbers remained low or marginal, the rest of the political community would treat him kindly and in fact welcome his down-home idealistic philosophy. But the minute a reasonable percentage of the electorate began to show more than a passing interest in what he had to say, the mainstream parties likely would dispatch their hired talking guns to "take him out."

While Wilton worried out loud about potential damage to the campaign and the Golden Eagles, and Billy quietly formulated plans for countering such attacks, Jack was calm as usual.

"I've been shot at and mugged. I've had loved ones taken from me long before it was their time," he said. "If talking ugly is the best these folks can do, then let 'em get on with it. Nothing they can say will ever add up to anything approaching my worst day."

Jack let the concerns of the others drift by like the telephone poles and mailboxes that raced past their windows as the campaign crossed Virginia on its way to the District of Columbia.

CHAPTER 12

Jack was in no mood to talk as Kevin pulled the RV off the Beltway and into the heart of the capital city. At seventy-one, Franky was chattering like a schoolboy, obviously excited about his first trip to Washington. Billy and Wilton sat at the table discussing preparations for the next two days of campaigning. Even Kevin, who usually remained silent unless spoken to, softly whistled "Yankee Doodle" as he caught a first glimpse of the Washington Monument glowing in the morning light.

Jack sat quietly, staring out the window. He had been to Washington just once before—as a soldier coming back from Korea. Back then, the city seemed clean, fresh, and full of the promise of democracy. It had been a fitting conclusion to his service overseas—a tangible reminder of what the fighting was all about. As Jack looked upon the symbols of freedom and sacrifice some forty-five years later, he couldn't help but feel small and insignificant—and a bit embarrassed.

The decision to go to Washington was accompanied by a substantial amount of debate. Wilton and the Golden Eagles had felt it was important for Jack to be seen near the seat of government. They thought the idea of Jack sitting in the oval office would seem less far-fetched to voters if he could be seen in the city itself. Billy was concerned that it was far too early to make a foray into the camp of the political establishment. Jack's objections were more about appearances than strategy. Surely the RV with its presidential slogans and flags looked like just another "wagon load of hucksters come from out there somewhere to beat a drum and throw rants up into the political winds."

In the end, the Golden Eagles won the debate because they were to a large extent paying the way. Jack agreed to honor their wishes, but he laid down the law on decorum. There was to be no silly stunts, no childish signs and slogans, no shrill chants, or anything that might be reported by the media as "gray-haired rabble rousing." They were going to conduct themselves with dignity, seriousness, and purpose. He was not going to be humiliated in this of all cities.

The first stop was to be on the National Mall, where a small rally was planned. After considering several sites, Jack had lobbied for the Korean War Memorial—a fitting site for a veteran of that conflict.

As Kevin pulled the RV up to the parking area, they were surprised and pleased to find a crowd of some one thousand people already gathered. Jack put on his suit jacket and straightened his tie and then turned to Billy who was standing in front of the door. "How do I look?"

"Like you belong here," he said, sensing Jack's nervousness. "Don't worry. Everything's going to be fine. Just be yourself."

Billy opened the door and stepped out into the sunshine. He was followed by Jack, which elicited a cheer and applause from the crowd. The sound melted the furrows in Jack's brow and a smile crossed his face. He made his way to a small podium, pausing to shake a few hands along the way. The crowd appeared to contain a wide mix of ages and skin colors. To the left side was a small contingency of media, made evident by the presence of video cameras.

"Well, thank you. This is certainly a delightful reception," said Jack. "We've come a long ways to get here, and we'd be tired and worn if it weren't for the way folks have received us up and down the highway. It's especially encouraging to be greeted this way here in Washington.

"There's a feeling out in America that this city is eaten up with scandal and hypocrisy. When we leave here in a few days and head back out, I'm gonna tell folks that there are still people in Washington who want to give rather than take. And that's what this campaign is all about: getting involved and giving something back. I'm not saying that all the politicians in Washington are bad, but I think too many have forgotten what they came here for.

"That wasn't the case with the soldiers portrayed in this beautiful memorial. I was there in Korea, and I can attest that those brave young men never once forgot what their job was. It was to fight for freedom and democracy. And they did it not by fighting with each other—they did it by working together. To do otherwise was to bring certain defeat.

"I realize that in government as in all aspects of life, there's always going to be some differences of opinion. But at some point, folks have to put that aside and pull together. In politics there's always going to be some in the majority and some in the minority. Those in the minority are going to have to work a little bit harder to get their ideas heard, but in the meantime, they've got to find some part of the majority view that they can work with. And those in the majority are going to have to lead graciously and fairly and honorably. Instead of running people over, they've got to work harder to bring them along. This is important business, and there's no place in it for bullying and ugliness, and certainly no place in it for slander and lies. As Abraham Lincoln once said, 'Nothing is politically right that is morally wrong.'

"So one of our goals in this campaign is to remind people of what they've come to Washington to do and to see if we can't become a part of the process. And with your support, I think our chances look pretty good. So we thank you, and God bless you all."

Jack stepped down, and as the crowd began to disperse, he and Franky were immediately approached by a small group of gray-haired men.

"Franky Parker, by God, is that really you?" said one of the men, busting through the pack and brushing past Jack to shake Franky's large hand.

"Yep, that's me. And who might you be?" Franky rubbed his chin.

"Well, there's no way you'd remember me, but I guarantee there's not a soldier who went through your chow line who doesn't remember Franky Parker," he said, with a couple of the others nodding affirmatively. "Out on the lines, they called you the 'Singing Slop,' 'cause you were always singing as you slopped that chow into our kits. You always gave us big helpings of the good grub, if there was any."

"Yep, I got in some trouble with a general over that," said Franky. "He said if I didn't hold back on the grub, there wouldn't be enough money left in the US Treasury for ammo. I told him that if he'd plan his battles a little bit better, maybe he wouldn't need so much ammo."

"That comment near 'bout got you sent to the front, didn't it?" Jack interjected.

"Yep, but then I showed him the pork roast I had saved out for him and his staff, and he let it slide. Kept coming 'round regular after that."

They all shared a big laugh, and then Jack, Franky, and the other veterans began moving down the sidewalk to get a closer look at the monument. A couple of television camera crews followed the vets, and Billy was pleased that they were getting some good pictures, even if the talk was a bit loose.

As they walked among the life-size bronze figures of soldiers on patrol, the chatter began to calm down, and the mood became more reverent. A jovial comment from one of the vets of, "Hey, Bob, this looks like you on one of your bad days," was answered by more hushed tones of, "This one looks like Walter, God bless him," and, "Wonder what ever happened to Ray?"

Some thirty minutes later, the men came back to where Billy and Wilton were waiting. They shook hands, patted backs, hugged, shared addresses, and made promises to stay in touch.

"You're doing a good thing, Jack Dodger," one of the veterans said. "You keep it up. You show 'em what you're made of. You show 'em what we're *all* made of."

"Thanks, fellas." Jack squinted to hold back a few tears. "We're gonna give it our best."

Jack and Franky watched the others leave, and then they walked back to where Billy and Wilton were standing.

"That was real nice," Jack said softly to Billy. "Nice of you to get them out here this morning."

"Wasn't our doing," said Billy. "Those men came on their own."

"Real nice," Jack repeated and turned to walk back to the RV.

They remained parked near the monument for the next several hours and entertained a steady stream of appointments with reporters and unplanned visits from casual passersby. The weather was mild, and so, they left the door propped open, allowing anyone who desired to step in and meet the candidate. Through the early afternoon, they were visited by reporters and cameras from two of the network primetime news magazines for stories scheduled to be broadcast that week. Then at mid-afternoon, Kevin cranked up the RV, and they made their way through traffic to three different network studios to tape interviews for the evening newscasts. One of the networks had planned to tape the interview but was able to coax Jack, with Billy's approval, to appear live on the evening news. Jack and Billy insisted, however, that the interview be conducted in the studio rather than in the RV. They wanted to present a more formal, traditional impression.

Following the evening news sessions, the campaign team went to Capitol Hill, where they had been invited by Jack and Franky's congressman to take a personal tour of the Capitol and then visit for a while in his office. The congressman had been in Washington for more than twenty years and was well known for his ability to twist arms and get things done. It didn't take long for his office tea party to turn into a full-fledged lobbying effort.

"Jack, I think you are doing a great thing," he said, "and I know the folks back home are real proud of you. I sure am. But you know, while independent campaigns get a lot of attention and sure add some interest to the political process, they seldom ever get any real percentage of the vote. Now, our party leadership has been talking, and we think your energy might be better spent under the sponsorship of the party. And, well, we're ready to swing the door wide open for you. You can continue as you have been, but as a sort of roving party spokesman and not as a candidate. We'll take care of all your expenses and in that way you will have—"

"While we appreciate the offer," Jack interrupted gently, "we plan to continue on our current course. We think we've got something to say that isn't being said, and we think this is our best forum."

"Well that's all well and good," the congressman said, "but you don't really think you've got a chance to win this thing, now do you?"

"And you didn't really think that we drove all this way to Washington just to turn ourselves over to you, now, did you Congressman?" Wilton countered suddenly.

Jack and Billy stared at each other, unsure of what their otherwise silent treasurer was going to say next. Wilton continued, "I don't know how long it's been since you've walked the streets of your district, but there's an appetite for change out there. Despite what your history book says, one of these days, one of these independent efforts is going to tip the scales and pull ahead. And the only folks that will be surprised will be you folks in Washington."

The congressman looked to Jack for some hint of a less strident view from the candidate. Jack just shrugged and offered, "As I've said, we plan to continue on our present course."

The congressman looked at his watch, slapped his knees, and apologized for the need to move on to another engagement. He showed his guests out of the office and into the hallway, shook hands with Jack, and only Jack, and then left them to find their way back down the corridor and out the door.

"Now that was very interesting," Billy said as they walked down the Capitol steps and back to the RV.

"Yes, it was." Jack chuckled. "Wilton, I think you've been hiding your real self from us."

"Well, I took offense to the whole notion that we'd just set aside all that we've been working toward," said Wilton. "That took an awful lot of nerve."

"And some planning too," said Billy. "That business about the party being ready to 'swing the door wide open'—I don't think that was something he came up with on the spur of the moment. It's rather obvious that someone somewhere is concerned about us making progress."

"Yes," said Wilton, "and I wonder what his other appointment was? Perhaps a meeting with his leadership to start working on a plan *B* to sink us."

"Oh, you with your plan *B*." Jack raised his hands in mock fear. "The way you tell it, they're huddled in a smoke-filled room somewhere trying to figure out what to do about Old Jack Dodger. I think the congressman is just worried about keeping things straight in his district back home."

Billy stopped walking and turned to face Jack head-on. For the first time since they met, the young reporter addressed the senior candidate with more than a little bit of impatience in his voice.

"Jack, your easy-going nature is without a doubt one of your most endearing characteristics and a big reason why we're standing here today. However, I sometimes wonder how seriously you are taking all of this. In case you didn't know, new poll numbers are going to be released tomorrow, and you're expected to have a much stronger position than you had two weeks ago."

"Well, that's great news," said Jack.

"Yes, it is," Billy continued, "but with the higher numbers is going to come more heat from the other camps. And I won't speak for Wilton or Franky or the board, but that has me just a little bit worried."

Jack smiled and put his hands on both of Billy's shoulders. "Billy, in case you haven't figured it out yet, you're getting paid to worry about those kinds of things. And as long as I know that I've got a bright young man like you doing the worrying and planning accordingly, then, I'm going to keep doing my part, which is to be upbeat and optimistic and easygoing. Now, speaking of planning, where do we need to be next and at what time?"

With the wind sucked out of his sails, Billy looked at his watch. "Well, it's nine now, and we need to be on the west steps at about ten thirty. So we've got a little bit of time. Why don't we go back to the RV and let you lie down for a few minutes and rest?"

"Now that sounds like a good Plan B," said Jack. They all walked back to the RV, except Franky, who said he was going to stroll along the Mall for a while and would meet them at the steps.

"Don't know when I'll be back here," he said.

Kevin dimmed the lights in the RV, and they all closed their eyes for a little while, with Jack stretched out on the bed and the others tilting back in their seats.

Jack tried to relax and drift off, but his mind would not stop working. He knew there was truth to what Billy said—to all of what he said. There could indeed be some heat ahead. And he admitted, to himself at least, that at some level he indeed was not taking things all that seriously. He could not rid himself of a lingering, nagging feeling that this whole enterprise was nothing less than preposterous. He was a retired accountant who owned a small house, a pitiful little barbershop, a blue pickup truck, and a black dog. There's no way on God's green earth the American people would be so silly or stupid as to elect such a person—or so the little nagging voice kept telling him.

Afraid that they all might succumb to fatigue and oversleep their appointment on the Capitol steps, Billy had set his travel alarm. When it went off, it surprised Jack, who in the midst of his worries had indeed drifted off. Jack jumped off the bed quickly, and as soon as he stood erect, his head became fuzzy. He swayed, and he would have fallen face down on the floor had the room been big enough for him to do so. Instead, he fell backward in a sitting position on the bed and waited for the blood to reach his head. Billy tapped lightly on the door. "Yes, I'm coming," Jack answered.

They started the short walk back to the Capitol, but Jack was lagging behind the others. The short nap had left him groggy and with a dull headache. Billy was leading the way, and when he turned to urge the others to quicken their steps, he caught Jack rubbing his temples and clinching his jaw.

"You okay?" he asked as he stopped to let Jack catch up.

"Sure, sure," he said. "Just got up too fast. Made me a little dizzy. I'll take some deep breaths as we walk and that should fix me up fine."

By the time they were within sight of the Capitol steps, they could see a large crowd already gathered and could hear a steady chant of "Grandpa Jack, we want Jack. Grandpa Jack, we want Jack."

As they approached, someone in the crowd shouted, "Here he comes!" The next thing Jack knew, he was surrounded and was being gently jostled. The night air had been cool and breezy, but in the midst of the crowd, it was warm and still, and the closeness of the bodies created a heat that quickly became stifling. Jack could feel beads of sweat forming behind his ears and running down his neck. A camera flashed not four feet from his eyes, and the smiling faces were replaced with dancing dots of light. Jack could sense hands reaching out at him from all sides, and he tried to reach out in return but his arms were numb and wouldn't budge. Then from somewhere in the crowd Jack heard Franky's voice, and when he turned his head to answer, the noise became muffled and the lights diffused. Jack felt his head roll backward on his shoulders, and then he felt nothing at all.

CHAPTER 13

"Mr. Dodger is healthy and fit and is in no way impaired by last night's incident, which we are satisfied was nothing more than a common fainting spell," a white-coated doctor said to the dozen media folks and a hundred or so concerned supporters gathered in the lobby of the hospital. A murmur passed through the ranks of the partisans, as the news was much brighter than the grim speculation that followed Jack's collapse nine hours earlier.

When Jack came to a couple of minutes after falling on the Capitol steps, he was immediately surprised to find himself lying in Franky's big lap, with his friend under him moaning in pain and others around him speaking in panicked tones and rushing about. It was as if he had awoken in the middle of some wild movie and had no clue as to the plot. Jack had heard Franky's voice just before he lost consciousness, but he missed the commotion that followed.

Franky had rushed up just in time to catch Jack and break his fall, but Jack's dead weight caused Franky to fall backward himself and bump his head hard on the steps, opening up a superficial but fluid gash. Franky bled all over himself and Jack, and when a doctor in the crowd rushed up and saw these two bloodied men heaped on the steps, his first instinct was to search them for gunshot wounds. That caused a panic among some in the crowd, resulting in people shrieking and running for cover.

By the time the paramedics arrived, the "assassination attempt" theory had been dismissed, and the attention was back on Jack. He was conscious but disoriented as he was carried to the ambulance, which had those who were left behind speculating about whether Jack had been felled by a stroke, heart attack, or some type of seizure.

The speculation was joined by others the next morning as the early newspapers and news broadcasts reported that Jack had collapsed and was in the hospital being treated for an unspecified ailment. So the impromptu press conference at the hospital was the first opportunity that anyone outside of Jack's immediate circle had to learn the true nature of Jack's condition.

"After giving Mr. Dodger a thorough exam, and after interviewing him and the people who he was with yesterday, we've determined that he has not been getting enough rest and nourishment. Yesterday, for example, he had a long busy day, and he failed to eat a full meal. Under those conditions and with the obvious pressures and stresses of campaigning, it is no wonder that he fainted."

"What is the long-term prognosis?" a reporter asked.

"Mr. Dodger is a healthy, vigorous man, and there should not be any lingering worries. Provided of course that he maintains some semblance of a healthy balanced lifestyle."

"Was age a factor in his collapse?"

"Absolutely not," said the doctor, "and I want to make this very clear. What happened to him last night could happen to anyone who is maintaining a fast-paced, high-pressure schedule. I would add, however, that if Mr. Dodger is prone to push himself beyond normal limits of activity, then it is incumbent upon his managers to make sure that he does not overwork himself."

Billy and Wilton were standing to the side, and they almost melted into the floor. The doctor looked over at them, signaling that he had no other comments, and Billy stepped forward to field any lingering questions.

"What are your immediate plans for the campaign considering what has happened?" asked a young woman from a television station.

"As the doctor said, Mr. Dodger is healthy and is fine, so the campaign will move forward," Billy said. "However, we do plan to take a couple of days off to do some planning as well as to allow Mr. Dodger some much-desired and much-deserved time with his family."

As Billy said that, almost on cue, an elevator opened across the lobby and a nurse stepped out, pushing Jack in a wheelchair. They were accompanied by Franky, who had a fresh white bandage on the back of his head. Their appearance immediately transferred the attention of the media from Billy to Jack. Seeing the waiting crowd and hearing a string of questions coming across the room, Jack asked the nurse to set aside hospital policy and let him walk the rest of the way. As Jack and Franky approached, Billy asked the media to hold back a bit, but they persisted and Jack stepped up to at least acknowledge their presence, if not to answer all their questions.

"Folks, as I believe the doctors have told you, and as I hope you can see, I am fine. We've been working real hard and we're gonna take a day or two off to catch our breath and plan the next leg of the tour, and then, we'll be off again. In the meantime, if you have any questions, just stick around and I'm sure Mr. Briar will be glad to fill you in."

"Mr. Dodger, are you going to quit the campaign?" shouted a reporter brashly.

"No, I'm certainly not," said Jack. "Are you?"

The reporter blushed with embarrassment as his colleagues laughed at Jack's quick response.

Jack smiled and waived good-bye, and then, he, Franky, and Wilton walked to the exit, went outside, and climbed in a car. Jack had spent the night in a private hospital room and was now being moved to a hotel suite in an undisclosed location.

All this activity had producers at the national morning news shows rushing to edit their reports. Tape of the bright, happy events of the previous day was merged with video from the confusion and uncertainty of the night before and the doctor's statements and Jack's exit from the hospital. The result was a report that was very different from what the campaign had worked for. The dominant image was of Jack being pushed in a wheelchair rather than standing and speaking from the Capitol steps. And despite the positive prognosis of the doctors, political analysts harped on the health and age issue for all it was worth.

And so the story rolled through the day's news cycles as Jack and his team made themselves at home in a hotel suite for a couple of days of R and R. They were joined in the early afternoon by Caroline and Wendy. Franky had called them immediately from the hospital, and while there was no pressing need for them to come, Caroline was determined to assess her father's condition with her own eyes.

With more time on their hands than originally planned, Kevin and Franky decided to continue their tour of Washington, and with Caroline's consent, they took Wendy along as well. Billy and Wilton monitored the news and huddled to discuss damage control and plan the next leg of the trip. It was decided that the best way to demonstrate Jack's health and resilience was to resume the tour as quickly as possible. With the Fourth of July fast approaching, they wanted to make sure the campaign was far from Washington and out in the heartland where patriotism still ran high. Looking at a map, they targeted St. Louis as the place to spend Independence Day. It was a city that had launched explorers and pioneers in search of opportunities out West, and for this pioneering campaign, it would mark the beginning of their westward push.

Meanwhile Jack and Caroline relaxed by the pool—he wore sunglasses and a ball cap in order to prevent unwanted attention. But his disguise did not hide him from a thorough dressing down from his daughter.

"Daddy, you really gave us a scare last night," said Caroline.

"I know, I know," said Jack. "I'm sorry to worry you, but it really wasn't anything at all. I don't know why everyone's making such a to-do about it. Heck, they should be doting on Franky. He got the worst of it."

"Well, they are making a to-do about it because you're no longer a private citizen. It's just like we warned you in Dallas. Once people discover you, they're going to hound you and focus on every little thing about you."

"Well, that's certainly proving to be true," said Jack.

"And what's this business of carrying on without eating or sleeping?" Caroline asked. "You should know better. And if these people aren't going to see that you're doing right for yourself, then I may just have to find someone who will."

"And who might that be?" Jack asked coyly, knowing where his daughter's train of thought was going even before she did.

"Well," she said, pausing and thinking. "Well … umm … well … there's always Franky."

"Franky? Not him. He eats like a hog and sleeps like a bear. Put him in charge, and I won't be able to get out the door of the RV."

"Well, then … maybe … I might just have to come along to make sure you behave."

"Now you're making good sense," Jack said, sitting up on the end of his chaise lounge. "You and little Wendy can just jump on the Jack Dodger Express and see the sights with us. I think that would be great."

"Well, I'm not sure it would be such a good idea," Caroline said, backpedaling. "There's probably not enough room, and I don't know if the others would like me breaking up their men's club."

"Don't worry about the others," Jack assured her. "If I want you to come, then, you'll come. And by gosh I *do* want you to come."

That evening when everyone had reassembled in the suite for dinner, Jack informed the team that Caroline and Wendy would be riding with them on the next leg of the tour and perhaps longer.

Nobody raised a complaint, but neither was there any jumping for joy save for Franky, who was ecstatic as usual and reached over to give Wendy a fond tickle. Wilton silently worried about adding two more people to their expenses, and Billy wondered whether having the women along would slow things down. After all, the campaign was more akin to a trail drive than a pleasure cruise, and their success depended on making good mileage every day.

Being familiar by now with the personalities and obsessions of his team members, Jack spoke up to ease their specific concerns.

"Now I envision Caroline taking on some of your lesser duties, enabling you to look even farther ahead as we get into the real crunch. And don't you worry, these gals are real troopers and they travel light. They'll be ready to go whenever you are."

After dinner, they watched the news shows to try to get some measure of the damage caused by Jack's fainting spell. While the analysts were still raising questions about Jack's age and health, the good trend was that the incident had finally moved Jack out of the oddity slot and into the main news segments. And surprisingly, the event also generated the first mentions of Jack by name from the other candidates.

"Jack Dodger is made of strong Texas stock, and I wouldn't expect anything less than for him to pick himself up and get back out there among the people," the governor said. "And by the way, I want to say that the man is a credit to his generation, and a credit to the great state of Texas. I look forward to our paths crossing very soon."

The vice president, who was lagging behind the governor in the polls, used the incident to make a policy point. "I'm glad that Mr. Dodger is feeling better, and I'm especially grateful that he was able to receive quick and competent health care. That is something that the American people—and especially our seniors—need to keep in mind when they go to the polls in November. Our administration will see that people like Jack

Dodger continue to get the best available medical care. Under another administration, there are no such guarantees."

Jack was asked about these comments during a brief session with a handful of journalists the evening before the campaign ended its Washington rest stop.

"What do you make of the vice president's use of your recent incident as a political tool?" a reporter asked.

"It seems he's used everything else for political gain. No reason why he shouldn't use me as well," said Jack. "I don't particularly think my fainting on the Capitol steps and the future of health care for seniors connect too well, but then maybe, that tells us something about the vice president."

"And the governor? What is your response to his comments?"

"I appreciate his kind thoughts, and I hope we do get to meet at some point. He seems like a nice young man."

"Mr. Dodger, it sounds like you have a higher regard for the governor than for the vice president."

"Oh, I don't know about that. I'm just responding to what they've said about me. I can guarantee that neither one of them will get my vote come November," Jack said with a sly grin.

Two mornings after Jack left the hospital, the campaign team loaded up the RV and departed Washington without fanfare, their numbers increased by two. Billy and Wilton set a course that took them to Charleston, West Virginia; Cincinnati; and Louisville. They continued their strategy of holding large rallies in the cities and impromptu visits in small towns. Wendy became a familiar sight and, without anyone planning it, she became a valuable asset for the campaign. With her at Jack's side, and quite often sitting on his shoulders, Jack's image was beginning to change. While the campaign never targeted senior citizens exclusively, Jack's age and his Golden Eagles sponsorship had initially attracted a predominately senior following. But now with his young family in tow, Jack was beginning to be perceived as representing all generations and not just his own.

Billy and Wilton began planning more rallies with a family theme. Local Golden Eagles members were encouraged to bring along their grandchildren, which in turn, would coax their voting-age parents to come. And rather than just stop in at diners when they rolled into small towns, they began targeting playgrounds, ballparks, and other places where the youngest generations—and their parents—might be found.

With each mile that they placed between themselves and Washington, the echoes of Jack's collapse and worries about his health and age became more and more faint. Caroline saw that he got more rest and plenty to eat, and the presence of her and Wendy meant that they spent more nights in motel rooms. But also, Jack just seemed more comfortable and at ease back in the heartland. Away from the monuments and the weight of history that he found so overwhelming in Washington, Jack again began to believe the plausibility of a common man being called to an uncommon purpose.

That was to be his theme for the day as the RV rolled into St. Louis on the morning of July 4 for a full day of events along the Mississippi River. The riverside parks near the Gateway Arch were bustling with tens of thousands of people attending the annual St. Louis Fair, and there were endless opportunities for Jack to mingle and be seen. The atmosphere was festive, and Jack couldn't help but be swept up in the spirit of the day. He and Franky challenged each other and anyone else who was willing to play skill games along the midway, but the highlight of the afternoon came when Franky dared Jack into taking the seat of honor in a charity dunking booth. Jack survived the throws of Franky, Kevin, and even his own daughter, but finally it was a little league champ from Springfield that plunged Jack to the bottom. Being a good swimmer, he sat at the bottom for a moment and waived at the crowd before rocketing to the surface to the sound of cheers and applause.

By late afternoon it was time to prepare for the rally to be held at the edge of the fairgrounds. Billy suggested Jack go back to the RV and get straightened up a bit, but Jack squelched the idea. "They've already seen me under water and soaking wet. It won't do any harm for them to see me a bit rumpled too."

Jack's face was sunburned, and his clothing was wrinkled as he stepped up to the microphone.

"When I was five years old, my parents took me to my first big Independence Day celebration, and the sights and sounds of that day are still vivid in my memory. Most of all, I remember sitting on a lakeside in my father's lap watching fireworks, and him telling me how ordinary people like us endured the danger and harm of real missiles and bombs so that we might enjoy the freedom and life that we have. That was during the Depression of course, but even then, my father said that the little we had could be measured as wealth compared to what some people had in other lands.

"That is still so true today. We have so much to be thankful for, and we owe so much of it to common people who accepted uncommon challenges. I believe America will continue to be great as long as people continue to step forward and accept challenges. Granted, we don't face threats from invading armies, but the strength and character of our nation is still being tested—from within, and in subtle, yet dangerous ways.

"So the question I have for you today is, how will you respond to these tests? When a new family down the street is harassed because they look or speak differently, will you go along with the crowd, or will you risk being humiliated to be their neighbor? When your boss oversteps his or her authority at the expense of others, will you play it safe and hold your tongue, or will you risk your job to stand up and say, 'That's enough'? When a friend makes a miserable mistake, will you turn your back and walk away, or will you risk embarrassment to help with their rehabilitation?

If *you* make a mistake and someone else is blamed, will you hide in the shadows, or will you step forward to accept the consequences?

"Now I know what you're thinking, 'Jack, these are of little consequence. None of these things is going to cause someone to be beaten or imprisoned, let alone killed.' Well that may be true, but we live in a culture of growing self-centeredness. And I fear that each time we, as individuals, take the selfish way out, we chip away at what's made our nation great—our collective moral character.

"So I'm asking you on this July Fourth to recommit yourselves to being good citizens. Remember what this day is about. Remember that the greatness of our nation was built by the greatness of individuals. Each of you, as an American, has inherited that legacy."

Jack's speech was well received by the crowd, and he found himself signing autographs and posing for pictures. Sensing that Jack's energy might be fading with the evening light, Caroline nudged Billy, and he in turn tried to bring an end to an autograph session that could have gone on for hours. Billy suggested that they retire to the RV, but Jack said no.

"I want to stay," said Jack. "I want us all to stay and enjoy the rest of the festivities. These are special times, and we shouldn't miss them. We should drink them in."

And so Jack and his family—Caroline, Wendy, Franky, Billy, Wilton, and Kevin—found a vacant piece of green lawn and sat down with the Gateway Arch towering gracefully overhead. There, Jack told Wendy about Lewis and Clark, who set out from St. Louis to explore the West, and how they too were going to cross the mountains and descend to the Pacific Ocean. Franky taught Kevin the words to military tunes as a band played nearby. Billy and Wilton set aside their schedules and plans and pressed Caroline to tell them what it was like growing up as the daughter of Jack Dodger.

The band struck up Sousa's "The Stars and Stripes Forever," and the sky blazed with fireworks. Little Wendy shrieked and ducked her head as the first rockets exploded, and Jack picked her up and cradled her in his lap.

"It's okay, Little Blossom," he said. "There's nothing to be afraid of. Cover your ears if you wish, but don't miss the pretty lights."

Wendy did cover her ears at first, but soon the "popping flowers in the sky" captivated her eyes, and she couldn't help but clap her hands with delight.

As the fireworks exploded overhead and cast their glittery reflections on the legs of the Arch, Jack felt more at ease than he had in weeks. The day had gone well, the reception had been enthusiastic, and nobody asked him about his age or his health or the seriousness of his intentions. He hadn't heard that nagging little voice of doubt either. Perhaps, it had finally gone away for good, or maybe, it had just been temporarily drowned out by the percussion of skyrockets. Jack was content. It felt good to be an American. It felt good to be alive.

CHAPTER 14

Billy Briar looked out the back window of the RV at the large passenger bus following them out of Des Moines. "Are they genuinely interested in covering us, or are they just waiting to see if Jack collapses again?" he said.

Several large newspapers and broadcast operations had pitched in together and chartered the bus to carry some twenty-five journalists and their equipment. The Jack Dodger campaign was headed across the Great Plains, and the media had come along for the ride.

While Billy was unsure about the media's real intent, he was certain that the campaign would be different from here on out. The constant presence of the press corps would add some new energy—and new pressure. On the positive side, Jack would enjoy unprecedented coverage from dawn to dusk. On the negative side, the campaign would have no down time; their every movement and activity would be captured on tape. To make sure that was so, the media provided Kevin with a two-way radio so that he could communicate directly with their driver. The result was that every place the RV stopped, the press was right behind them or, quite often, already at the specified location to record the moment.

Such was the case one morning in late July when the campaign pulled off the road in Douglas, Wyoming. Jack's gray hair was beginning to curl up around his ears, and he decided to get a cut from a local barber. The media was there to witness every snip of the scissors and record the conversation between Jack and the owner as they discussed the merits of the barbershop business.

Early that afternoon, the "Jack Dodger for President" caravan headed north across the Thunder Basin National Grassland and promptly drove into a heavy summer storm. Kevin had to slow down to a crawl to negotiate the narrow, two-lane blacktop road. After an hour at that pace, the two-way crackled with word from the bus driver that the media wanted to push on ahead to Sheridan. They were hoping to check into motel rooms and file their stories before it got too late. Unwilling to drive any faster and risk endangering his passengers, Kevin pulled over and let the bus pass. "Be careful out there," he told the driver as the bus topped a slight hill and then disappeared from view.

Kevin pulled back out into the middle of the road and resumed his slow but steady pace. The rain had let up a bit, but the road was still very slick and was holding several inches of water in the dips because the bar ditches were running full from the heavy downpour.

Franky had gone in back to take a nap, and Billy sat in his seat to help guide Kevin if needed while Wilton looked over their shoulders nervously. Caroline read a magazine, and Jack and Wendy passed the time playing checkers. Wendy had just commanded Jack to crown one of her pieces when the RV suddenly hit a pair of hard bumps, causing the red and black plastic checkers to slide off the table and onto the floor.

"Everything okay?" Jack shouted toward the front.

"No," Kevin shouted back as he gripped the wheel with both hands and struggled to keep the RV headed straight.

The RV had descended into a shallow valley where standing water hid a washed-out hole in the asphalt. After the back wheels bounced out of the washout, they spun wildly and failed to regain their traction, which caused the back end to begin skidding sideways. Kevin tried to steer out of the skid, but every turn of the wheel just created a new problem until they were completely out of control. They skidded sideways down the road for fifty feet until the back wheels caught a bed of gravel on the shoulder, causing the front end to become airborne and swing around 180 degrees.

The RV came to a sharp stop, and the last noise heard was the sound of Franky falling off the bed onto the floor. Billy quickly got up and checked everyone for injuries. Everyone was okay and accounted for. Franky came out of the back, rubbing his shoulder. "Heck of a way to wake a man." He groaned.

Caroline was shaken but okay while Wendy laughed with excitement. She stood on the seat and pressed her face against the window. "Look, Mommy, we made a bridge," she said.

"I better take a look," said Kevin.

He climbed out of the driver's seat and opened the side door. What he found was just as Wendy had described: the RV had come to rest straddling the bar ditch—the front tires on one side and the rear tires on the other. Looking straight down, Kevin watched as plant debris in the bar ditch floated out of view beneath the RV steps.

"So what's the story?" Wilton asked anxiously.

"The story is that we're stuck," said Kevin. "No way we can get out of this without a wrecker, and we're probably going to need one of those king-sized ones."

"Better get on the phone to the state police or someone and see if they can send help," Billy said to Wilton.

Wilton reached into his pocket and pulled out his cell phone. He pushed a few buttons, put it up to his ear, looked at it again, and then began shaking it.

"What now?" Billy asked.

"It's dead, or we're not in a cell zone." Wilton handed the phone to Billy.

Billy looked at it and, after fumbling with it a moment, came to the same frustrating conclusion. He asked Kevin to see if he could raise anyone on the two-way. Kevin tried, but nobody responded.

"Well, surely, someone will come along soon," said Billy optimistically. "Let's just sit tight."

And so they all busied themselves with little tasks and activities. Franky joined Wendy at the checkers table, and their chatter was the only sound inside the RV. Everyone else strained in hopes of hearing an approaching vehicle on the highway. Thirty minutes went by, and nobody came down the road. Meanwhile, the rain had stopped, and the sun began to peek through the clouds.

"Kevin, how far is the last town we passed?" Billy asked.

"About fifteen miles."

"And how far to the next town?"

"I'd guess about ten miles."

"I'm thinking that someone better start walking," said Billy. "Ten miles isn't so far, and there's bound to be a ranch house between here and there."

Kevin immediately volunteered. "Why don't you all just stay here and let me walk? I feel like this is my fault, and I should—"

"Nonsense," said Jack quickly, patting Kevin on the shoulder. "This couldn't be helped. We certainly can't blame you for the rain or the road conditions. I'd say your steady hands on the wheel probably kept us from ending up in even worse shape than we're in."

"I'll go," Franky said.

"No," said Jack. "I think you and Kevin should stay here in case help comes. Kevin may be needed at the controls, and Franky, you may be needed to help with towing or pushing. And, Wilton, you better stay here in case you need to write someone a check. Meanwhile, Billy and I will walk up the road and see what we can find."

Jack hadn't asked Billy, but he knew he'd come along, and indeed the young man nodded his head.

Caroline wasn't so sure about the arrangement. "Daddy, don't you think you better stay and get some rest?"

"Not at all. The exercise will do me some good. I feel like I'm growing cobwebs in here," he answered emphatically. "You ready?" he asked Billy.

"Let's go."

The two men swung open the door of the RV and had to make a short hop out to the side to clear the bar ditch, which was no longer carrying a rapid flow of rainwater but was still standing at least two feet deep. "Take good care of my girls," Jack called back to the others as he and Billy began walking north.

Jack and Billy hiked several hundred yards up out of the shallow valley and found themselves surrounded by rolling grassland that stretched out endlessly in every direction, with barbed wire fences lining either side of the road. Over this terrain the road gently rose and fell, and each time Jack and Billy reached the top of a rise, they stopped and strained in the hazy humid light for signs of a village or ranch house. And each time the view was the same: no manmade structures save for an occasional windmill surrounded by the fuzzy profiles of grazing cattle.

"Good grief!" Billy said after a dozen of these surveillance stops. "I've never been anywhere like this where you can see so far and yet not see anything at all. There's just nothing … nothing! I hope Kevin was right about the distance to that town."

"I trust he told us right," Jack said as the two resumed walking. "He's a smart, capable young man, and he's taken his responsibility for getting us around seriously."

Since Jack had invoked the nature of Kevin's character, Billy sensed that the time might be ripe to probe a little bit.

"Kevin's an interesting guy," said Billy. "Kind of quiet and serious. I've tried to get to know him a little bit better, but he doesn't have much to say."

"He's a very private person—more so than most," said Jack.

"Well, he sure seems to have taken to you."

"I suppose that's true," said Jack. "I guess you could say we've developed a relationship."

Billy let a few yards of blacktop fall beneath their feet before pressing further. "Have you and Kevin had any more discussions about the incident in Dallas?"

"No," said Jack. "There's nothing more about it for us to discuss. It's history. He's looking ahead now, and so am I."

"Hmm … " Billy's questions had hit the same stone wall that they hit in January, and unable to formulate in his mind another line of questioning that might reveal more information, he threw out one last comment to see if Jack would bite.

"I guess I'm just still curious about what happened that night—how a man points a gun at you, and then seven months later, he's driving you across the country."

Jack laughed. "Oh, come on now, Billy. That's not any more strange than me playing cards in a barbershop one night and then running for president, is it? And look at you, you were just a rookie reporter, and now you're running a national campaign."

"Okay, okay, I see your point," said Billy. "I guess we've all taken some pretty strange steps this year."

Without realizing it, Billy's inquiry had been turned back on himself, and now it was Jack's turn to probe.

"Given any thought to what you're going to do when this is all over?"

"No, haven't given it much thought," said Billy. "I do know that win or lose, I can't go back to the paper. Certainly not back to police reporting. I've seen and done too much. After all of this, I can't just go back and sit in that newsroom. But I don't have a clue as to what I could do."

"Don't think about what you *could* do," said Jack. "What do you *want* to do? What are you passionate about?"

Jack's question took Billy by surprise, and it was followed by a long pause, during which time they strode to the top of another rise and stopped to make another visual search for signs of life.

"Well, at the moment, I'd say I'm passionate about finding help and getting us back on the road." Billy shaded the sun from his eyes as he looked out over the horizon.

"Seriously," Jack said. "What are you passionate about?"

"Seriously, Jack? I'm not sure that I'm passionate about anything."

"Ha! That's a bunch of rot. I'd say you're more passionate than you think."

"Well, if you know so much, then, why don't you tell me," said Billy.

"Okay, I will," said Jack. "Let's see now … I'd say you're passionate about working hard. You're passionate about doing a good job. You're passionate about your responsibilities. But most of all, I'd say you're passionate about the truth."

Billy thought about that a moment as they resumed walking.

"Well, that's a nice list of work-type traits, I suppose, but I'm not sure that really says much about my talent or skills or abilities."

"I wouldn't worry too much about that right now," said Jack. "You've got plenty of time to find out what you can do and what you want to do. There's a whole lot of folks out there with great talent and skills, but who have no work ethic and don't have a clue about the truth. No, I think you've got things going in the right order at the moment."

They walked silently for a hundred yards or so, and then, Billy got up the nerve to say something that had been weighing on him for several weeks.

"Jack, I want to apologize for questioning your commitment back there in Washington. That was uncalled for. I don't know what I was thinking."

"Oh, you were just thinking the same thing I was thinking," said Jack.

Billy stopped walking and turned to Jack. "How's that?"

"Well, like we talked about earlier, it's a big jump from being a barbershop owner to running for president, and all the way into Washington, I had this nagging feeling that this whole effort was absurd, and that I have no business running for president."

"Do you still feel that way?"

"Well, it still seems pretty absurd to me. I mean, let's be honest. I don't have the typical resume. But as for having no business running, I have just as much business running for president as anyone else. That's what's so great about this country—ordinary people like us can organize a campaign and seek the highest office in the land. Now as for whether or not we can actually win, I'm content to leave that up to the will of the people and God—*look!*" Jack suddenly shouted, pointing out into the distance.

Shimmering in the late-afternoon heat waves was a small cluster of buildings and the bright reflection off the conical roof of what appeared to be a grain silo. Even though the village was still two miles away, Jack and Billy quickened their steps.

They found themselves in a refreshing shade of clouds with a light breeze for a quarter of a mile, and then the clouds spilled their load again in a brief but strong shower. With no cover to be found, Jack and Billy just kept walking and soon were soaked to the skin, though neither one was complaining after enduring the hot afternoon sun.

As they got closer to the village, they began to make out the details of the buildings more clearly. In addition to the silo and an adjoining mill, there were a couple of other buildings, a small tourist court with cabins and what appeared to be a diner. Scattered in the vicinity of the diner and the tourist court were a few pickup trucks and some grain trucks, one of which began to look more like a bus as they got nearer. Before long, it became clear that the latter was not just a bus, but the media bus that had pushed on ahead.

Inside the diner, a few of the media people were enjoying a cup of coffee and conversation when a photographer in the group stood up to get a better view out the window. He had seen what he thought were two backpackers, and thinking they might make an interesting addition to a photo essay on the American heartland, he had pulled out his camera and attached a 500mm lens. But as they got closer, the white hair, dress pants and dress shirt of one of the hikers was suddenly familiar.

"Good Lord, it's Grandpa Jack!"

The others jumped up to look out the window, and then, they scurried out the door and scattered—some to the bus and others to cabins at the tourist court. Within a matter of seconds, reporters streamed back out into the gravel parking lot with video cameras, notepads, recorders and 35mm cameras. They spread out in a wide line across the lot so that all could get a clear view of the approaching presidential candidate. The few locals in the diner and the lone waitress and cook stood inside and watched the whole scene unfold. By now, the media had filled them in on who they were and what they were about, and so they knew that Jack Dodger would probably follow them into the village, though nobody expected him to come on foot.

"Hey, Jack," one of the reporters bellowed, not quite in hearing range yet. "What are you doing?"

Jack and Billy couldn't make out the words, so they just grinned and waived. Camera shutters clicked and video cameras buzzed, catching the moment for the morning papers and newscasts.

When Jack and Billy got within twenty yards of the diner, the press broke ranks and encircled the two to get at the story, but Jack held up his hands to cut off their questions. "They'll be plenty of time for questions later, but right now we've got a bunch of folks stranded about ten miles back, and we need to tend to them."

"Ten miles back?" a reporter repeated, pointing back over the horizon. "You walked ten miles?"

"Is anybody hurt?" asked another.

"Billy will fill you in." Jack pushed his way through the reporters, with a handful of them following. Inside the diner, he asked a waitress where the nearest wrecker could be found, and he tried to recruit the driver of the press bus to go back to the RV and liberate its occupants.

"Can't be done," said the driver. "Got a flat rear inside tire. That's how come we pulled in here. Oughta be fixed by morning though."

"I can take you." Jack turned to find an attractive woman of about sixty years of age sitting alone in a booth by the window. "I've got a nice big sedan outside, and there's nothing I'd enjoy more this afternoon than to give the one-and-only Jack Dodger a ride up the road."

Jack was not a man who embarrassed easily. He spoke his mind and was comfortable when others did the same. But something about this woman elicited a response from him that was extremely rare: he blushed. It was a hot schoolboy blush that he could feel deep in his cheeks and that everyone else in the diner clearly saw.

Jack tried to speak but could manage nothing more than an awkward croak and a nod of the head. Taking that as an acceptance, the woman slid out of the booth and walked to the door with Jack following. Out in the parking lot, Billy was still talking to the reporters, but he stopped in mid-sentence when he saw Jack and the woman walk toward her Chevrolet Caprice.

"Jack?" Billy called across the lot.

"Going to get the others" was the reply. By then the reporters had turned their attention—and their cameras—to the Chevy and the woman at the wheel and followed both as they headed back down the road.

The ten-mile drive up the road took exactly fifteen minutes, and that was plenty of time for Jack to learn plenty about Opal Jenkins. She was a native of Michigan who met a Wyoming boy while on a school trip out west. She eventually married him and settled down on his family's ranch about twenty miles to the west of the village. He died in 1995 of a heart attack and left her alone without children or anyone else to help run the ranch. She sold it to a neighbor but continued to occupy the house and tend to a few horses and a small vegetable garden. She confessed that while she indeed knew who Jack was, she'd stayed away from politics all of her life and so didn't know anything about his positions or what he believed in, nor did she really care.

"So why did you volunteer to give me a ride?" Jack asked.

"Just seemed like the neighborly thing to do," she said. "And … we don't get many strangers out here, so I always enjoy talking to folks to find out where they're from and see what's going on out in the world. It's better than watching TV really."

When they arrived at the RV, they found the remainder of the campaign team no worse for wear. They all gladly squeezed into Opal's car for the ride back to the village, except for Kevin who volunteered to stay behind and wait for the wrecker. A wrecker did arrive about an hour later, accompanied by a state trooper who wrote up a routine incident report.

The RV was dragged to the village around dusk, where Kevin broke the bad news to the rest of the team: the axle was broken and the nearest mechanic who could handle it was in Gillette some forty-five miles to the north. Wilton called a number provided by the wrecker driver, and he got even more bad news: it would take at least a week to get a replacement axle.

With nothing else to be done about the RV until morning, the campaign team checked into the tourist court and then ate supper at the diner. As word spread throughout the area that Jack Dodger was in the village, they were soon joined by several dozen people who had come to see the candidate in person. The crowd was more than the cook could handle—in fact more than he had ever seen at one time—so Franky put on an apron and hat and jumped behind the counter to lend a hand. Wendy joined in the fun too, helping the waitress carry water and place settings to the tables. Woven throughout the crowd were media people, taking it all in.

Jack tried to stay out of the way and blend into the crowd, but that wasn't going to happen. People had come to find out what he was about, and they were prepared to stay all night until their questions were answered. When it became evident that most had come with the same questions, Billy coaxed Jack into sitting on top of the counter and conducting an impromptu town-hall meeting. And so for two straight hours, Jack was asked about his perspective on everything from government subsidies for ranchers and farmers to home schooling and price relief for gasoline and diesel fuel. And in between their questions, Jack asked a few of his own.

"The problem with most presidents is that they think it's just about leading," he said. "They forget that it's also about serving, and you can't do that without listening to folks."

By ten o'clock all the questions worth asking had been covered, and family-by-family, the crowd faded into the cool dark Wyoming night. Even the media retreated to their cabins, leaving Jack and his extended family to help clean up the diner and put things back in order. Opal kept company with Wendy, and eventually, she invited Jack to sit down for one last cup of coffee.

"Well, Ms. Jenkins, I believe you're the only person here tonight who didn't have something to say, so I think I'll ask you a question. Do you think we'll get any of their votes?"

"Oh, I think you'll do okay with most of these folks. Can never tell about some of 'em. Depends a lot on the weather and the economy."

"Does that include you?"

"Now, Mr. Dodger, you should know better than to ask a woman about her politics," Opal said in mock disdain. "However, since you asked, I must confide that I may just have to drive up to the county seat and get myself registered."

"Umm, Jack," Billy interrupted, approaching the booth. "We're all going to turn in now."

Jack looked up to see his entire entourage gathered at the door, with the owner ready with key in hand to lock up.

"Why don't you folks come on out to my place," said Opal. "I've got plenty of room, and it'll be more comfortable than those musty old cabins next door."

"Thank you, Ms. Jenkins," said Billy, "but I think it would be best if we all stay here tonight. We've still got a lot of arrangements to work out in the morning. But we certainly appreciate your hospitality."

Jack looked at Billy and then at Opal. "He's the boss, so I guess we better do what he says."

They all filed out the door and began walking toward the cabins, except for Jack who decided to hang back and walk Opal to her car. Caroline and Franky turned to see if he was coming, and he waved them on. "Be right there," he said.

Jack and Opal stood outside her car and chatted for another twenty minutes before finally saying good night.

"It's been a pleasure meeting you," said Opal, extending her hand for a polite handshake. "I hope our paths will cross again some time, although I can't imagine you'll ever have a need to come back through this dusty crossroads."

"Well, then maybe, you'll just have to find a reason to come to Big D," said Jack.

"Or perhaps Washington?" Opal asked slyly.

Jack stood alone in the parking lot and watched as the big Chevrolet rolled slowly onto the highway and then disappeared over a hill. He started to walk to his cabin when something moved in the corner of his eye and he turned to look. A curtain blew in the open window of a cabin down the line, but there was nothing more.

Billy and Wilton were up at dawn and on the phones, and by nine o'clock, they met the others at the diner with an alternative plan. The press bus was not full, so the campaign team would ride with the media north to Billings, Montana, where they would board a chartered airplane and fly west to Seattle. There, they would resume their campaign activities, either on board a new RV or bus, or by plane.

Wilton practically glowed as he reported the next bit of news: the trip west from St. Louis had stimulated substantial contributions, and the campaign treasury was now flush with cash.

"We can travel like the major boys from here on out if we wish," he said. "And Billy, we've even got enough cash now to produce a national television ad."

So with spirits running high, Jack and his crew boarded the press bus and headed northwest to Billings, followed by the wrecker pulling their damaged RV. With the candidate captive for several hours, the reporters took turns following up on some of his comments from the previous night. Wendy worked the aisle, engaging reporters in conversation and, if they let their guard down, a game of checkers. With nothing else to do, Kevin and Franky camped out on the back row of the bus and were soon sound asleep.

Through the course of the day, Jack had the opportunity to spend time with all the reporters on the bus—all except for Howard Hickman, a reporter from the *Houston Journal*, who had opted to get off in Gillette when they stopped to deliver the RV to the mechanic for repairs. Hickman said casually that he had some business to attend to and that he would rejoin the campaign in California.

Billy didn't give it much thought at the time, but by the time they boarded the plane in Billings, he had an uneasy feeling in his gut. Hickman had a reputation for finding and chasing offbeat stories, sometimes with damaging results. He was known in Texas media circles as "the Houston Hound," and Billy worried about what kind of bones he might be digging up.

CHAPTER 15

By the time the Jack Dodger campaign charter touched down in Seattle, news of Jack's ten-mile trek across the rolling Wyoming grasslands was plastered all over the newspapers and television. Images of him walking into the village, and the story of how he took charge and "rescued" his associates painted an all-new picture of the seventy-year-old. He was no longer the tired, feeble old man who had collapsed in Washington and had to be carried away on a stretcher. He was once again the hero of New Year's Eve—a vigorous, resourceful man who faced trouble head-on and took care of things.

The result was a tremendous crowd waiting for the candidate at Sea-Tac Airport. Extra police were dispatched to the private terminal to make sure the throng didn't get out of hand, but they were as well mannered as their candidate and expressed themselves with their voices rather than unruly actions. When the plane rolled to a halt and the door opened, the familiar chant of "We want Jack, Grandpa Jack" rose above the whine of the engines. And from one quarter came an all-new chorus that for the first time placed Jack into the thick of the presidential contest: "Keep the governor out, don't send the VP back, cast your vote for Grandpa Jack!"

Indeed, with the first of the major party conventions underway in Philadelphia, the relatively docile summer campaign season was getting ready to turn the corner into the serious, pointed, and heated fall push. Analysts were expecting the vice president and governor to begin tearing each other down, starting during their respective conventions and on into the fall. And many were wondering how Jack would fit into this mix if he were to fit in at all.

Even more pressing was choosing a vice presidential running mate. The topic had come up on a few occasions during the summer, but for the most part, a serious discussion was postponed until it couldn't be avoided any longer. That discussion came late one night in their hotel suite after a long day of campaign events in Seattle. Jack sat down and turned on the television in time to see the governor campaigning with his freshly chosen running mate.

"You know, Jack, we can't hold off much longer," said Billy. "With the governor naming his choice, and the vice president planning to do the same soon, we better get our business in order."

Admittedly, Jack had given the process little thought, and he wasn't anxious to do so now. Things had been relatively uncomplicated before this, and he knew that adding another personality would change the chemistry of the campaign and might even undo the progress that had been made. His first inclination was to choose someone he knew well and was comfortable with simply to comply with the constitutional requirement that a vice president be elected alongside a president. In terms of comfort, Franky was the obvious choice, and if it was just about picking an assistant, there would be no problem in selecting him. But Jack knew better; choosing a running mate was about choosing someone who could step in and be the president. While Jack had come to grips with self-doubts about his own abilities, there was no doubt that Franky was not up to the task.

"Wilton, is there anyone that the Golden Eagles would like to recommend?" Jack asked. "Do you have an officer or a board member that might fit in well with what we're doing and also generate some national interest?"

"No, I can't really say that there is anyone like that," he said. "We've got a lot of good people, but nobody who could be vice president—or president."

"I can do it, Grandpa Jack," said Wendy, who was coloring at a desk next to the window. "Let me be your ice president."

"There's nothing I'd like more than for you to be my *ice* president," said Jack, patting her on the head, "but you're going to be starting school in a few weeks, and I think that's going to be a lot more fun. I don't think the ice president gets recess very often."

The room fell silent again for a moment, and one could almost hear the wheels turning as everyone twisted the vice presidential question around in their mind like a Rubik's cube.

Then Franky spoke. "You could always advertise."

"What? Advertise? You mean like in the want ads?" said Wilton, who after all these months still could not comprehend Franky's odd view of the world. "We're not selling a bass boat, we're looking for someone to help run the country. Good grief, Franky!"

"It's just an idea." Franky shrugged.

"And a pretty good one too," said Billy, who caught the attention of everyone.

"What?" Jack, Wilton, and Caroline said in unison.

"Well, I don't think we should advertise quite in the same way Franky is talking about, but if we choose our words right, we might be able to bring some good candidates forward," he said.

As luck would have it, the question came up the following day at a briefing with the media. The press and pundits, if not the electorate, were abuzz with the whole running mate process, and the question was put to Jack. "When will you announce a running mate?"

Jack provided the answer that Billy had carefully crafted to generate interest: "We're giving that a lot of thought, and while we've already spoken with a candidate, there are still some others that we've not heard from, and so we're not ready yet to single one out or even give you a list of possibilities."

Jack did not like playing verbal games and initially he was uneasy with the implied meaning of the statement—that they had talked to a "real" contender. But Billy reasoned that they had indeed spoken to a candidate—even though she was just in grade school—and in truth they had not heard from others yet, though they had no idea who those others were.

❦

That evening in a little houseboat docked near Rolling Bay across Puget Sound, Hamilton Lee watched the news of Jack's Seattle campaign visit, including a report on the status of his search for a running mate.

"Seems like folks would jump for the chance to work with a good man like Jack Dodger," he said.

"Oh yeah?" came a voice from the bedroom. "Then why don't you jump up off your lazy butt and go join him. Maybe he'll make you vice president—maybe secretary of state or something."

Hamilton's relationship with Marsha was fading after just six months, and her mocking tone stayed with him all night long. He got out of bed at four thirty, looked at himself in the bathroom mirror, and quietly said, "Why not?"

An hour later, he emerged from the bathroom in his army dress uniform, which, after hanging in his closet for a decade, still fit his thin frame well.

"Where you going?" Marsha asked when she opened her eyes and saw him standing at the mirror, brushing the top of his hat. "And what's that you're wearing?"

"I'm going into town—for a job interview," he said.

"Well, it's about time," she said, and rolled over.

Hamilton Lee looked at himself in the mirror one more time. At fifty-eight, he was a bit grizzled, with salt-and-pepper hair and the dark skin and deep creases that come from ten years of working outdoors. He didn't look much like the officer who last wore the uniform a decade earlier, but beneath the dark green wool, he was the same man. He had always been one who did whatever he put his mind to, and today was going to be no different.

Two hours and a ferry ride later, he found himself in the lobby of a downtown hotel. With the rank of a major general still showing on his uniform, the young concierge did not hesitate when Hamilton asked for the room number of Jack Dodger.

It was a toss-up as to who was more surprised when Hamilton knocked on the door and it swung open: Jack, at the sight of a soldier standing outside his door, or Hamilton, at the sight of the presidential candidate in his robe and slippers.

"Hello?" Jack asked, a bit confused. "Did I … was I … did we have an appointment?"

"Oh no, sir, not at all," said Hamilton. "But I can come back at a better time."

"No, no, that won't be necessary. How can I help you?"

"That's what I came to ask you, Mr. Dodger. Is there something I can do for you?"

Jack scratched his head for a moment. "Come on in, and let's find out."

∽⸌◯⸍∾

When Hamilton didn't come home that evening, Marsha thought nothing of it. She figured he was just having a cold one with some of the boys, but when she turned on the television to catch the late news, what she saw and heard rocked her back on her heels.

Jack Dodger was speaking in the hotel lobby. "Ladies and gentlemen, I'd like to introduce my running mate." The camera panned to Jack's left to reveal a uniformed soldier. And as it zoomed in, it showed that soldier to be Hamilton Lee.

What was absurd to Marsha and puzzled most everyone else watching the announcement made perfect sense to Jack Dodger. In a full day of conversation, and with the help of a quick background check by Billy and Wilton, it was revealed that Hamilton Lee was a highly decorated veteran of the Vietnam

War who had stayed on in the army and served in a variety of roles, most notably attached to foreign diplomatic missions. In that duty, his counsel was sought by presidents and secretaries of defense and state. In 1990, he retired from the military and was offered a job as an under secretary of state, but he respectfully declined. And then for reasons that left his former colleagues bewildered, he dropped out of sight.

"After thirty years in the service, I wanted to enjoy a little bit of the life and liberty that I had helped preserve," he explained to Jack. "I was tired of wearing green, brown, and khaki. I wanted to see what blue and red felt like."

And so he moved to the Pacific Northwest. While he could have traded on his military service and government contacts to get a high-level white collar job at a defense contractor, he decided instead to make a living outdoors with his hands. He worked as a fisherman, lumberman, and carpenter, and often, all at the same time. It was rough and rugged, and it made him feel alive.

"So why give it up? Why come knock on my door? Why aren't you out right this minute on a boat chasing the catch of the day?" Jack asked.

"You," he said flatly. "You, and what you've been talking about. How we all have the responsibility to give something back, to leave this country better than we found it. So I decided I'd come over here and see if I could pitch in somehow."

"Are you married? Do you have a family?" Jack asked.

"No, I was married once in Georgia, just before I left for Southeast Asia. But she got interested in someone else while I was away. She filed for divorce before I got home. And, well, I wasn't exactly in the best frame of mind back then, so I just signed her away."

"Were there any children?"

"No. I did hear that she had a child while I was overseas—a boy, they said—with the guy she started seeing while I was gone. But they left Georgia, and I never saw or heard from her again, so that's all I know about it."

Jack ended the interview with a final question. "Why the uniform?"

"Oh this? I don't own a civilian suit. Never have. I've been wearing uniforms ever since I turned eighteen."

"I was in the same situation a few months ago," said Jack. "We'll see that you have at least one good suit. You're gonna need it, because I do want you to work with us. I want you to join our team."

"You just tell me where you want me and what you want me to do, and I'll do it," said Hamilton. He didn't know at that moment what Jack was going to ask him to do, and what might have appeared as naiveté to some observers was recognized by Jack as a deep commitment to service. He knew that whether he asked Hamilton to carry his luggage or stand beside him as vice president, Hamilton would do it with conviction and dedication.

By the end of the day, Jack announced to the world that Hamilton Lee would not be merely carrying his luggage.

The announcement rolled across the political landscape like a strong wind, blowing the media and pundits off their current stories and angles. They were just beginning to understand who Jack Dodger was, and now, they had this new man to figure out. Who was this Hamilton Lee? Where did he come from? And what did this choice mean for Jack Dodger's chances?

Researchers worked overtime trying to find the answers to these questions and more, and much to the relief of Billy and Wilton, the story they compiled was basically the same story that Hamilton had told Jack, but there was more to it.

Hamilton's military record was even more heroic and impressive than he had revealed, and likewise, he had understated his responsibilities and influence during his diplomatic tours.

Those who worked alongside him described him as exceptionally competent, highly intelligent, thorough, thoughtful, extremely loyal, and a bit of a loner. It was this last trait that seemed to explain his self-inflicted exile to the Pacific Northwest. And while Hamilton's story became sketchy at that point, there was no record of any troubles with the law, alcohol, creditors, the IRS, or even neighbors. From all indications, he had been a model citizen.

With nothing sensational to report about Hamilton Lee, the media focused on Jack's unusual but shrewd choice for a running mate. And with his sterling military and foreign affairs credentials, Hamilton single-handedly bumped Jack's polling numbers into the upper teens. While Jack continued to have a strong following among Korean War vets, Hamilton was now pulling in many Vietnam vets who couldn't identify with the "light duty" of the vice president and governor during the war.

"Jack, you just seem to be followed by a lucky star," Wilton said the night before the campaign left Seattle. "To find a man like this—his combination of modesty, commitment, and an outstanding record of service that nobody can fault—we couldn't have done better had we interviewed a thousand people. I can just hardly believe it."

"Sometimes, things happen in a way that can only be attributed to some kind of divine guidance," Jack said, "and I think this might be one of those times."

Billy wasn't so sure. Howard Hickman had flown back into town that afternoon to rejoin the press corps, and talk was getting around that he was following some interesting new leads. And they had nothing to do with Hamilton Lee.

CHAPTER 16

What had arrived in Seattle as the "Jack Dodger for President" campaign left for San Francisco rechristened as the "Dodger-Lee 2000" campaign. And they rolled south out of town aboard a brand new RV donated by a Seattle computer software entrepreneur. Hearing about the accident in Wyoming, the businessman donated a rig for as long as it was needed. He even provided a credit card with which to buy gasoline and take care of any repairs that might be needed out on the road.

When the media asked if the use of the RV constituted an endorsement, the businessman said he was intrigued by Jack's patriotic naiveté, his bottomless optimism, and his seeming lack of a false veneer or ego. "We need someone who is not obsessed with himself," he said. "Good leaders don't keep looking in the mirror. Their eyes are always focused on the horizon. That's what has made companies like ours successful, and that's the kind of man I'm going to vote for."

News of the endorsement ricocheted across the country and especially through the business community. Within a couple of days, the *Wall Street Journal* had dispatched a reporter to the West Coast to follow the campaign, which by now was being trailed by two busloads of media.

For the next three days, the campaign rambled south down the coast, sometimes traveling on Interstate 5 to make strategic stops in cities such as Portland and Salem, and at other times clinging to the rugged shoreline on the Pacific Coast Highway. The crowds were enthusiastic, and the combination of good will and spectacular scenery invigorated everyone—even the most cynical of the media who had come along for no other reason than to be on hand should Jack make a mistake.

They rolled along without incident, making good time until the unexpected happened just north of Redwood National Park. Wendy climbed into Jack's lap and whispered into his ear, and Jack in turn walked up to the front of the RV and asked Kevin to pull off at the next available roadside turnout. Kevin followed his orders and brought the caravan to a halt beside a little cove that was framed by tall cliffs on the left and a cluster of windblown cypress trees on the right. Between the guardrail and the ocean surf was a slope scattered with large rocks and tufts of vegetation, and then a brown sand beach dotted with small rocks and shells.

Jack asked Billy and Wilton to go to the two buses and gather everyone on the roadside. Not knowing what was happening, the media sprang forth with their cameras, microphones, and notepads, ready for action.

When everyone had been assembled, Jack stood on a rock and explained the reason for the sudden detour. "Friends, after a brief discussion with my chief morale officer, I do hereby declare a temporary moratorium on politics and campaigning. For the next hour, there is to be no discussion or work of any kind even remotely related to this campaign."

"For what reason are you calling this moratorium?" asked someone in the crowd.

"The reason? Why don't you tell them, dear," he said, lifting Wendy up on his shoulders.

"We're going to swim in the ocean!"

Wendy's announcement was greeted with cheers and laughter from the media, with only a few moans and groans.

"Now I realize that many of you did not come prepared for this," Jack said, "but you can at least take your shoes and socks off and get your feet wet. Might do you a bit of good to cool your dogs and get some of the blood out of your head and down into your feet. Oh, and your bosses would probably appreciate it if you leave that expensive equipment on the bus."

For the next hour, the cove resembled a school field trip for grown-ups who had forgotten how to relax. Reporters with khaki pants rolled up to their knees walked around in the shallow water, their loosened neckties whipping about in the brisk sea breeze. Some of the less adventurous sat on rocks and absorbed the warm sunshine or walked at the edge of the wet sand in groups of two or three, bending down to pick up shells or pieces of starfish. The few who had brought swimsuits to take advantage of hotel hot tubs howled and shrieked as they took tentative steps into the chilly surf.

As for the Dodger crew, Franky made a headlong charge into the water without testing the temperature or the depth. He ran as far as he could and then plunged from sight, reappearing a moment later, choking and gasping but displaying a hearty thumbs-up. With Franky's assurance that all was okay, Jack walked quickly into the water with Wendy in his arms until only their heads could be seen.

Hamilton Lee, the veteran outdoorsman, contributed his own touch of practicality to the affair. Knowing that the swimmers would be chilled by the breeze once they came out of the water, he foraged around for driftwood and straw, built a little teepee stack and, then, set it ablaze with matches he produced from his pocket.

Caroline and Wilton sat on the rocks and watched as Jack, Wendy, and Franky played in the water. The two men took turns rocketing the little girl out of the water and into the saving arms of the other.

"Your father is something else," Billy said as he sat down next to Caroline. "He's got such a gift with people."

"Yes, he does. And he's having such a wonderful time. I kind of worry about him. This has all been such a special time, and I hope he can adjust when it ends."

"When it ends?" Billy asked.

"Now come on, Billy. You don't really believe he has a chance to be elected do you?"

"Well ... " Billy paused a moment, not sure whether to tell her what he really thought, what he really wished, or some combination of the two. "I could tell you exactly what I think, but I'd be in strict violation of Jack's orders. Remember? No campaign talk."

"You wouldn't be the only person in violation," Caroline said, pointing around them.

Billy looked around and indeed there were plenty among the media who were still busy at work. A few had their video cameras trained on Jack out in the surf, and one reporter was even recording a stand-up camera take against the backdrop of the beachcombers. Billy smiled, knowing that Jack's impromptu beach party, though not meant to be a photo opportunity, had become exactly that, and a good one.

But then he turned to look over his left shoulder, and he saw something that erased the smile from his face. Howard Hickman was sitting on a rock next to Kevin Walker, and the two were talking.

"Who is that man?" Caroline asked, seeing Billy's frown.

"He's a reporter from Houston. A tenacious reporter," he said.

"What are they talking about?"

"I don't know, but I sure aim to find out." Billy stood up and walked through the rocks to where the two men were talking.

"Kevin, why don't you go up to the RV and give us a good honk on the horn. I think it's time to get everyone up out of the water and back on our way."

Kevin climbed up the rocks toward the RV as instructed, leaving Billy behind to see if he could get anything out of Hickman.

"Well, Howard, did you get your business taken care of in Wyoming?"

"Sure did," Hickman said, tapping his notebook with a pen. "In fact, I got more taken care of than I had anticipated. It was a very, very successful stay for me."

"And was there something I can help you with?" Billy probed. "You know, Kevin is just our driver, and you really should come to me if you need anything."

"No. I've got everything I need. And don't underestimate your driver. He's more helpful than you can imagine."

Billy stood up to confront Hickman face-to-face. "Okay, Howard, you want to tell me what this is all about—what you were talking to Kevin about?"

"Now that's interesting," said Hickman. "I can't imagine that you don't know what I was talking to Kevin about? Oh, wait a minute. No, surely Jack Dodger hasn't kept some secrets from his own press secretary. That would be awfully careless of him."

Just then the horn on the RV sounded.

"Would love to talk more, but looks like it's time to go," Hickman said as he stood up and walked back toward the buses. Jack, Franky, Wendy, and the others tromped out of the water and stopped by Hamilton's fire to dry off before going back up to the RV.

Billy stepped into the RV and found Kevin sitting in the driver's seat. "Kevin, I need to see you outside a moment."

Standing in front of the RV, Billy asked Kevin about Hickman's questions.

"There wasn't much to it," said Kevin. "He only wanted to know how long I had been with the campaign, where I was from, that sort of thing. Oh, and where I first met Jack."

"And what did you tell him?"

"I told him that we met at his barbershop. I didn't say anything about how we met. Why? What's wrong?"

"I don't know, Kevin. All I know is that man is a snoop, and it's best if you don't speak to him."

"Okay, I won't. I'm sorry. I hope I didn't do anything bad."

"Oh, I doubt that you did," said Billy. "Don't worry about it."

Jack walked up to the RV. "Is there a problem?" he asked Billy after Kevin returned to the driver's seat.

"I don't know. And *that* may be a problem—that I don't know what the real problem is," said Billy helplessly. "Jack, is there anything about Kevin that you haven't told me? Anything that might be a problem if it were made public?"

"Of course not," said Jack. "What's this all about?"

"I wish I knew," said Billy. "I wish I knew."

The campaign caravan rolled across the Golden Gate Bridge and into the heart of San Francisco late that night. With the vice president's party holding its nominating convention in Los Angeles, the Dodger-Lee campaign moved quietly into its hotel, observing the custom of suspending major campaign activities during an opponent's convention. A few of the media flew down to Los Angeles to join their coverage teams, while others lounged in their rooms or huddled in the hotel bar to watch the speeches.

Jack, Hamilton, and Wilton spent the next couple of days visiting Golden Eagles chapters, community centers, VFW Halls, and other "friendly" locations. The events were personal and low-keyed, with no formal speeches or fanfare. So low-key, in fact, that when Jack and Hamilton walked alone into a retirement center, the receptionist at the front desk assumed they were there to inquire about rooms and began loading them down with brochures and fact sheets.

"Uh … that's not really necessary," Jack said with a wry smile. "We've already got our eyes set on a nice little place in Washington, DC. We're just in town to visit some friends."

The receptionist looked up at Jack, then at Hamilton, then down at the newspaper on her desk. When she saw the picture on the front page of the men now standing in front of her, she blushed beet red. "Oh my," she said.

"Don't worry about that," Hamilton said. "I was just as shocked as you to see my picture in the paper today."

On the Friday morning after the convention concluded in Los Angeles, the Dodger-Lee campaign shifted back into high gear with rallies at Fisherman's Wharf and Golden Gate Park. With the major party conventions over, the media was back in full force and eager to get Jack's assessment.

"What'd you think of the conventions?" they asked him.

"I think they were marvelous," he said. "The candidates spelled out who they are, their philosophies, and what they want to do. The commentators griped that the conventions are too staged, but I believe they are still very important to our process. I hope everyone took the time to watch them or read about them in the newspapers. It's important to know what the candidates stand for."

"Do you feel at a disadvantage not having that type of national exposure?"

"Oh, I don't know. We're working hard in our own way to meet people. We don't have a big show, but I'd say we're still reaching a lot of folks with our message. At least, when I'm speaking to a group in person, I know I've got their attention. They're not switching channels or slipping out to the kitchen for a sandwich."

The day was long and full, and Jack was showing signs of fatigue when Billy announced that they had one more engagement. Jack let out a deep sigh. "Who's the audience? What's the topic?" he asked.

"Don't know yet. Actually, it's more of a Q and A type event."

"How many folks you expecting?"

"Don't know that for sure either. Could be a handful, or could be thousands."

Jack looked at Billy with a puzzled expression. "Do you at least know where it is?"

"Sure. It's at UC Berkeley, in the main library," said Billy.

"Oh, well that sounds nice. It'll be good to see young folks in the audience for a change."

That's when Billy laid out the rest of the plan. "Actually, you won't be seeing anyone. You're going to talk to college students online."

"Online? You mean in one of those chatterboxes?" Jack asked.

"Yes." Billy laughed. "And they are called chat rooms, not chatterboxes. It'll be fun. All you have to do is sit in front of a computer and type answers to questions that come across the screen."

That evening Jack, Billy, Hamilton, and Wilton crossed the bay to Berkeley where they were directed to a computer terminal in the library. A student facilitator helped Jack get situated in front of the monitor. The others stood behind him or pulled up chairs to watch over his shoulder.

"I'll get you started," the student said, and with a few quick keystrokes and mouse clicks, the terminal was connected to the Internet and, then, to a Web site that had been set up for the event.

"There you go," he said. "Just start typing."

"But … how do I know there's anyone out there?" Jack asked.

"Oh, you'll know," said the student, who patted Jack on the shoulder and then disappeared into the stacks.

Jack looked at the screen helplessly for a moment, and then he began typing.

> Jack: Hello?

> hello
> hi
> hey
> howdy
> what's up

> Jack: This is Jack Dodger.

> hey, jack
> good evening
> Hello, Mr. Dodger.

the jackster
what's up

Jack: Sorry, I'm a little slwo at theis. Hope you cand read my poor typng.

itz cool mr jack just let your fingers fly
yeadon't worry about it out here on the web spelling and punctuation don't matter
Oh yes it does!
no it dosn t susie q. short and sweet is key
and fast. very fast. donmt back up to fixit just keep moving
just let it come and will know what you say

Jack: Well, that's very interesting. Is it just on the web that spelling and puncutatiun don't matter, oris it that way every where you go?

we gotta spell right in shcool of course, but then we get out here and life is too fast toi worry about it
lets just say we're more informal than the oldies and iut spills over to a lot of what we do
I try to spell correctly always.
who asked you

Jack: I believ I did. So whty are you so informal? What's different about life today that makes you so?

everything is sped up
Its fastpaced.
No time to lose
snooze & lose
go slow and grow mold
our lives are moving at 56k+, our folks had it more like 14k
mine move at 1k

Jack: Does that bother you? That life is so fast?

no
Yes!
No
don't know any different
who really cares anyeway
I do!
hey jack I thought you were dead, thought you died in DC or something

Jack: No, I just fainted. But thanks for asking.

oh
gotta read the paper guy

Jack: So what else are you wiorried about?

getting a job
gettin a good job
being successful
Having what my parents have.
like a new car
making it to 30

Jack: 30? Really? just 30?

i'd settle for 27
you from the hood?
no i'm from burbia
then whats your beef
its all out of control

Jack: Out of control? Do you really feel that way.

yes
sometimes
mostly
often
Yes

Jack: That's interesting. You see, when I was growing up …

you walked 20 miles in the snow right
don't be rude

Jack: As I was saying, when I was growing up, I had much of the same kind of feeling.

oh sure
Let the man talk!

Jack: Seriously, I did. I came up at a time of high anxietry and uncertainty. We weren't worried about life moving too fast; we were worried about life grinding to a halt. People couldnb't find jobs. Couldn't feed their families. Some people liveds on the street or itn their cars, if they ahd one. It was tough. people felt they had nbo control.

i slept in my car once
No, he's serious, I've read about this. It was hard.
would you please go away
yea but it was different, not at all like us

Jack: You're half right. It was very different, and yet it was the same, because the emotion was the same. Just like tyou, people lived with a lot of anxiety and uncertainty.

really?

Jack: Really.

so what you do
yea what
tell it preacher

Jack: We just kept pushjing and working and moving forward one step at a time until we climbed out of the hole we were in. Some folks even figured out new and better ways to do things. Main thing is we nevber gave up. We just kept trying. We helped each other along. And you can do the same.

why should I try when dropouts are becoming dotcom zillionares every day
That's part of the problem—incentives are all cock-eyed. Why spend years studying in school to get a degree not worth the paper it's printed on
really

Jack: Now I'm not just talking about being financialluy successful. Nothing wrong with that. Gotta feed yourself and your family. What I'm talking about is learning how to be happy and confident wherever you are, whatever you do.

i don't care too much for money, cause money cant buy me love
where'd that come from
Beatles, ever heard of em, or is your cd stack two weeks old like you
oh yeah the FABasauruses give me a break those guys are older than my dad
Why are you so rude?

Jack: The Beatles were after my time, so they're not so old. But the words you quoted are on target. Money can't buy love.

or happiness
health
peace of mind

Jack: Exactly. And money isn't the reason you shoudl stay in school. You should stay in school to find out whoi you are, what you canm do, what you like and don't like. Then you focus in and build on your natueral skills so that you can go out and do something meaningful and exciting with your life. And that's how where you find happiness. Not in what is printed on a paycheck, but in the quality of way you spend your time.

The chat rambled on for an hour in which Jack sought answers to as many questions as he was asked. It was organized chaos, with the topic changing rapidly and people logging on and off all the time. Jack was in the middle of an explanation of his philosophy of public service when the student facilitator suddenly reappeared and tapped on his watch.

Jack: Looks like our time here is about up.

any last ideas for us rookies?

Jack: Yes. This computer and this web is a wonderful tool. It's amazing what we can do with it. It's amazing what we've been doing here tonight. But try to remember that it is just a tool. Don't let it become your life, don't let it become your only contact with the world. Use it as you need to, but then push away and turn it off. Go outside and watch a sunset, read a book, go to a museum, visit family and friends, help a stranger. Life's too short and precious to waste it sitting in front of a computer. Lastly, never go to bed angry, and never start a day without thanking Almighty God for another chance to give it another try, another chance to use the extraordinary gifts he's given you. Every new day is a blessing, and every new day should be treated as such.

amen
yo Jack
Thank you Mr. Dodger
bye
later

Jack: Goodnight.

And just as quickly as it started, the chat ended, and the nameless participants disappeared into the cyber void. Jack leaned back in his chair and rubbed his fingers. "I'm exhausted."

The student facilitator leaned over him and clicked through a few menus until he opened a diagnostic screen. "I'd say you did very well tonight, Mr. Dodger."

"How so?"

Looks like you had about nine thousand people log in.

"Nine thousand? Are you sure? It felt like less than twenty."

"No, nine thousand, and that's just the live chat," the student said. "We'll post a transcript on our website by morning, and people worldwide will have access. Could be hundreds of thousands ... even millions."

"Remarkable!" said Jack. "Simply remarkable. Maybe we've had our own convention after all."

Jack went to bed that night uplifted and with a sense of peace that win or lose, he was indeed part of an extraordinary process.

***

When Jack awoke the next morning, his prayers of gratitude for "another day" and "another try" were interrupted by a rude revelation. Franky had been downstairs already and came back to the suite with a newspaper tightly rolled up in his big hands.

"Jack, you're not going to like this." Franky, with hesitation, unrolled a copy of the *Weekly World Inquirer* on the table in front of Jack. On the cover was a grainy picture of Jack and Opal

Jenkins, standing outside her car in Wyoming, with the headline: "Grandpa Jack Interviews Potential First Lady."

As Jack stared at the image, he suddenly recalled the flicker of movement that he saw that night from the corner of his eye.

"How dare them," he said. His voice possessed a sharpness that he seldom expressed. "We were just talking, and they knew that. This is totally absurd."

"Well, of course it is," said Franky, trying to calm him. "It's in the *Inquirer*. The whole world knows everything they print is totally absurd. It's not a problem for us."

"I'm not worried about us, Franky. I could care less about what they say about me. It's Ms. Jenkins I'm worried about. All she did was show us kindness, and this is what she gets? We invade her town and her life, and now she's on the front of a piece of trash like this."

Caroline came in from her room, looked at the paper, and shook her head, but she was not as aghast as her father.

"It is shameful, I agree completely," she said. "But I wouldn't worry too much about Opal. She seems to be made of pretty tough stock."

"Well, that may be so, but that still doesn't make it okay," said Jack. "If I find out who took that picture, I'm gonna see that they don't take any more pictures for a while."

"Whoa Jack," said Wilton, who had entered the room with Billy in time to hear the candidate's surprising show of bravado. "Last thing we need is for you to be making threats."

"Oh, Wilton, I'm just talking. But I sure might put 'em off the bus and make 'em walk back home."

"Billy, got any idea who did this?" Wilton asked.

"There's no byline or photo credit, but I've got a good hunch."

Billy left the room and went downstairs where he found a group of the media gathering in the lobby for breakfast. Sitting off to the side by himself reading the morning paper was Howard

Hickman. Billy walked right up to him and thrust the tabloid under his nose.

"Are you responsible for this?"

"That piece of trash? Of course not," said Hickman. "It is a clever piece of fiction, but you should know, Billy, that I don't deal in fiction. I deal in cold, hard facts. And facts, as you know, are a lot more dangerous than fabrications. Facts can weigh on a man, can crush his dreams and the people who believe in him. Facts have a funny way—"

"Oh, cool it with the pompous sanctimony," Billy said and then walked back to the elevators.

Back upstairs, Jack's anger had subsided, but not his sense of responsibility. He fumbled through his wallet and found a slip of paper with a phone number scrawled on it. He stole away to the bedroom and dialed the number. After a half-dozen rings, it was answered.

"Hello," came a soft, warm voice.

"Hi, Opal? This is Jack Dodger. Listen, I'm sorry but—"

He was interrupted by uncontrollable laughter at the other end.

"Opal? Have you seen the story in the—"

"Yes! Yes!" she gasped between fits of laughter. "Oh yes! Isn't it a hoot?"

Jack was astonished and relieved. Caroline was right: Opal Jenkins was no wilting violet. She took it all in stride. Her hearty laugh melted Jack's concern and before long he was laughing too.

CHAPTER 17

Jack Dodger couldn't stop big teardrops from rolling down his rough cheeks as he stood in the airport terminal with his arms wrapped around Caroline and Wendy. School was starting in a week, and it was time for Wendy to go home and get ready to join her classmates.

"I'm going to miss you, Little Blossom," he said, drawing Wendy close. "Is it okay if I call you sometime and let you help me decide what to do? Like going swimming in the ocean?"

"Oh sure, Grandpa Jack, just call—I'll tell you how to have fun," she said.

"That'll be great." He turned his attention to Caroline. "Gonna miss you too, sweetheart. These weeks have sure been special."

"Oh, it's been a wonderful time, Daddy, a real adventure!" said Caroline. "Now we want you to remember, we'll be with you every day in spirit, and we'll be watching you every night on the news. And we're always just a phone call away if you need anything at all."

Then Caroline looked deeply into Jack's silver-gray eyes and added, "Remember, whatever happens over the next two months, whatever happens in November, win or lose, you'll always be my father, and you'll always be Wendy's Grandpa Jack. We'll always be proud of you, and above all else, we'll always love you."

That was more than Jack could take. The teardrops became a stream as they shared another round of hugs and the time came for Caroline and Wendy to board their flight.

"You take good care of him," Caroline shouted to Billy as they walked toward the Jetway. "You make him behave."

"I'll try," shouted Billy, the only member of the campaign team to go inside the airport with the Dodgers. The hope was to avoid a lot of attention and let the family share good-byes as inconspicuously as possible. Even the media had been asked to stay away and respect their privacy during this moment, and so they had pushed on ahead in their buses.

※

The drive from San Francisco to Sacramento was quiet, and Jack took the opportunity to nap. He and Hamilton Lee were to appear at a rally that afternoon on the steps of the state capitol, and he wanted to recharge his batteries—both physically and emotionally. As he stared out the window at the changing scenery, he had a feeling of dread at continuing without Caroline and Wendy. Their presence had added a comfortable family quality to the process, and he knew that life would be different without them. He also knew that the tone of the campaign was going to change right after Labor Day, although he didn't know to what extent. He knew that up to this point, the media and the other candidates had given him a relatively easy ride. But beginning soon, the compliments would probably be fewer and the criticisms more pointed and personal. He was nervous, not about what others might say, but about how he might react.

If the inevitability of the serious campaign season made Jack uneasy, it made Billy and Wilton downright anxious. Wilton still had ambitions of the Golden Eagles gaining a strong political foothold, and he knew they were about to face the real test of the organization's strength. As the main candidates firmed up their support, the "other party" candidates—Jack included—would be scrambling to gain the attention of anyone who was still uncommitted. Wilton was not worried about not winning it all; he was worried about making a weak showing. Pre-Labor Day polls showed Jack to be getting a nod from 24 percent of likely voters, with an overall favorability rating of 59 percent. Wilton hoped they'd come out of the election with those numbers intact, if not better.

Billy, on the other hand, was more concerned about the smaller daily battles that likely lay ahead. He had already caught whiffs of smoke, and he knew that a fire could break out at any moment. What's more, though he had no proof, he already suspected that Howard Hickman was carrying gas cans and matches.

The campaign rolled smoothly through Sacramento and on across northern Nevada, where Jack's conservative leanings, common sense, and practicality played well with ranchers and farmers in the northern end of the state. However, he ruffled some feathers in Reno and Elko when he spoke out against the waste of gambling.

"Want to hit the jackpot?" he asked. "Invest in yourself and your family. Go back to school so you can get a better job. Give your children what they need to become smart, happy adults. Find someone down the street who's fallen behind and help them get caught up. Sitting on a stool and throwing your money down some machine—is that really the best you can do?"

Jack's words fell on deaf ears in the casino towns. The gamblers couldn't hear over the clatter of the slot machines or the boos and hisses of the casino and resort workers who rejected him loudly. "Go back to the old folks home," they shouted. "This is our livelihood. It's none of your business."

"Well, fine," Jack retorted. "Then you go ahead and take these folks' money, and then be prepared to give it back to them in taxes for welfare programs."

Up until this time, the media hadn't seen Jack so openly opposed, and they were eager to get the most out of it. "Mr. Dodger, are you bothered by this rebuke of your position on gambling?" he was asked at a briefing.

"Rebuke?" Jack said. "That's a pretty strong word. I thought we were just having a difference of opinion. Nothing wrong with that."

"And what about your own history of gambling?" asked Howard Hickman, getting the attention of not just the candidate but also his fellow journalists. This was news to them, and they were eager to learn more. "What about your famous Friday night poker games at the barbershop?"

"What about them?" Jack responded.

"Aren't you being a bit hypocritical? Telling these folks they shouldn't gamble, and then doing it yourself."

"Our poker games? Hypocritical? That's nonsense," Jack laughed. "For starters, we don't play with money—we play with chips. We play until one man has all the chips, and then, he gets a free lunch later in the week. Actually, it's not entirely free. He puts his lunch money in one of the charity cans up there on the counter, and then, we pick up his lunch tab. The game's not about money, it's about a bunch of old men getting together and yapping. Now does anyone else have a question?"

"What about your poker games in Korea?" Howard persisted. "The games run by your friend Franky Parker? Didn't that land him in trouble a few times, and you along with him?"

"Now those games—I've got no excuses. Those were real poker games. We played for money, cigarettes, matches, cookies, shaving soap, postage stamps—whatever had value at the time. Mostly small stakes. We were young and foolish and scared, and it kept our minds off our fears. Sure, it got us into trouble, but we had bigger worries at the time. Anyone else have a question? If not, then, we best load up. We need to make Salt Lake by morning."

Jack headed for the RV and the media disbanded, leaving Howard standing alone. He was clearly put out by being made to look foolish among his peers, and Billy couldn't resist the opportunity to rub it in a little.

"Better do a little more homework next time, Howard."

"Oh, I have been, I have been," said Howard. "To use Jack's own words, this was just 'small stakes.' The high stakes game is coming up soon, and you better be ready to play, cause it's gonna be winner take all."

Three days later in Denver, Howard began to show his hand. During an afternoon break, he called Billy's hotel room and asked him to meet him in a sitting room off the hotel lobby.

"We're prepared to go to press in two days with a story about Jack," said Howard. "We've uncovered some details that we think the electorate will find provocative and probably even troubling, and we—our lawyers, that is, I could care less—they think I should give Jack the opportunity to respond."

With that, Howard pulled a folded piece of paper from his shirt pocket and handed it to Billy. Billy unfolded it, read it and reread it for a full two minutes. Then he folded it in half and handed it back to Howard. The information was indeed provocative, and for the first time since the campaign began, Billy didn't know what to do.

Billy went down the sheet in his mind. Some of it was clearly misinformation, some of it had the smell of fiction, and some of it … well he just didn't know for sure. Clearly, he didn't know everything there was to know about Jack Dodger. All he knew about Hamilton Lee was what they had heard from him and discovered from their background check. As for Kevin, he knew what Jack had told him, and Jack told him Kevin was entirely trustworthy.

The broader decision to consider was even if the "facts" on the sheet were pure fiction, would a response from Jack lead to an endless series of nit-picking questions that could completely swamp the campaign? And if he did not respond, would that lead people to think that the allegations were true? Even more uncertain, was Howard just bluffing? Were the allegations completely false, and was Howard just trying to trap Jack into revealing something else, or at least provoke his anger and create a scene? If Jack refused to respond, would Howard's editors kill the story?

"Need to look at the paper again, Billy?" Howard asked in a condescending voice as he reached for his shirt pocket. "Need to run it upstairs and see what the boss says?"

"No ... No! Keep your damn paper," said Billy angrily. "I speak for Jack, and I say this is a bunch of garbage, you know it's garbage, and we're not going to play your game of 'gotcha.'"

Howard was astonished. "My God, Billy, are you sure about this?" For the first time he spoke with a tone of concern in his voice, but Billy saw it all as just an act and he strengthened his resolve.

"Yes, I'm sure. Now, if you'll excuse me, I've got some *real* issues to deal with."

Howard's smart-aleck tone quickly returned. "Well, now, looks like I was wrong after all. It's not Jack who's the big gambler in this campaign."

Indeed. Billy gambled that the story would die, and two days later while the campaign was in Colorado Springs, Howard showed his hand. He was not bluffing. The *Houston Journal* published his story, which was copyrighted and quickly picked up by the wire services and, then, every major paper in America. It landed in Jack's lap on the Sunday morning of Labor Day weekend as he relaxed on a chaise lounge on the verandah at the Broadmoor Hotel.

This time it was Billy and not Franky that brought the bad news. The local paper had reprinted Howard's story in its entirety, including the headline and the editor's note.

Jack Dodges Truth
By Howard Hickman

> *Editor's Note*: As the result of a lengthy investigation, we have assembled facts and details that call into serious question the honesty and integrity of the Jack Dodger campaign. In fact, the information we have uncovered may very well reveal a level of hypocrisy that is unequaled in this election year. It also reveals a candidate whose judgment of character is seemingly in opposition to his recent calls for the importance of character in public life. Let us make it clear that we allowed the campaign to respond to these allegations, but they declined.

What followed was a list of allegations and then details, some more complete than others, related to those allegations:

- ❏ Jack Dodger and Franky Parker have been involved in business dealings that might best be described as "shady." Most notably, they operated a diner that was known as a hangout for an unsavory clientele, many of them known hoodlums, and where cigarettes and alcohol were sold in the presence of minors. The diner was closed in 1990, and the property was seized by the city.

- ❏ Kevin Walker, the driver for the Dodger-Lee campaign, in January was arrested and pled guilty to charges of burglary, aggravated kidnapping, and illegal possession of a firearm. What makes this revelation all the more unusual is that it was Jack Dodger and his associate, Franky Parker, who were the target of Walker's crime. Nonetheless, Walker was released after serving a brief sentence. From all accounts, he was unemployed until he was hired by the Dodger campaign. In the interim, he received a number of payments by check from Dodger.

- ❏ A further investigation of Kevin Walker's background reveals that prior to the burglary-kidnapping incident in Dallas, he was fired from a previous job for "unauthorized internet activity."

- ❏ Hamilton Lee, while claiming to have never fathered a child during a brief marriage, in fact did have a son who he has never supported. Furthermore, his departure from public life and his isolated existence in Washington State appear to have been an attempt to further remove himself from contact with and responsibility for his son.

Jack studied the article carefully while Billy watched nervously from the foot of an adjacent chaise lounge.

"Well, that's just nuts." Jack folded the paper and laid it at his side. "There's explanations for most of this, and the rest just isn't true. They'd know that if they'd given us the chance to respond, which they clearly did not despite their little note there at the top."

Billy cleared his throat and then made one of the most difficult confessions of his life. "Jack, they *did* offer us the chance to respond."

"What? When?" Jack sat up and faced Billy knee-to-knee. "What are you telling me, son?"

"Howard showed me these allegations a week ago. I knew most of this was bogus, and I didn't think his editors would go to press unless we responded. Obviously, I made a terrible misjudgment."

"Yes, I believe that's right," Jack said. He leaned back on the chaise and closed his eyes. Billy sat beside him, watching helplessly, not sure whether to say something or keep quiet. Jack's eyelids twitched for a moment, and then he opened his eyes and stared across the Broadmoor's small lake at the towering mountains.

"Go on up to the suite and get everyone together—including Kevin. Tell 'em what's happened … and why. I'll be up in about an hour. I'm gonna take a walk around the lake."

Billy sat still for a moment, waiting for Jack to get up.

"Well, do as you're told," Jack said with rare impatience.

"Yes, sir," said Billy quietly, springing to his feet. He took one last look at Jack lounging in the chaise, arms folded across his chest. Then he walked back into the hotel to gather the team.

Jack did finally get up. He stretched in the morning sunlight, and then began a leisurely walk around the small lake. The mountains above the hotel glowed with the rising sun, casting light back down onto the lake and filling its surface with reflections of the hotel, the towering trees, houses up in the foothills, and the mountain itself. A couple of dozen people were scattered around the lakeshore path: young couples jogging, children playing, others just strolling after breakfast or before brunch. All were in a cheery mood and greeted Jack with a nod of the head or a simple "good morning" as they passed by. If they recognized Jack, they weren't bothered by him. It was the kind of morning when sunshine and rich mountain air were more important than celebrity. Jack too was drawn into the moment and the worries of the morning went away.

At the far side of the lake, just off the hotel property, he spotted a little church and crossed over to look inside. It was between services and the sanctuary was quiet. Jack sat down on the back row and looked one by one at the stained-glass windows down the sidewalls and above the altar. As he did so, he prayed silently. He thanked God for another morning, for his family, for his campaign team, and for the many nameless people who had wished him well over the months and across the miles. He ended with just one thought for himself: "Lord God, grant me the wisdom to know your will, and to follow it without question, wherever it may lead."

Jack returned to the hotel suite to find Billy, Wilton, Hamilton, and Kevin all assembled. They were sitting around on various sofas and chairs, and Jack's entrance caused them all to jump a bit. They watched with anticipation as he closed the door, walked into the bathroom to wash his hands, came back out, and sat in a large, stuffed chair in the middle of the room.

Billy finally broke the uncomfortable silence. "Well, Jack, what did you decide?"

"Didn't decide anything," Jack said, drumming the armrests with his fingers. "Just took a walk. Beautiful morning for a walk."

"Well, Jack," said Wilton impatiently, "while you were out enjoying the beautiful morning, I was taking phone calls from headquarters in Kansas City and other Golden Eagles locations. People want to know what's going on. We're getting calls from all over the country. Everything is in disarray. Some big donors have threatened to withdraw their support. What are you gonna do about it? Well? What are you going to do about it? What?"

Jack looked at Wilton a moment, and then he looked at Billy. His eyes spoke to Billy with a clarity that only he could understand. Billy had gotten them into this, and now, Jack was trusting him with the responsibility of getting them out of it.

"Listen, everyone," said Billy, "I made a serious misjudgment. I've put you all on the spot. I'm terribly sorry, and I take full responsibility for it." He paused a moment to shift from a confessional state to one of action. "Having said all that, I believe the allegations must be addressed quickly and firmly. All of them."

"Good," said Wilton. "The sooner the better."

"I think we should call a press conference this evening," Billy continued. "Until then, nothing should be said to anyone. There should be one concise answer to each of these points and, then, nothing more. The media will try to ask the same questions over and over again in different ways, but there should be only one answer to each question, and then, we should move on. We can't allow them to stay parked on this."

"That sounds fine," said Jack, confident in Billy's plan. "I'll answer all the questions that pertain to me, and Hamilton will have a chance to address the question that relates to him."

"What about Kevin?" said Wilton. "Is it true? Were you fired?"

"Yes, but it's not what you think," Kevin answered.

"Kevin is not to be drawn into this. Neither is Franky," said Jack. "They're not running for office, and if someone wants to question my judgment in having them here, then, they can and I will address it."

"Well, you've got to say something," said Wilton.

"I'll handle it," Jack said firmly.

⁂

That evening, the press was called to a hotel ballroom, and their numbers had swelled in anticipation of Jack's response to the allegations. Jack didn't wait for questions; he addressed the allegations one by one.

"On the matter of my business dealings in Dallas, it is true that Franky Parker and myself have made some mistakes. And the diner was probably the biggest. We weren't serious enough about it, and we gave away more food than we sold. As for the character of our clientele, we never pretended to be a country club. We were a short-order diner. We served folks and didn't ask them what they did. Sure, some of them probably had a bad reputation, but as long as they kept that outside, it was no bother to us.

"As for serving cigarettes and alcohol in the presence of minors, we had a cigarette machine at the door, and I wouldn't doubt that a few kids probably bought some. That was more than a decade ago, so there wasn't the stiff laws that we have today, though we did try to police it. Don't know what this business is about alcohol. Might have happened under the previous ownership, but not us. We never had a liquor license. Never wanted one. That's a dangerous business to be in.

"Now, about this notion that the property was seized by the city. That never happened. About the same time that it became clear that we weren't going to make any money in the restaurant business, the school board was in need of opening more preschools, but were strapped for cash. So we gave them the property. It was a nice write-off for us, and the district built a preschool. It's still operating there. It's understandable that Mr. Hickman didn't get that straight because the donation wasn't in the records that way. We didn't want any attention."

At that point, Jack turned the microphone over to Hamilton Lee to answer the allegation against him.

"My wife divorced me while I was serving in Southeast Asia," he said. "And I didn't fight it. I was not only too far away to stop it—I also wasn't able emotionally to deal with it. Seeing good men die, facing death myself, I just let her go. It was just part of the miserable package."

Then looking straight at Howard, Hamilton said, "If you're saying that I have a son, then mister, you know more than I do. My wife left no forwarding information of any kind. No, sir, she ran out on me. She sold our house and took my car. She was the one who never made any contact, she was the one who left and never looked back. If she needed my help, she never asked for it. If she—if we had a son, I never knew about it. If she wanted financial support, all she had to do was contact the Pentagon or the State Department. I had an office there with my name on the door. I wasn't hiding from anybody."

Hamilton gave Howard one final glare and, then, stepped aside. Jack returned to answer the final allegation.

"About Mr. Walker, yes, he was involved in an incident in Dallas that was stupid and reckless and that he likely will regret the rest of his life. But he paid the penalty required by the courts, he personally apologized to me, and I forgave him that very night. As far as I'm concerned, the slate has been wiped clean. Since then, he's driven me and my friends and family thousands of miles, and our lives have been safe in his hands. He's worked hard and earned our trust—and our respect."

Kevin was standing in the back of the room, and Jack gave him a little nod. Others in the press corps who weren't familiar with the story looked over their shoulders and were surprised to see the familiar figure of Jack's driver.

At least one reporter wanted to know more and pressed Jack further. "What about his previous employment situation, and what about the money you paid him?"

"That's his personal affair. He's not running for any office, and we're not going to talk about it. It has no bearing whatsoever on this campaign and is of no relevance to the voters."

Then Howard, seemingly defeated and deflated, stood up to play one last card.

"Well, then perhaps you would like to address this question, which was not covered in our story, but it will be in tomorrow's paper. We have it on good authority that you met your wife, the former Claire Budrow, in a dance hall—"

"That's enough," Jack interrupted, holding up his hands. "Please, that's enough."

"And that she was a frequent guest of that dance hall, or was she an employee—"

"Enough!" Jack said loudly. "Please, stop now!"

"And that she was well known by many different men at that dance hall, an establishment that was the scene of occasional shakedowns for various morals violations—"

"Enough, I said. Stop it, now!" Jack shouted.

"And furthermore, there is reason to believe that your daughter was born a bit sooner than expected and that—"

Jack exploded in anger. "You pompous, arrogant—for the love of all that is good and decent ... how dare you even attempt to blemish the memory of the sweetest, most precious, most gentle person I have ever known! How dare you!"

"Do you not then deny what I'm saying?" asked Howard.

"Deny? Deny? I won't dignify with a response this trash you've hauled in here. How dare you. You've been given the unique privilege to report on some of the most important issues of our day, and instead you crawl off down some back alley and drag out this sack full of half-truths and flea-bitten innuendo?"

Jack was on the verge of hyperventilating and he stopped for a moment to catch his breath and regain his composure. Billy stepped over to help him, but Jack stuck out his arm and stopped him in midstep. And, then, he resumed in a quieter voice, speaking to everyone in the room.

"People, yours is an important, and in fact a constitutionally blessed calling, but this one here has brought disgrace and shame to your profession with his shoddy research and baseless fiction. And I'm afraid that some of you have let yourself be duped by this man and have bought into his lies and have begun to repeat them, and you do so at great risk. I can't believe you would even want to associate with a piece of—"

Howard suddenly growled and lunged headlong at Jack, and would have caught him in a waistline tackle and thrown him to the ground had Hamilton not stepped in front of Jack and sent Howard headfirst into the floor with a perfect varsity counter-tackle.

As Howard and Hamilton sprawled out on the ground, they rolled into several reporters, knocking them off their feet and into the rows of metal folding chairs. Others in the room pushed forward with cameras in an attempt to get it all on tape, and several more fell. Billy leaned down into the pile to try and pull Hamilton off of Howard, and when he pulled backward on Hamilton's belt, he hit his head on a camera lens and recoiled in pain. Afraid that someone else might be on the attack, Franky jumped out in front of Jack and spread his arms out to catch any comers, while Wilton and Kevin dashed out of the room in search of a security guard.

Jack felt his muscles cramp in his right arm, and he looked down to find his fist clinched tightly with his fingernails digging into his palms.

"No … no … this is all wrong," he said in disbelief at the chaos now before him. "This isn't right. This isn't right. No!"

Jack pushed Franky out of his way and stumbled over bodies to the door. "I've had it with all of you … the whole damn lot of you."

"Jack, wait!" Billy shouted, his head still pulsing with pain. He tried to push his way out of the middle of the room, but Franky reached out with one large hand and held him by the upper arm.

"Let him go, Billy. Just let him go."

CHAPTER 18

It was Jack's fate—and his fortune—that after eight months in the national spotlight, he was still not immediately recognizable whenever the spotlight was turned off. Dress him in a suit with an American flag pen on his lapel, surround him with media, let his resonating voice be heard, and people would gather around, nudge each other and say, "Look, it's Jack Dodger," or, "Hey, there goes Grandpa Jack!" But dress him casually in slacks, a striped dress shirt, slightly worn loafers and a cardigan sweater, and he was just another senior citizen on a golf vacation. And so it was that Jack was able to slip out of the Broadmoor Hotel with nobody paying him the slightest bit of attention.

Jack left the hotel at full stride, propelled by raw emotion. All he wanted to do was get as far away as possible, as fast as possible. His feet carried him quickly out of the hotel and down the street to a corner, where he found a woman waiting for a city bus. He asked her where she was going, and she said downtown. That suited him, and he waited with her. The bus came and fifteen minutes after leaving the ruckus at the hotel, Jack was on the sidewalk in downtown Colorado Springs.

He wandered around for a few minutes with no particular destination in mind until he found himself at a coffee shop attached to the Greyhound bus station. Jack stepped inside to get out of the chilly mountain air, ordered a cup of coffee, and sat down at a table where he could watch the people coming and going. He sipped the hot, stale brew and thought about mostly nothing until his eye caught a glimpse of the bus station's electronic destination board. Anaheim, Atlanta, Baltimore,

Boston, Chicago, Cleveland, Dallas, Denver, Detroit—Jack read about halfway down the list, and then, he backed up again. Dallas. The bus for Dallas was leaving at nine. Jack patted his pocket. Good, he thought. He still had his money clip with the "walking around" cash that Wilton had given him, and there was enough to get him home if that's what he wanted to do. Jack put aside that decision and went back to sipping his coffee. But when he heard the first call for the Dallas-bound bus, he got up from the table without hesitation and walked to the ticket window.

"Where you going tonight?" the ticket agent asked.

"Dallas."

"Round trip?"

"No, sir. One way."

"Any luggage?"

"No, sir."

"That'll be sixty-nine dollars."

Jack pulled out his money clip, unfolded several bills, and slid them across the counter.

"Bus leaves in fifteen minutes. Won't be full, so you've got your choice of seats."

"Thank you." Jack took the ticket and walked out into the garage, where a half-dozen silver buses were lined up waiting to go. Jack scanned the front windshields till he found the one that said "Dallas." He climbed up the steps and found just a handful of people inside. Jack walked about halfway down the aisle and slid into a window seat. The interior lights were not on, and the darkness of the bus and the quiet vibration of the engine were soothing compared to the bright glare and commotion of the hotel ballroom. Jack leaned his head against the window, closed his eyes, and relaxed until the closing of the door and the hiss of air brakes roused him.

The bus made a series of slow turns out of the station and through downtown on its way to Interstate 25. Jack hadn't really gotten to see Colorado Springs, so he looked attentively at the shops and buildings and homes as they passed. As the bus turned onto the interstate and began to pick up speed, Jack began to settle back into his seat when a line of four police cars sped by on the right with lights flashing and sirens moaning. The cars exited at the next off-ramp and then turned toward the mountains. Jack craned his neck a moment and could see the police cars streaming up the broad avenue toward the silhouette of the Broadmoor. Jack leaned back in his seat and looked straight ahead again. Within a few more minutes, the bus had left the lights of town and Jack slipped into a deep, marrow-soothing sleep.

The scene back at the Broadmoor was not so peaceful. Hotel security guards held Howard Hickman, Hamilton Lee, and Franky Parker until the police arrived to sort out the details of who had manhandled whom. Because nobody was injured and no property was damaged, no charges were filed by the police or the hotel against the key parties, although Howard insisted that the lawyers at his paper would have the last say. The rest of the media were either standing at a distance, recording this final action, or were up in their rooms on their laptop computers cranking out the next day's headlines.

The only unresolved issue was the whereabouts of Jack. Billy, Kevin, and Wilton fanned out across the vast hotel acreage in search of Jack, but they all met back at the suite without any news of a sighting.

"Don't worry," Wilton said, his hands clinched together. "He's probably just out blowing off steam. Might have taken a cab into town. I'm sure he'll be in before too late."

By dawn, however, Jack had still not come back to the suite, and nervousness had grown into near panic. Caroline called early after seeing the report on the morning news, and Billy had trouble hiding his own fears.

"I'll be straight with you. Your father's been out all night, and we don't know where he is," he told her. "Yes, I'm worried about him. We're all worried about him."

Caroline became hysterical at the other end of the line and gave Billy an earful of childlike distress over her missing father mixed with anger at their carelessness for letting him slip away. Unable to calm her, Billy asked Franky to take over.

"Don't you worry about a thing," Franky said firmly. "Your father's a smart man, but he's also his own man. It was a mess last night and I just think he's looking for a little air. He'll be back."

About ten in the morning, Jack woke to find sunlight streaming though the bus windows. He stretched his legs forward and then rubbed his eyes and face, which by now was covered with a day's worth of gray stubble. He sat up straight and looked out to the left and right and then stretched his neck to see out the front window, trying to get his bearings.

A girl of about twenty was sitting across the aisle, and when he saw that she was watching him, he asked her where they were.

"Just west of Amarillo," she said. "You've been sound asleep all night long, through all the stops. You must've been really tired."

"Yep, I was." Jack yawned and looked around the bus and noticed there were more passengers than when he had boarded. "I don't remember seeing you in Colorado Springs. Where did you get on?"

"I got on in Santa Fe," she said. "I went out there for the weekend. Now I'm heading back to school in Canyon. How about you? Where are you going?"

Jack sat back in his seat and looked out the window again. "Home. I'm going home."

Jack got off the bus in Amarillo to catch the connecting bus that would carry him down US 287 to Dallas. With time on his hands, he got on the phone and made one call—to Caroline. He knew his daughter would be worried, and he didn't want her to be upset for a moment longer.

"I think it's all over," he told her. "It got out of hand, and I don't know that I can fix things. I'm not sure I should even try. I don't think I'm the right person for this—it's tougher, uglier than I imagined. I'm gonna spend a little time away. Maybe I can figure something out."

When pressed to tell where he was, Jack didn't break down. "I'm safe and in good health, and I think I'll just leave it at that. If I tell you, folks will be bugging you to tell them, so it'll be easier if you don't know. I suspect it'd be good for you to call Billy and let him know I'm okay, but I think it's best for everyone if I don't say where I am right now. I think they probably need a break too. I'll call again in a day or two. Now give my Little Blossom a big hug and tell her that Grandpa Jack hopes to see her real soon."

Caroline made the call to Billy, and soon the word was dispersed through the media that Jack was taking "a well-deserved break before the final push." The same word was relayed back to Golden Eagles headquarters by Wilton, but Hank Simmons and the board were upset about what they were seeing on the news, and Wilton was told to get back to headquarters right away for an emergency board meeting. Wilton, Billy, Franky, and Hamilton loaded up the RV and left for Kansas City.

The Greyhound bus rolled into downtown Dallas around five in the evening, and Jack was glad to see the familiar sights of home. But that familiarity also posed a problem. Aware that he might be more recognizable in his hometown than he was elsewhere, Jack stepped into the restroom at the back of the bus to adjust his look. He combed his hair straight down on his forehead, pulled part of his shirttail out and misbuttoned his sweater so that one side hung clumsily over his lap. The result was that when he stepped out of the bus onto the sidewalk, he looked more like a street person looking for a meal than a presidential candidate on the run.

Twenty minutes later and a dozen blocks up Live Oak Street, Judson was trimming his last customer of the day when Blackie suddenly awakened from her snooze in the corner and growled. Judson stopped snipping as he heard the door to the back alley open, and then, the shuffle of feet across the storeroom floor. His memory flashed back to New Year's Eve, and he froze with fear as the back door opened ever so slightly. But fear turned to surprise when he saw the familiar face peek through.

"Jack! What the—"

"Shhhh," Jack hissed and beckoned him with his index finger.

Judson dropped his comb and scissors on the counter and walked quickly into the back room, pulling the door behind him.

"Jack, what are you doing here? They said on TV you were taking a vacation."

"That's right," Jack whispered. "I am. I just stopped by to get my keys and my truck."

"Well, sure, Jack," said Judson. He rummaged through the top drawer of a file cabinet and produced Jack's keys.

"I got something else you might want," he added, and went back to the door, opened it, and gave a little whistle.

Jack heard the sound of toenails clicking across the tile and in seconds he was kneeling on the floor enjoying a full welcome from Blackie.

"Caroline and Wendy brought her back last week," Judson explained. "With school starting and all, they needed a break, and so I've been watching her."

"Well, if you don't mind, I think I'll take her with me," said Jack. "I could use a little company for a few days."

Jack stood up and before he and Blackie left, he put his hands on Judson's shoulders and looked him squarely in the eyes.

"Now remember, Jud, I'm just taking a few days off, and I don't need anyone to know that I've been here. Not even Caroline or Franky. I'll let them know where I am tomorrow. Okay?"

"Sure Jack, sure," said Judson. "I haven't seen you since spring. But if I had seen you, I'd have told you how much we've missed you around here." He paused and looked Jack over from head to toe. "And I'd probably have told you that you were looking a bit raggedy, but that's only if I had seen you, which I haven't."

"Thanks." Jack laughed. "See you soon."

Jack and Blackie climbed into his blue pickup truck parked out back and headed east toward Lakewood. Jack turned cautiously onto his street, knowing that there might be media staking out his home. There was no sign of trouble, so he pulled into the driveway and on into the garage. Twenty minutes later, he pulled out again with a small satchel of clothing, a sleeping bag, an ice chest, a frying pan and a few utensils, a tackle box, and a fishing pole in the bed of the truck.

With Blackie sitting quietly at his side and the sun setting in his rearview mirror as he drove toward the Piney Woods of East Texas, Jack began to feel the tension of the past twenty-four hours flow out of his body. The muscles in his arms and legs loosened, his breaths became deeper and slower, the furrows across his brow melted away, his jawbone relaxed, and his teeth unclenched. Without thinking, he reached over and turned on the radio, only to be startled by the sound of music. It had been months since he had heard music that wasn't being played by a high school band. He twisted the knob a few turns and found a station in Shreveport playing old country standards. Before long, he was strumming the edge of the steering wheel with his fingers while Blackie beat erratic time with her tail.

That night, the two travelers bedded down in the back of the truck near the shores of Lake O' The Pines. They'd gotten in too late to find a campsite, so they just parked and went to sleep. Jack awoke at dawn with the sensation of wet dew on his face.

"Come on, girl," he said, rousing Blackie from a deep dream. "I got a feeling the fish are biting this morning."

And indeed they were. Jack pulled in a trio of nice-sized bass, and he cleaned them and cooked them with eggs over a small wood fire. Like the sound of music on his truck radio, Jack had forgotten how healing a morning in the woods could be.

For Wilton Harris and the rest of the campaign team, the new morning was not so pleasurable. They were already tired from traveling, and when Wilton arrived at the closed-door board meeting, he was immediately peppered with questions: What about the accusations? Was Kevin really a criminal? Didn't they check Hamilton Lee's background? How could Billy let things get out of hand? And most important, where is the candidate?

"Like we've said, he's taking a break," Wilton said helplessly.

"From what I've seen and heard, he walked out," said a board member.

"He didn't take any of our money, did he?" another asked loudly.

"No, of course he didn't," said Wilton. "Please, people, he didn't even take any of his luggage. Truth of the matter is, I don't know exactly where he is, and I'm worried about him."

"Well, has there been any contact with him?" asked another.

"He's been in touch with his daughter, so we know he's okay," said Wilton.

"Well, that's all fine and good that *he's* okay," said Hank Simmons, "but what about us? What about the Golden Eagles, the folks that have been supporting him all these months? We're not okay. That fiasco in Colorado Springs is an embarrassment to our organization. Not to mention these unanswered questions about Jack and his friends."

A board member leaned forward and spoke slowly and deliberately. "Folks, considering what has happened, and considering all the uncertainties that still linger, I believe it is in the best interest of this organization that we end all financial support of Jack Dodger immediately, and that we make a public statement as soon as possible announcing that we have severed our ties to his campaign."

There were nods and murmurs of agreement around the table, with the exception of Wilton, who could not believe what he was witnessing.

"Do I hear a motion that we disassociate with Jack Dodger and his candidacy?" Hank asked.

There was a motion, and a second, and then a vote. All but one hand was raised in support of the action.

"Very well, then," said Hank. "I will instruct the finance staff to close the campaign bank account and to pay all outstanding bills. Wilton, I need you and Billy to draft a statement for the media and then arrange a press conference for later this afternoon. Something real simple and to the point so ... "

"No." Wilton stood and moved toward the door. "*No!* You write your own statement. You talk about being embarrassed? I'm embarrassed, but not of Jack. I'm embarrassed to be a part of this organization. I'm resigning—immediately."

Wilton started to open the door then paused and walked back to the edge of the board table.

"You know something ... I've spent the better part of eight months with Jack Dodger. In that time I've come to know a man of unquestionable honesty and integrity, with stamina and strength beyond his years. And while he's also a man of great courage and patience, he's also human. Like all of us, he can be pushed too far, and that's what happened in Colorado Springs. If I had heard those kinds of things said about my family, I'm not sure how I would have reacted. Yes, it's true, he walked out. But there's one more thing I know about Jack, and this is key: he's a man who always finishes what he starts. Always. As bad as it might get, as deep as it might hurt, he's not a quitter. Not like the people sitting in this room. So I intend to help him finish what's been started. Keep your money. Keep your organization. Keep your precious name. It's not needed any longer. The only name that is needed is that of Jack Dodger."

"For God sake," Hank shouted as Wilton left the room. "You don't even know where the man is!"

∽⊙⊙⊙∾

But Franky knew. While Wilton was in the meeting, Franky had called Caroline, and she reported that her father had phoned again and that he was okay. "He said something like, he's in a place where there's fresh air, cool water, and … and something about 'fish jumping over the pines.' Do you know what he meant by that?"

"Yes," said Franky. "I know exactly what he meant by that."

CHAPTER 19

Hank Simmons was grim as he read the statement that officially severed the ties between the Golden Eagles and Jack Dodger. It was not completely unexpected, but the news still hung in the throats of most who heard it.

"We are deeply sorry that it has ended this way, and I would like to personally apologize to Golden Eagles across the nation, and to the American people as a whole, for our role in perpetuating what has sadly been revealed to be a horrible blunder. Still, the democratic system is alive and well, and we encourage everyone of voting age to let their voices be heard in an appropriate way on election day."

There were many questions that followed, but Hank simply folded up his script and walked from the room. There would be no answers to their questions, and especially not those asking if there might be some form of reconciliation. The bond with Jack Dodger had to be broken—quickly and completely. From here on out, there was to be no mention of Dodger or the campaign, officially or unofficially, by the officers of the Golden Eagles. The whole matter was to be struck from the records, as if it never happened.

Of the press that had been traveling with Jack, only about a dozen made the trip from Colorado Springs to Kansas City for the announcement. The rest had dispersed to new assignments once it became known that Jack had slipped away and the campaign was "over."

Likewise, Jack's campaign team did not stay to see the curtain pulled down. Billy, Wilton, Hamilton, and Kevin had all ridden together to Kansas City for the board meeting. When it was clear that the Golden Eagles were withdrawing support, Kevin turned in the keys to the RV, and he, Billy, and Franky rented a car for the drive home to Dallas. Hamilton flew back to the misty hills of Seattle, his brief day in the sun over. Wilton was the only one to stay in Kansas City, but just for a few days to close out his affairs with the Golden Eagles. Then, he would follow the others home to Dallas.

Despite what Wilton had said at the board meeting about helping Jack finish what had been started, that idea now appeared far-fetched at best. Any flickering hopes that the campaign could be salvaged were quickly doused by reading the newspapers or turning on the television, where the analysts and pundits cried "quitter" and "charlatan." The press conference had ended the rumor that Jack was "taking a few days off," and the dispersal of his campaign team was a clear sign that the show was over and the tent had been folded.

The US Debate Commission, which unbeknownst to the campaign had been on the verge of offering Jack a place on their stage due to his high poll numbers, now stated that would never be the case.

"His credibility has been shattered, the support of his sponsors and his public has crumbled, and he's nowhere to be found. Hardly a good resume to warrant an invitation to talk with serious people about serious issues," they said.

All of this negative press, this dramatic shift of the wind after a summer filled with such unforgettable moments and great promise, was almost more than Billy could take. He still blamed himself for letting Howard Hickman's story get into print without a proper rebuttal.

"This is my fault," he kept saying during the long drive back to Texas. "I should have stayed at the paper where I belonged. He should have had a pro handling this. A pro wouldn't have let this happen."

"It's not your fault," comforted Kevin. "You did what you thought was best. And that's all Jack has ever asked of any of us. 'Just do your best,' he would say."

"Then, he was naive to trust me or any of us for that matter," said Billy angrily. "And we were all naive to think we could do in one summer what others have spent whole lifetimes learning."

"But that's what got folk's attention," countered Franky. "We weren't playing by the regular rules. We were just doing it our way."

"Well, that's all well and good," said Billy, "but the problem is that everyone else is still playing by the regular rules. And I guess we proved once again that no small party candidate has a chance unless they get organized and operate like a big party."

The conversation ended there, and the car was silent for a dozen miles until Kevin, who was driving, decided to change the subject.

"You know, we've been talking about how we failed and all, but maybe we should put that aside and worry a little bit more about Jack and how he's doing. He's the one who really got beat up in this thing. So, Franky, got any ideas where he is?"

"I can't say I know where he is, but I'd bet money that I know what he's doing."

"And what's that?"

"Fishing. Just fishing. And if you want my opinion, that's exactly what he should be doing. A man should spend his retirement sitting beside a nice cool fishing hole. Figuring out where they're biting—that's the only pressure us old men should have to deal with."

Franky looked out the window as they crossed the Red River into Texas. He tapped his fingers nervously on his knees because he hadn't been completely honest with Kevin. Not only did he know exactly what Jack was doing, but he also knew exactly where he was doing it.

On the evening of the third day of his exile, Jack left the fishing hole that Franky knew all about and drove up out of the lake basin with Blackie to a little country store and bait shop to pick up some supplies and borrow a telephone to call Caroline. As he made his way through the store picking items from the shelves, he came upon a group of four old-timers sitting around a butcher-block table, drinking coffee and talking. Behind them on a little table was an old black and white television. The volume was hardly audible, but the picture screen showed the vice president chatting with an afternoon talk show hostess about his plans for the nation if elected president.

"I'll sure be glad when this nonsense is over," one of the old-timers said. "These candidates are all the same. They just make up a bunch of promises they can't keep."

"Yep, and they keep on doing it year after year," said another. "Must be some mighty powerful ego to make a man do that."

"Except for that Dodger fellow," said the third man, who, by his position at the table—back to the wall so he could see the entire store—seemed to be the leader. "He's different, that one. I think he's got folks' best interests ahead of his own. He's not boastful or prideful like some of these others. He speaks plainly and directly, but without pushing too hard."

"Well, Roy, I'll agree with you on part of that," said the fourth man. "He *was* different, until he run off like a rabbit. Seems to me he was thinking about himself when he done that."

"Well, I'm not so sure I wouldn't have done the same, considering what they were saying about his family," said Roy.

Jack heard his name in the conversation, and he couldn't hold back his curiosity. He moved a little closer, with his back to them, so he could hear better.

"Heck, where have you and this Jack Dodger been the last twenty years," said the first man. "That's just the way they do it now—ugly and personal. He should've known that going into it. It weren't no secret. Seems a bit naive if you ask me."

"Well, that's all over now," said another. "He's buried himself. He could come back tomorrow and I don't think folks would give him another look. I sure wouldn't. Had me thinking about voting for him, but I wouldn't do it now. Gotta be tougher than that to be president. Shoot, in this town, you gotta be tougher than that to be mayor."

Roy had seen Jack looking around while they were talking, and he turned his attention from the others for a moment.

"Finding everything okay?" he asked. "Care to join us for a cup of coffee? Best free brew in town."

Jack was startled and dropped the can of tuna that he had balanced on top of a loaf of bread. He reached down to pick it up and then turned cautiously toward the men.

"Um … thank you, yes I've just about got it all," said Jack. "Appreciate the invite too, but I better move along. Got my dog waiting outside in the truck. She don't like to be kept waiting too long. Thank you anyway."

Jack nodded at the men and then began to move away when Roy interrupted him again.

"Wait a minute," he said. He looked closely at Jack's face. "You look kind of familiar. Have we met somewhere before?"

"Don't know," Jack said cautiously. "Could be. I grew up over here at Marshall. I live over in Dallas now, but I've been fishing out here all my life." Jack adjusted his cap, pulling the bill down a little more over his eyes.

"Hmmm," the man said, giving Jack another close look. He stared intently into Jack's eyes, and Jack looked back at him in quick little glances. And then suddenly, in that moment, Roy made the connection. He knew exactly whom he was talking to, and he also read in Jack's eyes that he wanted to leave with his privacy intact.

"Yes, maybe that's it," Roy said slowly. "So how long you out here this time?"

"Oh, just a few days. Probably go back tomorrow."

"That's the problem with city folks," said one of the men. "Always rushing back to town. Always got big important things to do. Gotta go make another million."

"Well, now, maybe we shouldn't judge this gentleman so quickly," said Roy. "Could be there's people waiting on him who really need him, who are depending on him. Can't fault a man for keeping up with his responsibilities."

Jack smiled slightly.

"Besides," Roy continued, "he said he grew up in Marshall. That pretty much means he's got some good in him somewhere."

By now, Jack knew that his secret was safe with Roy, but he wasn't so sure about the others. He felt he better get out before one of them recognized him. "Thanks. You gentlemen have a good evening now," he said.

"You too," said Roy. "And good luck to you. Remember, fishing isn't just about catching fish. It's about watching and listening, it's about being patient. Most of all, it's about knowing when it's time to move on, and knowing when you need to hang in a bit longer."

"That's good advice," said Jack.

Jack paid for his groceries at the counter and then slipped out the door and climbed into his truck. It was beginning to get dark as he returned to the campsite, and with an early fall chill in the air, he arranged some kindling and small branches in the circle of stones he had built and used his receipt from the store to light the fire. He pulled a tarp and his sleeping bag out of the back of the truck and spread them out, upwind from the fire. He and Blackie had slept in the bed of the truck the previous night, but tonight, they would stretch out next to the warm embers.

Jack stoked the fire a moment, added a couple of larger logs, then sat down on a fallen tree trunk that he had dragged up to use as a camp seat. Blackie lay at his side, her tail sliding back and forth along the sandy ground.

Jack hadn't thought much about the campaign for the past two days—had not really thought about the consequences of his departure, or whether or not he would try to complete the journey. But as he sat quietly and stared into the growing flames, he reflected on the conversation he had heard in the store, and he began to feel the full weight of his actions. A lot of people had depended on him. Many had invested the better part of a year in the campaign, just as he had. The Golden Eagles and their supporters had invested millions of dollars in the effort. Billy and Kevin had looked to him as a father figure. Wilton and Hamilton had tied their reputations to his. And with one mighty surge of temper and ego, he had spoiled it all. Worst of all, he had embarrassed his family. *Poor little Wendy,* he thought. *Someday she'll read in a history book how her Grandpa Jack squandered the opportunity of a lifetime.*

"Good gosh, what have I done?" Jack asked aloud, his chin resting on his knuckles. Blackie heard him speak, got up, sat right in front of him and nosed his hands. Jack looked into her dark brown eyes, and she stared back intently, her furry brow rising slightly as if to ask, "What's wrong?" She gave him another nudge with her nose, and Jack reached out to caress her large, strong head.

"Girl, I think you're the only person on the planet who doesn't think I'm a big ol' fool," Jack said, stroking the sides of her head and her ears. "You may be the only friend I've got."

"No, you've got at least one more," came a familiar voice from the darkness behind him.

"So you found me." Jack turned around on the log to see Franky coming from the darkness of the brush into the circle of campfire light.

"Yep, I just followed you to where the fish are 'jumping over the pines.'"

"So you got my little clue."

"Loud and clear," said Franky. He was carrying a small knapsack, and he set it down and plopped down on the log next to Jack.

"So what took you so long?" Jack asked. "I figured you'd be here at least twelve hours ago."

"Oh, we had a little unfinished business to take care of in Kansas City. In case you hadn't heard, they've cut you off."

"Hadn't heard it, but it doesn't surprise me. It's just as well. Probably best for them to not waste any more money."

"Why, Jack Dodger, I can hardly believe what I'm hearing," said Franky. "Doesn't sound like the Jack Dodger I've always known—the Jack Dodger who never quits, who never gives up."

"Well, Franky, it's the Jack Dodger that's sitting here tonight, and that man believes that it's time to be honest and admit that it's a lost cause. Common sense tells me that this thing has come to its end. Not necessarily its logical end, but its end just the same."

"Lost cause? Oh boo-hoo," said Franky with all the sarcasm he could muster. "The only thing that got lost is your temper. And in case you'd forgotten, the cause isn't yours to lose. You're just the spokesman. The cause belongs to the people."

"Their cause? Well, then, the people can just go on without me," said Jack with a level of belligerence to match Franky's sarcasm. "Let them answer the media's questions. Let their families be insulted and derided."

"Now you see, Jack, that's what's got me really baffled. The Jack Dodger I used to know not only would not quit, but he wouldn't do it just cause some starch-shirted newspaperman from Houston said some bad things about him."

The wind changed direction slightly, pushing the smoke toward the two men, and Jack covered his face with his hands. The smoke burned his eyes, but the recollection of Howard Hickman's words burned even more, and he hung his head and began to weep. He tried to muffle his sobs with his palms, but the emotions of the last few days welled up and shook his entire frame.

Franky placed a burly hand on Jack's shoulder, which triggered even stronger shudders that shook the tree trunk they were sitting on. And, then, the tide of emotion seemed to ebb, and Jack rubbed his face with his hands and lowered them into his lap. Blackie leaned forward to lick the salty tears off of his fingers.

"Franky," Jack sighed, "I just couldn't stand what he said about Claire. It was just so awful. I hated like anything for Caroline to hear those kinds of things said about her mother."

"Then, don't let his words be the last words," Franky said strongly. "You make it right—not because you want revenge, but because it's the right thing to do for Claire."

Jack nodded. "And then what?"

"And, then, you get back to work on this campaign. You finish what you started. You keep your promises."

Jack turned his head to look at Franky. It was one of those rare moments when Franky's hidden eloquence was pushing through, and Jack just sat there taking it in.

Franky, feeling Jack's stare, looked back at Jack. "What? What?"

Jack reached over and gave Franky a tap on the knee. "We better get some rest."

CHAPTER 20

"Billy, gather the troops. It's time to get back to work."

With that short directive from Jack Dodger, the campaign was back on. Billy called Wilton and Kevin in Dallas, Hamilton in Seattle, and Caroline, Don, and Wendy in Austin. They gathered at Jack's little house in Lakewood and laid out a strategy for the final month of the campaign.

Billy, Hamilton, Franky, and Don sat at the dining table, poring over a map and planning where they needed to go and who they needed to see during the final weeks. Wilton was down the hall in the bedroom making phone calls to Golden Eagles chapter leaders around the country. The answer was the same from everyone he spoke to: "We're still ready to work for Jack, regardless of what they say at headquarters."

Caroline played with Wendy and Blackie in the backyard, while Jack and Kevin drove down to the barbershop to check out a vacant storefront next door to serve as a campaign headquarters. It was an unusually base task for a candidate to carry out himself; most would have sent a low-level staffer so they could stay and huddle with their top advisors. But Jack had sensed that Kevin had something on his mind ever since the team reassembled, and he thought the time alone might open him up. He wasn't disappointed.

As they drove down Live Oak, Kevin confronted Jack for the first time since New Year's Eve. "Jack, we need to talk. There's something we've got to get settled before tomorrow."

Jack was driving his pickup truck, and he pulled into Exall Park where he had played during his earliest boyhood days in

Dallas. The two men climbed out and talked as they strolled around the park's square, urban perimeter.

"Jack, you don't need to protect me any longer," Kevin said. "I don't want to be a problem for you, and I think at this point I am."

"But I made a pledge to you—"

"Yes, you did," said Kevin, "but pledges should be broken if they are harmful and if both people agree. At this point, neither my privacy nor my foolish pride are as important to me as seeing you go ahead and finishing this race without folks doubting you because of me. So I want to release you from our pledge."

"Are you sure about this, Kevin?"

"Yes, I'm sure. You need to go ahead and explain."

Jack nodded and put his hand on Kevin's shoulder. "Okay then."

They looked at the building and then returned to the house where Jack, inspired by Kevin's openness, had one last piece of personal business to resolve. Caroline and Franky were making dinner, and Jack asked his daughter to go outside with him for a few minutes, alone. There, sitting on the edge of the porch, Jack unloaded the last of his earthly worries.

"Caroline, I'm so sorry about what was said … what was suggested … about your mother. It just pained me so bad for you to hear that, and I don't want to hurt you any more. But I think I need to set the record straight about your sweet mother. I think I owe it to her to not let there be any hanging questions about the kind of person she was."

"Daddy, I'll tell you something," Caroline said. "Before I left for college, Momma sat me down one afternoon, in this very place. She told me that she had some rough times before she met you. She didn't have any family to help her, and she said she did some things she wasn't proud of. She didn't give me any specifics, and that wasn't her point. Her point in telling me that was to say that I should never let things get so bad before asking you and her for help. And there's something else she said: she said everyone makes mistakes, but there's forgiveness for those who ask for it, especially from those that truly love us."

Jack looked at his daughter in silence. He had never heard these things before. But then again, this was the type of honest, straightforward, loving advice that had made his wife so special. As he pondered Claire's words, delivered through Caroline, he found it remarkable that a lesson passed from mother to daughter years earlier was now shaping his own actions. He too had made mistakes, and it was time to ask for forgiveness.

***

The next morning as Jack faced a gathering of media and supporters at a downtown hotel, he felt a lightness of spirit and purpose. If the past several months had been propelled by naive enthusiasm, and the past several days propelled by hurt pride and emotion, the final month would be propelled by openness and honesty.

"First off," Jack said, "I want to apologize to the American people, and especially to those who have supported us over these past months, for my behavior up in Colorado. I got angry, I lost my temper, and I ran away from the fight. It was a childish reaction, and certainly not one befitting someone who wants to help govern. I can't undo what I did, and I fear that I've lost the confidence of a whole lot of folks. I reckon I'll regret that for the rest of my life. I'd like to ask for your forgiveness.

"I also want to address some of these comments that upset me so. I think you have a right to know. Regarding Kevin Walker, it is true that Kevin was fired from a previous job, for what they called 'inappropriate' use of the Internet. Well, in our society today, a lot of folks hear that and think 'pornography,' but that's not at all what it was about. You see, Kevin has a boy with a very serious illness, and his income and insurance were not going very far in getting him the medical help he needed. So Kevin sat down at a computer in the office one night to look for other sources of help.

He wasn't trying to run some kind of illegal business. He was just trying to do right for his boy.

"Well, he sat down at the desk of the wrong person, and he gets fired for it and has no income or insurance at all. He's desperate at that point, and so he does something borne out of that desperation: he robs a shop. My shop. It was a stupid, stupid thing to do, and I wish he hadn't done it. But he wasn't out to buy drugs or a fancy car—he was simply trying to help his child. Now Kevin has a lot of pride, and as a man, he was embarrassed about not being able to do right for his family. And so I told him that night that I would respect his privacy so long as he paid his debt for the crime and he didn't do anything stupid again. I also told him that if he ever got into a bind again, to call me and I would help. No questions asked.

"After he served his time, he went back out and tried to work, but it wasn't enough. He kept his word and called me for help, so I sent him some money, and then when a job opened up to drive us across the country, I gave him the job. He's done an excellent job of it, he's sent every penny he's earned home to his wife and son, and I couldn't be more proud of him.

"I wasn't going to tell you any of this, because, like I said, Kevin is a man of unusual pride and humility, and we had a promise that I wouldn't talk about it. But he's also a loyal man, and a decent man, and he chose on his own to release me from that promise so that there would be no more questions about whether or not we were running some kind of scheme."

Jack paused and took a deep breath.

"Now, the more serious issue, regarding these questions about my dear wife. The night I met Claire was the first time I had ever seen or heard of her, and I fell immediately in love. I knew nothing of her past, and to be honest, I wasn't interested in her past. I was only concerned about her future, and whether or not I was going to be a part of it. She told me that she had been through some hard times, as a child and later as a young adult, but many of us did, and so I didn't press her about it.

"But I want to tell you that the Claire Budrow Dodger that I knew for twenty-two years was the sweetest, loveliest, most decent, most caring person that God ever put on this earth. I miss her more than words can express, and I look forward to seeing her again some day. This version of her that some of you put in your papers is completely foreign to me. I never knew that woman. The woman I knew was an angel, straight from heaven, and that's where she is now."

Jack's chin trembled, and he had to pause for a moment to hold down the lump that was rising in his throat. He hadn't wanted to get emotional, but Claire was a sacred subject with him. He pulled himself together and made a final statement with a little more fire.

"As for when our daughter was born—that's nobody's damn business, and as casual as our society has become, I'm surprised that anybody would want to make a big deal about that." Jack paused again for a moment, but this time it was for pure dramatic affect. "Still, in my day we cared enough to do things in the proper order, and I'm proud of the fact that we did just that. Now, that's all I'm going to say about that. Any other questions?"

"Yes, Mr. Dodger. What are your plans now?" a reporter asked.

"Who do you plan to vote for next month?" asked another.

Jack was surprised by the questions. He looked at the reporters a moment, then at Billy. "Didn't you tell them what this was about?"

"I just told them we were having a press conference," Billy said with a grin. "I thought I'd let you break the news."

"Well, now," Jack said, turning to the audience with a new smile on his face. "Seems to me that it would be highly unusual for a candidate for president to vote for someone other than himself."

Now it was the media's turn to stare at each other in surprised silence. They had thought Jack had come out of hiding and called the conference to formally end his run for office.

"But the Golden Eagles … they've cut you off," one said.

"Yes, the board has cut me off, said they won't provide any more money, and I certainly understand their reason for doing that," said Jack. "But at this point, we don't need money. We need votes. And the individual members out there each have a vote to cast next month, and that's what we're going after. Anything else?"

"Yes—where'd you go last week?"

"I went to get myself straight," Jack said. "Sometimes life bends and twists you into knots, and you have to go straighten yourself out again."

"How'd you do that?"

"Fishing. Just fishing. Maybe some of you folks should try it some time. Now unless there is something else, we best get going," Jack said. "We've got a whole lot of work to do."

Jack made his way to the back of the room, stopping along the way to speak with some of the other interested people who had come to see what the story was. As the crowd began to thin, he caught a glimpse of a gray-haired woman standing near the door. He leaned on his toes to get a better look at her, and when he finally got a clear view, he almost fell over. It was Opal.

"Lord have mercy, Opal, I'm so glad you came." Jack was unable to hide his enthusiasm as he sauntered over to greet her. He reached out for a friendly handshake, but she pulled him forward into a big, warm hug.

"When Billy called to tell me what was happening, I just couldn't stay home," she said.

"Well that's just—," Jack started to say, but Opal placed a finger on his lips and whispered so that only he could hear.

"I said to myself, there's a crazy old fool in Dallas who would give up the chance to be president to defend the memory of a dear, sweet woman. Now that's a man I'd like to get to know a little better."

Jack's face turned bright red under his gray scalp, and Opal let out a giggle at the site of this big strong man blushing like a schoolboy. "Oh look at you." She laughed.

Jack struggled for a response but was rescued by Billy and Wilton, who walked up and ushered them to the door.

"Did you find everything okay," Billy asked Opal as they left the room.

"Oh yes, just fine," said Opal.

Jack stopped and looked at Opal and then Billy, his mouth open.

"What?" Billy asked. "She wanted to come, and I made sure she got here. Anything wrong with that?"

"No," Jack said. "No, of course not."

By the end of the day, the newspaper headlines and broadcast anchors were shouting the news of Jack's return with words like: "Jack is Back," "Grandpa out of Retirement," and "Dodger is Revived."

The pollsters quickly added Jack to their questions, and his approval numbers promptly bounced back up out of the cellar and into double digits again. Moans of annoyance came from the camps of the vice president and governor, while the pundits and analysts were thrilled. After three debates, the two mainstream candidates were locked in a seemingly unbreakable tie for the hearts of the electorate, and the consensus was that the return of Jack Dodger to the race would help siphon supporters from one of the leaders, at long last leaving a clear-cut front runner.

Jack, aware that this scenario was being forwarded, gamely promoted his own version of what was going to happen. "I agree. I think I *will* pull votes from the other candidates," he told audiences. "I'll pull votes from both of them—enough to win!" It was bold talk from a man who had quit and gone fishing, but the crowds loved it.

Without the financial support of the Golden Eagles organization, the campaign no longer could travel at will, nor could it travel with a large group. For that reason, the campaign was divided into two teams. Caroline, Don, Wilton, Kevin, and Franky made up the "home team," charged with running the campaign headquarters. From there, they made arrangements for rallies and speeches out in the field, and coordinated the activities of campaign volunteers in all fifty states, including local Golden Eagles members who still supported Jack.

The road team consisted of Billy, Opal, and, of course, the two candidates. Billy's role was to manage campaign events at the local sites, while Opal took on the job of road secretary and liaison between the home team and the road team.

While money continued to come into the campaign from all over the country, it was more sporadic in the absence of the Eagles' national administrative machine. While previously, the Eagles forwarded money to the campaign team out of its treasury with the faith that it would be replenished by donations, the campaign now could only spend what it had on hand.

As a result, the movements of the road team were patched together as funding allowed, and often without much advanced planning. They might fly a commercial airline one day, and hitch a ride on a private jet with a traveling business executive the next. Sometimes they rented a car, and on a few occasions found themselves being shuttled across a state by a volunteer with a van. Their sleeping accommodations were equally unpredictable: hotels, motels, volunteers' guest rooms. They spent two nights in Wisconsin on a houseboat, and a weekend in Arkansas in a trailer park.

No two days or nights were ever the same, and Jack worried at first that the campaign's relative poverty would be a hardship or at least an embarrassment to Opal. But she was spunky and unpretentious and quickly became the chief architect of the campaign's eccentric style.

"This is good for Jack and Ham," she would say, using the nickname that she quickly pinned on Jack's running mate. "It keeps 'em bright and alert. When you wake up in a hotel room day after day, you begin to forget where you are, and then who you are, and what you're about."

Perhaps Opal's theory was valid, or maybe the candidates were just getting a strong dose of end-of-the-race adrenaline. Whatever the reason, Jack and Hamilton in these final weeks reached a level of comfort and ease that was noticeable in everything they said and did. While the vice president and governor waged a battle of words that grew darker and heavier with every passing day, Jack spoke and moved with the lightness of a man who carried no weight of concern about the outcome. He was living in the pure joy of the moment. His message of caution and concern about the state of the nation was replaced with an earnest, evangelical call to join in the Great American Dream.

"Friends, there's never been a better time to live in America," he told a crowd at a bowling alley in Nebraska. "We've got so much to live for, so much to gain. It's out there, and it's yours if you want it. But you can't just wait for it to come to you, you can't just wait for someone to toss it in your lap. You've got to pick yourself up and go get it. You've got to join the march, join in the great parade. This is no rehearsal, you know. This life that you are living is the only one you get. There's no turning back the clocks, there's no starting over. So why waste another day, why waste another minute. Won't you join us, today, right now?"

CHAPTER 21

With a week to go in the campaign, the polls were showing that 25 percent of the electorate was ready to pull a lever for Jack Dodger. Demographic analyses indicated that his supporters represented a broad spectrum of the public. Certainly, he had captured a majority of the senior vote, but he also was doing well with conservative-leaning independents, and surprisingly, young first-time voters who had little respect for, or interest in, mainstream politics.

Jack's call for people to take responsibility for their own lives was resonating with many young people intent on casting off their parents' expectations about education and careers. They saw their futures not in walking down traditional career paths but rather in the new world of information technology, where the ability to think quickly and innovatively was more important than what degree you had or what zip code you came from.

The Dodger campaign was greeted by five thousand of these young people when they rolled onto the campus of a small university in western Oklahoma. Their numbers were greater than the enrollment of the university, and Jack was delighted when he learned that most of this enthusiastic crowd of young people had come by car and bus from dozens of colleges and universities in ten states.

"When you go back to your campuses and your classmates tonight," he told them, "don't just tell them that Jack Dodger is counting on them. Tell them that their nation is counting on them to learn and grow and absorb all that they can during these school years. Yes, it's important whom you vote for on Tuesday, because the president carries important powers of democracy. But more important is how you go about becoming adults. The president is just one man, but you—you are a generation. It's generations that move this nation forward in big steps, and it will be your generation that decides what the future will be like."

It was a great moment for Jack and the campaign because the coverage he got from the newspapers of all those individual schools was read by people in those communities and picked up by the local community papers and state papers and on to the wire services and across the nation. Jack had not received such widespread coverage since he dropped out of the race and then returned, and in this final week, it was sorely needed.

But as good as the coverage was, there also was a backlash. Because the race was churning on toward the closest finish in decades, and because the Dodger-Lee ticket threatened to pull votes away from the governor and vice president, the campaign attracted heat from partisans on both sides. While the other candidates never uttered a harsh word about Jack other than to question his experience, their supporters in the field were more direct in their opinions. Jack was heckled severely during a rally at a shopping center in Georgia, and when it became clear that he was not going to be heard over the noise, he decided to engage the hecklers directly.

"What is your problem?" Jack asked. "Why are you so angry?"

"You're busting up the race," one of the detractors shouted. "We've got two serious men who need to be heard, and you're just a distraction. You're not a serious choice. You don't have any experience. You should go home."

"I disagree," said Jack. "I *am* a serious choice. I've been campaigning seriously all year long. I'm serious about what I'm trying to accomplish. I'm serious about wanting to help lead this country. And besides all that, our constitution allows me to do this. I have every right to be here."

"You may *have* the right, but that doesn't *make* it right," the man shouted back. "There's no way you're gonna win. You were never gonna win. You're just wasting everyone's time."

"Let's just wait and see," said Jack. "Let's wait and see what happens Tuesday. If I lose as you predict, you can come down to Dallas and remind me how wrong I was. Just give me a call, and I'll send you a plane ticket, and you can come tell me face-to-face. But until then, I'm going to continue talking to those who care to listen."

Jack faced another unruly crowd the next night in Tennessee. While the other candidates had the time and money to stage events loaded with supporters, the Dodger campaign often did not know where it was going next and, thus, often arrived in a town unexpected, and in this case, unwelcomed. The team had hitched a ride out of Atlanta on a private jet with a corporate executive friendly to the cause. They were trying to get to Arkansas, but the executive was only going as far as Memphis. As soon as word got around that Jack Dodger was in town, staunch supporters of the vice president descended on Jack's motel late at night, chanting and taunting until Jack, Hamilton, Billy, and even Opal came out of their rooms. Dressed in pajamas and a robe, Jack made a plea for peace.

"I certainly understand that you'd prefer that we not be here, and to be honest, we were hoping to make it to Arkansas tonight. But we're sort of stuck here until morning, so we'd be appreciative if you'd let us get some rest."

"There won't be any rest until you drop out and leave politics to those who are experienced and qualified," said a man who appeared to be a spokesman for the rabble.

"Well now, that's interesting that you should say that," said Jack sleepily. "If I remember correctly, the constitution allows us to be doing what we're doing, and that same document allows you to vote for someone else if you wish. You also have the right to voice your opinion, but it seems to me there might be a better time and place to do that than at midnight in a motel parking lot."

Jack's constitutional lesson didn't play at all with this audience.

"Get out of town, Dodger," came an angry voice from the back of the crowd, and before Jack or any of his team could respond, they were bombarded by raw eggs. One caught Jack on the knee, and another smacked Opal in the center of her forehead. She let out a yelp and then began laughing as she pulled the dripping residue off of her face.

"Now that hasn't happened since I was in school," she said.

Jack turned to make sure Opal was okay, and then, wide awake by now, he began walking straight toward the assailants, some of whom backed up as he approached with head up and shoulders back.

"You know," he said, "if I were the governor or the vice president, the secret service would be putting you in handcuffs about now and dragging you off to face federal charges." Jack paused and looked the leaders of the gang in the eyes. "But seeing how I don't have their protection, that's not going to happen here tonight. So, you have a choice. You can continue this ugly display and see what does happen, or you can go on home and let us get some rest."

Surprised by the crusty civility coming out of this gray-haired seventy-year-old man, the crowd quietly disassembled and drifted off into the night.

Jack stood in the parking lot until all were gone and all was quiet. Then, away from the lights of the motel, he instinctively looked up at the stars. He turned his body a moment until he found and oriented himself to Orion. The great hunter was there, changeless and timeless. He thought about fishing trips long ago with his father and later with Franky. Orion had always been there high above their campfire, and he was there again on this night.

"Jack, you coming back to bed, or you gonna stay out here and wait for sunrise?" Billy asked.

Jack's attention was drawn back to the scene of the melee. "What a night," he said quietly as he walked back to his room.

On the Sunday evening before election day, the road team was settling in to a hotel in Phoenix when Jack called everyone to his room. He had Wilton and the headquarters team in Dallas on speakerphone, and when everyone was assembled, he announced his desire for the final twenty-four hours.

"I know it's become sort of a tradition for these things to push on until midnight on Monday, but I don't believe we're going to do that," said Jack. "We've worked hard, we've talked to a lot of folks, and I think we've gotten our message out loud and clear. I think most of the hard work is behind us, and it's all up to the people at this point. So what I want now is for everyone to start making their way back home to vote. Hamilton, you and I will make one last big pitch in the morning, and then, you best head on back to your district in Seattle. Caroline, you and Don go ahead and cover the phones there in Dallas until mid-afternoon, but then it'll be time for you to go home to Austin so you can vote. Opal, we'll put you on a plane back to Wyoming in the morning. Billy and I will fly back to Dallas in the afternoon. Perhaps we can put together a last little event there at the airport, but by the time the sun goes down, I'd like everyone to be home with their families."

"What about election night?" Billy asked.

Wilton came across the speakerphone with the answer. "For Tuesday night, we've got a watch party arranged downtown at the Majestic Hotel. Everything's in place, and we're expecting a good crowd. It should be a nice time."

"Good," said Jack. "We need to thank a lot of folks for their efforts. It's important that we do that."

Jack adjourned the meeting and signed off with the team in Dallas. Billy, Hamilton, and Opal all said goodnight and wandered down the hallway to their respective rooms. By the time Opal got inside her door, the phone was ringing, and it was Jack. "Can you meet for breakfast, about six a.m.?" he asked.

⸎

The next morning Jack and Opal quietly slipped out of their rooms so as not to wake anyone else. They met at a table in the back corner of the coffee shop, and Jack sat with his back to the rest of the tables. He wanted to visit without generating any attention.

"So, Mr. Dodger, what is it you wanted to see me about?" Opal asked playfully in her best "young campaign volunteer" voice.

"I didn't want to see you about anything in particular. I just wanted to see you," Jack said.

Opal took a sip of coffee and waited for Jack's blush, but it didn't come this time. But that was because he knew what he was going to say; he had been planning this moment in his head for weeks.

"No, I just wanted to be able to spend a little quiet time with you before you catch your plane," he said. "With all the work and traveling, we haven't really had a quiet moment alone since we stood outside your car in Wyoming."

"Yes, that's right, but as you'll recall, we weren't really alone then either." She pretended to scan the restaurant for hidden photographers.

Jack took a glance over his shoulder too, but he turned back around as soon as he felt Opal's hand on his.

"Oh stop that, Jack Dodger," she said. "There's nobody here but us, the waitress, and the cook. Don't tell me you're worried that we're gonna be seen together again?"

"Oh no," said Jack. "No, I just … I just don't want anyone to bother us. Like I said, I just wanted to spend some good private time before—"

"Well, we've got it, so let's not waste it," Opal said.

And led by her assurance, they didn't. For the next hour they talked about life and events that had nothing to do with their current business but everything to do with who they were. They talked about the things that they were proud of and the things for which they held regrets. They laughed at each other's silly mistakes and comforted each other as they shared their losses. And then when it seemed there was nothing more to say, Jack said what had been forming in his mind gradually ever since he first saw Opal sitting in that booth at the diner in Wyoming.

"Opal, I think by now you know how much Claire meant to me. You know how much I still love her, and that I always will."

"Yes, Jack, and I think that is just so lovely, so very special," she said softly. "That's what real love is all about: loving someone long after they're gone. I hope that you will just go on loving her forever."

"Yes, I think I will," Jack said. "But while I know that nobody can ever replace her, I've sort of come around to the idea that my old heart is not so small and tired as I once thought it was. I think there's room enough in my heart for my memories of Claire … as well as for new memories."

Jack slowly slid his hands across the table, past the salt and pepper, coffee mugs, and jelly caddie. He was within a precious half inch of Opal's waiting fingertips when Billy suddenly walked up.

"Hey, you two, up awfully early aren't you? I called your room Jack but—" Billy stopped. In a flicker of a second he assessed the scene: four hands on the table, Opal grinning like a teenage girl, and Jack glaring at him with fire in his eyes.

"Oh … I'm sorry … Jack … Opal … I didn't mean to … I'll just go across the way and see if I—"

"Oh, hush and sit down, Billy," said Opal. He did reluctantly, and within five minutes they were joined by Hamilton, and Jack wondered if he'd ever get to finish his sentence.

After breakfast, Jack and Hamilton made one last appearance together at a local high school, and then the team members went to the airport to send each other off, with a small cadre of local media standing by.

"Thanks for everything," Hamilton said, shaking hands with Jack and then giving him a bear hug. "I don't know how it will shake out tomorrow, but win or lose, it's been an honor and a privilege. If the folks out there don't send us to Washington, then I can say that you're sending me back home a much better man than you found me. I've spent the past decade trying to lose myself, but you've helped me find myself again, and so I'm going to try to do something good with the years I've got left. Maybe even try to find that boy that they say I have."

"You do that," said Jack. "I think that'd be more important than anything you might accomplish in Washington."

Hamilton turned and walked down the concourse to catch his flight. It was now time for Jack to say good-bye to Opal, but with the press watching, his instincts told him he had better keep things casual.

"Opal, it's been a pleasure working with you." Jack took both of her hands. "We've traveled a lot of miles together, and I hope there's going to be more in the future." To the media watching and listening, Jack's statement sounded political. *More miles together? Might this woman have a role in a Dodger administration?* But Opal knew better; she knew Jack wasn't talking politics, and neither was she.

"We'll just have to make it so," she said. They hugged, and she too was on her way.

Hamilton and Opal flew home on commercial flights, but she made it her last task as campaign travel arranger to see that Jack and Billy flew home to Dallas on a small private charter. While Jack was pleased with the opportunity to have some quiet time and even catch some sleep, the reason for the charter became clear to him only when they taxied to the private terminal in Dallas.

At the hotel the previous night, Jack had described a campaign that was winding down to a quiet conclusion. But when he stepped off the plane in Dallas, he was met by the largest crowd he had encountered since he gave that first speech in Kansas City months earlier.

"What's all this?" Jack asked as he was greeted by Wilton on the tarmac. Billy stood behind him, offering Wilton a big thumbs-up.

"It might have been fine for Douglas MacArthur to fade away, but we thought we'd end this campaign with a big bang," Wilton shouted over the noise.

Jack was moved by all that he saw, and he blinked in an effort to absorb the tears that were forming in the corners of his eyes. He saw Wilton smiling at Billy, and he turned around to see Billy give one of his now familiar shrugs of innocence.

"Well, you better say something," Billy said to Jack. "They didn't come here to just look at your back."

Jack brushed a hand across his eyes to blot the moisture, and then, he turned to face the crowd, which sent them into a new session of chants and cheers. From somewhere obscured off to the side, a band began to play a patriotic march, and Jack just stood and took it all in. He didn't try to quiet the band or the crowd's enthusiasm. This was their moment too, and he let them have all of it.

When the band came to the end of their tune and the crescendo of the crowd began to taper, Jack gave his final speech as a candidate for president of the United States. He hadn't prepared what to say, but the words came naturally, straight from his heart.

"Dear friends, I can't begin to tell you how much this reception means to me. What a wonderful way to come home to the people and city I love so much. When we left from this airport six months ago, I didn't know what to expect. I didn't know if people would listen. Heck, I didn't know if people would even care. But we got out into the countryside and into the communities and what we found was that people did want to listen, and they really do care. We had the opportunity to visit with a lot of folks, and I want to tell you that despite what you hear on the news and read in the papers, this is a kind and generous nation. It's a nation full of people who really do care for each other, who really do want what's best for each other. If there is a conflict, then, it's about how best to go about making things right.

"And that's what tomorrow is all about. This campaign journey has come to an end. Our work is done, and now, it's time for you to decide how you want this nation to move forward. It's time to decide who can best lead us in taking care of things.

"Now, a good number of people think that I might be that person, and it goes without saying that I'd like to have that opportunity. But this isn't about what I want, or what the vice president or the governor wants. It's about you, your families, and your neighbors, and what you need. So when you go into that voting booth tomorrow, don't think about us. Think about yourselves and the people you care about. Make a decision that will be best for you and those folks close to you. And then when the votes are counted tomorrow night, get behind whoever comes out on top. Give them your full support and attention. And while you're at it, say a little prayer for them every now and then."

On the morning of November 7, Jack slept later than he had in months, crawling out of bed at nine. He and Blackie went out into the yard to get the paper, and then, he fixed himself a couple of eggs, a few strips of bacon, and two slices of toast. While Blackie scarfed down her morning bowl of dog chow, Jack ate quietly and looked at the newspaper. The headline across the top of the front page declared: "Day of Decision." The headline on a sidebar to that story asked the question: "Dodger Saga Ends?"

"We shall see," Jack mumbled aloud to himself.

Since the campaign was officially over at seven in the morning when people began to cast their votes, Jack had told his team to take the day off. "Go about your business, spend time with your families, and of course, vote at your local precinct," he told them. "Then we'll get back together at the hotel to see what happens."

Jack had purposely not told Billy when he planned to vote, and he asked that the media not be told when he might vote.

"I don't want to make a show of my voting. People should have their minds made up by now, and those that don't shouldn't be swayed by some kind of media circus at the precinct," he told Billy. "This is an important process, and it should be treated with dignity and respect."

It was a cool, overcast day, and Jack decided to walk with Blackie the half-mile to the fire station. Wearing tennis shoes, blue jeans, a dark gray sweatshirt, and blue ball cap, he and Blackie wove their way through the neighborhood. After stopping at a little park to let Blackie take care of business and chase a pair of squirrels, they rounded a corner and arrived at the fire station.

Despite his best efforts, Jack could not keep the media away, but their numbers were small: two local television crews and a very young-looking newspaper reporter-photographer. Election laws required that they keep their distance, and with the television crews set up next to their vans across the street, Jack was able to slip by them unnoticed.

The newspaper reporter, on the other hand, was standing on the curb near the fire station driveway. He made eye contact with Blackie, and before Jack could make the turn up the drive, Blackie pulled Jack toward the reporter, eager to meet this new friend.

"Hey, girl, how ya doing?" the reporter asked, slinging his camera back on his shoulder to give Blackie a two-handed head rub. "Who ya gonna vote for, girl?"

"Aw, she'll just go with whoever I pick," said Jack.

The reporter looked at Jack and laughed, and Jack quickly became aware that the reporter didn't recognize him. It might have been his scruffy attire, or his thirty-two hours worth of gray stubble. Jack decided to make the most of it.

"Since the two of you seem to get along so well, you mind keeping an eye on her while I go inside and vote?" Jack asked, handing him the leash.

"No, sir, be glad to." The reporter knelt down to play with Blackie while Jack walked between the fire trucks and into the fire station garage where the voting machines were set up.

The precinct was staffed by the regular crew of senior citizen volunteers, and they all knew Jack well from his decades of local business activities and, now, from his candidacy. But when he stepped up to the table to show his voter registration card and sign his name, there was not the least little bit of fuss made over him. He was just a local citizen at this moment, and they treated him as such.

"Here you go, Mr. Dodger," said a woman, handing him back his card and a punch-card ballot. "Just slide this card into the machine over there and make your choices, and then bring it back over here when you're done and put it in the box."

Jack nodded and walked over to the machine. A little more than two minutes later, he returned to the table and slid his ballot into the box.

"See you next time," said the woman.

"See you then," said Jack. "Y'all have a nice day."

Jack walked back out to the curb where the reporter and Blackie were waiting.

"She treat you okay?" Jack asked.

"Oh sure. She just sat here and watched you go in and then watched you come back out. She sure loves her master."

"Yes, she's a good loyal friend. None better really." Jack took control of the leash. "Have you voted yet?"

"Yes, sir, first thing this morning."

"Good for you. Good for you. Well, thanks again for holding her for me."

"No problem," said the reporter, giving Blackie a last pat on the head.

Jack began walking away from the fire station, when a firefighter sitting on the back bumper of his engine finally broke Jack's cover. "Hey, Jack, we're pulling for you!"

Jack turned without breaking stride. "Thanks, I appreciate that," he said and gave the firefighter a smile and a wave.

Seeing the man with the dog from a distance that way, the newspaper reporter suddenly recognized that he had been talking to Jack Dodger the entire time. He fumbled for his camera, but before he could pull it up and focus, Jack had turned his back and was moving on down the street with Blackie at his side.

"Oh no," the reporter groaned, kneeling down and shaking his head. "All I've got is small talk about a dog. They're going to kill me."

CHAPTER 22

By seven o'clock on election night, the big hotel ballroom had filled up with friends and supporters of the Dodger campaign. Some were there to see if Jack might pull off a miracle, while others were there just for the party. It was impossible to tell one group from another because it was clear that everyone was having a big time.

The media were on hand in numbers that had not been seen since after the scuffle in Colorado Springs, including the major networks. The consensus among the reporters on hand was that it would be a short night in Dallas, with a few taking wagers as to how early Jack might concede defeat. It was their way of making the most of being dispatched to what they believed would be a dull loser's party.

Meanwhile, as had become tradition for these affairs, the candidate was sequestered upstairs in a suite with his family, campaign team, and close friends. In a corner of the room, three televisions were tuned to three different channels where the pundits and prognosticators slowly dished out the numbers and their projections for the popular vote and electoral vote.

The evening moved at a torturous crawl for Jack, and the pressure of the night—if not the past few months—was beginning to show on his face. Inside, he felt as if he was on the edge of an emotional breakdown. Yes, he wanted to win, and yes, he would be disappointed if he lost. At the same time, the thought of actually being elected president was frightening, and a part of him hoped the final results would cast him back into retirement where he really belonged.

By ten o'clock, with none of the candidates yet claiming the prize, Jack had to get away. He backed his way across the suite and slid into one of the bedrooms. He turned on the television in the room but kept the volume at a whisper, and then, he turned off all the other lights and plopped down on the sofa.

He was staring blankly at the screen, his mind retracing many of the events of the past year, when the television screen suddenly flashed with new numbers, and the news anchor declared the race over. Jack fumbled on the couch for the remote control, and a quick scan of the channels showed the news to be the same. It was over.

The flashing television screen—combined with his own dancing thoughts—made him dizzy, and he closed his eyes for a moment. As he did, he heard the door open, the noise from the next room spill in after it, and then the door shut again. Then there was the soft sound of small feet on the carpet, and the sensation of a tiny body sitting on the sofa beside him.

"What's the matter, Grandpa Jack?" implored the tiny voice beside him.

With his eyes still closed, he reached to his left and raised the warm little frame onto his lap. He opened his eyes and was met immediately by a wet kiss from Wendy.

"Oh, nothing, Little Blossom," he answered. "I was just thinking about all the nice people I've met in the past year, and how I'm going to miss seeing them."

"But me and Mommy will always be with you," said Wendy.

"That's right, that's right, Wendy." He smiled down at her little face. "And you know what? We're going to have a lot more time to spend together than we've had in a long while."

As he said that, the door opened again, and this time, it was Billy Briar. He closed the door quietly behind him so as to keep the noise outside for a moment longer.

"Is it time?" Jack asked, already knowing the answer.

"Yes, Jack, everyone's waiting for you. The hall is bursting at the seams with your friends. And all the networks have their people in place. All that's missing is you."

"Well, then, I suppose I shouldn't keep them waiting any longer. That wouldn't be right," he said. He took one glance back at the television screen then lifted Wendy off his lap and back onto the sofa. "Why don't you stay here, and you can watch me on TV," he told her. "Then you can tell me how I did. Just like always."

"Sure, Grandpa Jack. Just like always."

With that, he leaned down and kissed her on the forehead and then walked the few paces to where Billy was waiting.

"What will I say, Billy?"

"Just go down there and tell them what's on your mind. Just like always."

As Jack reached for the doorknob, Billy put his hand on his shoulder. "You'll do just fine."

Jack nodded appreciatively and pulled open the door, walking into the light and noise. Billy gave a little wave to Wendy and then followed Jack out of the room. They walked silently through the sea of well-wishers gathered in the outer room, then down the elevator, around a corner, and down a service corridor.

Just as they reached a side door leading onto the ballroom stage, a man in a dark suit suddenly stepped out of the shadows and held out a cell phone. "A call for you, Mr. Dodger," he said quietly.

"Not now, please," Jack said. He was nervous and in no mood to take random phone calls. "I need to get on out there. Billy, why don't you take it?"

"Jack, I believe you better take this call," said Billy.

Jack looked at Billy and, then, the stranger who nodded and pressed the phone into his hand. Jack put it up to his ear.

"Uh … hello … this is Jack Dodger." Jack spoke with caution, but the voice on the other end came roaring through the earpiece like a freight train.

"Hey, Jack, this is, um … I guess I'm supposed to say the president-elect, I don't know. Still getting used to that. Anyway, I wanted to call you tonight and tell you how proud I am of what you have done for Dallas, Texas, and the nation."

Jack was dumbstruck, but he managed to get out a few sentences.

"Well, that's very nice of you, but isn't it me who's supposed to be calling you to congratulate you for winning the election? And now that I've got your ear, I would like to say that and offer you my best wishes for the future."

"Thank you, Jack, I do appreciate that. It was a long, drawn-out deal, a real marathon, as you well know. And I think all of us can be proud of how we conducted ourselves, and a lot of that's because of you. I'll be honest and tell you there was never a day when I wasn't aware of what you were doing and saying. And I have to say that your down-to-earth, honest approach helped keep us sharp and on message."

Jack tried to think of something to say, but before he could get anything out, the president-elect jumped back in.

"Anyway, Jack, the reason I called is I have a proposition to make. You've made some very important points during this campaign, and it's clear that you have a wonderful connection with the people. And so I was wondering if you might consider a role in my administration. I don't know what it might be yet—perhaps an undersecretary for senior affairs in Health and Human Services. Haven't really thought it all through yet. But I wanted to plant that idea with you before you got busy with other things. I believe we could benefit from a man like you on our team."

"Well now, I don't know," said Jack. "Yes, I'll have to think about that. To be honest, I hadn't given much thought to what I might do next. I'm just trying to get through the next hour or two."

"Well, that's fine, Jack. You go and tell those good folks in Dallas how proud you are of them, and while you're at it, tell them how proud I am of them too. They represented you with honor and dignity, and that's something that's sure worth being proud of. And then, you think on this idea for a while and give me a call in a few weeks. I'll make sure someone gives you my direct line."

"That'll be fine," said Jack. "I'll do that. Well, congratulations again."

"Thanks again, Jack. Good night and God's blessings to you."

"And to you."

Jack handed the phone back to the man and then stared at the floor. He tried for a moment to process what he had just heard, but then, the noise of the waiting crowd brought his attention back to what he now needed to do. He looked at Billy and nodded. "I'm ready now."

Jack stepped through the door, and the waiting throng screamed and cheered and waved as Jack hesitated in the back corner of the stage. Any weakness he had felt coming to this place was vanquished by the buoyancy of the people who surrounded him.

Back in the quiet of the hotel room, Wendy watched as her grandfather approached the podium. Just then, Caroline came in and sat down beside her. "Oh look, Mommy, it's Grandpa Jack. He's on TV tonight."

"Yes, honey, he sure is."

They watched as he waved appreciatively at the ballroom crowd. Even with the sound turned down, they could read his lips as he said over and over again, "I love you. I love you."

Jack was anxious to say his peace and leave the spotlight, but something inside him still hated to see it all end. It was as if the entire nation had become his family, and he was afraid to tell them good-bye and return to his quiet life. But he knew that was what this night was about, so he raised his hands in an attempt to suppress the noise so that he could get on with his final speech.

As the crowd took his cue and began to settle down, Jack looked around at those who had joined him on the stage. Franky, Billy, and Kevin who had brought his entire family. Judson and Paul from the barbershop. Even Hamilton had flown all the way back from Seattle, unable to keep himself away. Only one person was missing, and Jack knew she was probably sitting at the diner in Wyoming watching with her friends. Surrounded by this group of strangers who had become family, Jack said good-bye to America.

"Dear friends, I want to thank you for this wonderful reception. This past year has been a remarkable experience. A humbling experience really. Over these months, over these countless miles, I've come to know how vast and enormous this nation is, and how numerous our people are. And yet, I've come to understand what 'nation' really means. It's not about states, borders, cities, rivers, or natural resources. A nation isn't just a mass of land on a map. It's a people who, while living lives as different from each other as night and day, share a common history and a common hope and dream for the future.

"That's what this past year has been about. It's been about the people of this nation becoming reacquainted with the common dream of the future that we share and, then, picking leaders who can help guide us toward it.

"I've just been on the phone with the president-elect," Jack said, which drew hoots from some in the crowd. "Now before you do that, you should know that he very graciously thanked you for your contribution to the political process. He said, 'You tell those people how proud I am of them.' And I agree—you should be proud of yourselves. You did what many said was impossible, and you did it with honor and dignity.

"And that's the way I hope you'll carry on under this new administration. We've chosen a good man to lead us—an honorable man who I believe will do an outstanding job. We need to get behind him, all of us, because he's got a tough job ahead of him. We should keep him to his word and tell him when we disagree, but we should never lose track of who he is and who we are. He's an American, just like us, and he deserves our respect as well as our prayers.

"I'd like to close by saying that when I celebrated my seventieth birthday last December 31, I had no idea that I was entering the most exciting year of my life. It's been an incredible ride, and I'll never be able to thank you enough for making it possible."

Jack's emotions bubbled to the service, and he hung his head a moment to regain his composure.

"Grandpa Jack in 2004," someone shouted, which broke up the crowd.

"No, I don't think so," Jack said, laughing through moist eyes. "I've had my go at this, and I think I'll sit back and watch next time. Besides, I've got a lot to catch up on—my family, my business, a little fishing. And there's a gal up in Wyoming who's not gonna rest until we finish the conversation we started.

"So I thank you one and all. God bless you, and God bless America."

Jack backed away from the microphone and out of the glare of the spotlight for the last time.

The party continued well into the night, and Jack was determined to mingle with the guests until all were gone or he fell asleep, whichever came first. He made a special point to spend time with those who had ridden the long hard miles with him, and especially Billy Briar.

"Billy, I know what I'm going to do tomorrow. How about you?" Jack asked with his big arm around Billy's shoulders.

"Well, by the strangest of coincidences, I got a call tonight too from the president-elect's press secretary. He asked if I might meet with him next week and talk about a job in the White House. He said he had gotten a very good recommendation on me a few days ago. Imagine that."

Billy scanned Jack's face for a wink or some other sign of a conspiracy, but Jack didn't give anything away.

"No kidding? Well that's just wonderful," Jack said. "See, I told you that you might discover that you have a future in this business." Then, he pulled Billy close. "I just want to tell you, Billy Briar, that I couldn't be more proud of you, and proud of our friendship."

Billy was going to answer but was interrupted by a new voice.

"Excuse me, Mr. Dodger."

Jack turned around and was surprised to see the same young reporter that he had eluded that morning at the fire station.

"You finally caught me," Jack said. "We had a bet going that you'd track me down eventually."

"Yes, sir," the reporter said nervously. "I was wondering if I could get a few comments from you."

"Be glad to," said Jack, "but then you might want to spend a little time with Mr. Briar here. He can tell you all about the dangers of getting too close to your story."

"Oh, yes, we really must talk about that." Billy gave Jack a playful punch on the shoulder and walked off into the crowd. Jack and the reporter found a sofa against the wall, where Jack gave the last interview of his life.

A while later, Jack was sitting quietly, alone, almost hypnotized by the motion of people walking back and forth, when he became aware of a little figure rushing toward him.

"Grandpa Jack, Grandpa Jack!" Wendy jumped into his lap with a hard thud. "Can we go home now?"

"Yes, Little Blossom. Yes, we can."

Jack hoisted Wendy up on his shoulders, and together, they drifted through the ebbing waves of revelers, across the confetti-strewn floor, away from the fading chatter and music, and out the door.

Some men would have turned to take one last look at what might have been, but not Jack Dodger. He was content. Another man would be president for a season, but he would be Grandpa Jack … always.